Good Vibrations

Book One of the HaChii Concatenation

A Science Fiction Novel of Cosmic Integration and Intolerance

This is a work of fiction. Any resemblance between the characters in my stories and real people is unlikely to be taken seriously by anyone with similar names. None of my acquaintances have developed the capacity to turn invisible, nor have any become counterterrorist agents, to my knowledge. So there. The 'disclaimer' thing has been done, and in the improbable event that I have accurately revealed any of their superpowers by mistake...Sorry about that!

GOOD VIBRATIONS

Table of Contents

GOOD VIBRATIONS

PROLOGUE

Between the orbits of Mars and Jupiter, amidst the myriad fragments that constitute the Asteroid Belt, (4147) Lennon is a rock in space with the same surface area as the City of New Orleans, if neither the population nor the climate. It was named after 20th century composer John Winston Lennon, known for such compilations as *Sergeant Pepper's Lonely Hearts Club* Band and songs like *Lucy in the Sky with Diamonds* and *Imagine.*

Late in the 21st century, the robotic survey probe *Donald Johanson* surveyed this body and reported back a spectroscopic signature that aroused minor interest back on Earth. It was catalogued as a possible source of gemstones, filed as "Mineral Exploration Desirable" and forgotten.

As the next two centuries passed, humanity acquired its first knowledge of other races in the Galaxy. In particular, the discovery of communication channels using quantum entanglement opened a whole new realm of SETI contacts. Among these was the HaChii Confederation, a group of three planetary systems 50 parsecs away, not that distance mattered to entangled-particle communicators. The sole sentient species were blue-green, biped, tentacled, quasi-cephalopod humanoids with a slightly higher technology level than humans.

The first diplomatic and physical contact between the humans and HaChii took place on Earth. HaChii diplomats and scientists had taken well over a century and a half in deepsleep to arrive, so the meeting was groundbreaking, but also intensely anticipated. Yes. It was humanity's first face-to-face with people that were not humans, but it was not as jarring as encounters with other peoples were later. If anything, it was like meeting old friends.

The meeting began with speeches, diplomatic and scientific panels. Both races were oxygen-breathers, ate, spoke, and breathed through their mouths, and "walked" upright on two lower limbs while two upper limbs were used for gripping and manipulation.

Some details were different, of course; for instance, inhaled air passed through HaChii bodies and exited through spiracles on the sides of the torso, so there was no huffing and puffing. The word "walked" was euphemistic for a form of locomotion that involved the two lower HaChii limbs sidewinding across the countryside like a pair of desert snakes. And skin color was a matter of mood, not racial ancestry.

HaChii were clearly invertebrates, but like some Earth cephalopods, had a cuttlebone-like internal shell along their backs, including a structure enclosing the brain. Eyes had evolved that were remarkably like those of cats or goats, according to mood. For the most part, HaChii physiology had evolved to be uncannily similar to that of humans, even though it had started from very different ancestral origins.

Although the HaChii home world had weaker gravity than Earth, HaChii females were built more robustly than most humans and had remarkable strength in their gripping arms/tentacles. HaChii males were smaller than the females--about the size of human 12-year-old boys. In HaChii society, leadership roles seemed to gravitate disproportionately toward the females.

To the eyes of the human participants at the conference, HaChii locomotion seemed sinuous and serpentine, though graceful; to HaChii eyes, humans' jointed skeletons made their movements awkward and gawky. The hinges--joints--in the four human tentacles, and within the strange branchy things visible at the ends of the arms, seemed to restrict freedom of movement ridiculously, compared to the unlimited degrees of freedom in a tentacle.

Dr. Rii Ix Klii, a biologist, was overheard at the opening ceremonies, questioning how Cha Iz DaWii, the HaChii biologist who first proposed evolution a thousand years ago, would have explained a planet dominated by endoskeletal beings. "How could you 'vertebrates' succeed with such restricted motions?" she asked Dr. Kim Barcacs, a human biologist.

HaChii diplomats present feared this gaffe would spark a disastrous interstellar incident, but Dr. Barkacs just laughed it off with "Oh——We manage to elbow our way through." The diplomats, not expecting her sense of humor, were both pleasantly amused and greatly relieved.

In the evening after the first meeting, human and HaChii scientists put on a talent show, to entertain the guests. Humans marveled at the fluidity of HaChii dancers; HaChii winced to watch human dancers, although acknowledging that their speed often camouflaged the natural rigidity of their motions. *"But then--what could you expect of beings with such a structure?"* one speaker was heard to remark.

Then the stage ninjas rolled out a piano. HaChii looked at each other. What was this? They had only seen keyboards, briefly, when human scientists keyed something into a computer or calculator, and there obviously wasn't much entertainment value in ***that***——

But Dr. Jan Bukowski, the pianist, walked in, sat down, and began a piece representative of his native country--Chopin's *Polonaise in A flat, No. 53*.

The HaChii delegation, who had been chattering to each other throughout the dance presentation, became silent. Their arms went limp. As one, their skin color shifted from its normal cyan to a pale violet, then as Bukowski romped and pranced across the keyboard with both verve and skill, the HaChii shaded to a bright lilac color. Grippers began to wave in the air. By the end of the performance, the entire HaChii delegation was--"on their feet" isn't exactly the right expression--but they were definitely upright. And making loud un-coordinated sounds. "I think they're screaming and yelling," the human interpreter explained to the head of the Earth delegation, "in a good way, I mean. I think they are very, very excited and pleased."

A news reporter pushed a microphone in front of Dr. Rii. After babbling in HaChii for a moment, he realized his audience wouldn't understand a word, and re-stated himself: "I take it all back. Even if endoskeletons were evolved for ***no other purpose*** than this, Cha Iz DaWii would be fully vindicated. Those branchy things on the end of your gripping limbs are amazing!" He made one more HaChii remark that was later translated as *"Who'd have thought?!"*

After the piano recital, the juggler who rode a unicycle onstage with a cascade of twelve balls under control sealed the deal. What the HaChii had taken for a handicap had turned out to be an advantage. Every HaChii with an entrepreneurial bone in her body (figuratively speaking) began thinking of ways to use these differences for entertainment, fun, and above all, profit.

With the first meeting an unqualified success, a second round of meetings between business and industrial representatives of both species was scheduled. A hundred fifty years of technological improvement made it possible for the second delegation to arrive in less than a year. This led to trade and business partnerships, including a very profitable association between human and HaChii mining companies. Both races had complementary strengths that made the whole greater than its parts, and one area where they worked together especially well was the asteroid mining business.

Within twenty years, human-HaChii companies were exploring and developing mining operations jointly in five star systems within the human and HaChii spheres of influence. Small teams of miners worked best, supported by industrial firms from a dozen worlds.

And that is how a human-HaChii team came to the asteroid (4147) Lennon four centuries after the report recommending "Mineral Exploration Desirable."

Federated Minerals sent up Dorm Room L (for Lennon), a module about twice as big as a city bus. It contained bunks with sleeping cushions for four, shower and bathroom with space for one at a time, a place to eat, and few other amenities. The first team, two HaChii, were to break ground and do preliminary assays. If the gemstone prospects looked good, more mining and blasting equipment would be supplied, and two more miners would join them.

The rotation of (4147) Lennon was adjusted to 21 hours, mid-way between the human home world's 24 and the HaChii home world's 18-hour days. This had worked well for other crews, and was one of the standard setups for these small mining outposts.

The first day, HaChii prospectors NaDii Ix ChiBii and MeBlii Ix BaShii headed out to gather samples. By the end of their 7-hour shift, they had assay samples which proved to contain diamonds, garnets, and a few other gem stones. The industrial-and-gem grade diamonds found in the assay were enough, alone, to justify staffing the outpost.

More significant mining equipment arrived over the next few weeks, and at the end of the month, two more miners, Greg Firestone and Rob Harker, joined the crew. Greg had worked asteroids for five years, Rob for twenty.

Every day, there was one seven-hour shift where all four miners worked together, then two other shifts where two miners worked and the other two had time to sleep. Usually, whatever team was outside working consisted of one human and one HaChii. There were scheduled days off, of course, but not much to do in what was essentially a slightly oversized camper. And the mining teams' contracts were for a full year before any 'shore leave' or off-asteroid holiday time was scheduled.

Federated Minerals had learned over the years, that the four-person mining setup suffered from both isolation and at the same time, lack of privacy. Human miners were almost exclusively male, while the HaChii teams, there being an even greater difference in size and strength between the two HaChii genders, were always female. That left the miners with very little outlet for certain needs. Federated Minerals had also learned to implement a policy that "looked the other way" if one of the miners asked for an hour or two off alone, during a regular four-person shift. Requests of this nature were expected at least once a week, and it was actually institutionalized, to the extent that employees who didn't ask for a break every few days were often asked if everything was OK, and a checkup ordered if the situation persisted.

CHAPTER 1 -- Low Batteries

One morning in month seven, Gregory and MeBlii were in the pressurized control cabin of the grab crane, using its drill to make holes for the blasting charges, while grappled to the rock face Gregory had dubbed "Lucy." Every surface was a "rock face," because with less than a thousandth of a 'G' of gravity, it would take about 10 seconds just to find out which way was down if you dropped something. So they followed precautions and procedures as though they were in zero gravity or working on a sheer cliff. Most of the time it was safest to think that way.

"You humans love to name things." MeBlii said. "But sometimes you choose names that make no sense. For instance, you named this rock face 'Lucy'--that's a name for a human female. Was she a girlfriend of yours?" she asked.

"Not at all." Gregory answered with a twinkle in his eye. "She lived almost five hundred years ago."

"Old, for a girlfriend." MeBlii quipped. HaChii life span was about the same as human, so Gregory knew she wasn't being serious.

"If she was anybody's girlfriend, she was Julian Lennon's." he explained.

"The guy this piece of rock is named after?" MeBlii inquired.

"His son." Gregory replied, "John Lennon wrote a song about her--*Lucy in the Sky with Diamonds,* when his son brought home a picture from school."

"So we're on John Lennon's asteroid, mining diamonds——" she paused for a beat. "Oh——you're awful! Do you mean to tell me that this place where we're mining is 'Lucy'——in the sky——with diamonds? *Groan* "

HaChii physiology meant she couldn't really groan, but she knew Terran English and expressions well enough to say the word——

"I'm not the first person to name a discovery 'Lucy.'" he said, apologetically. "There was an ancient hominid fossil."

"Named after the song?" she asked. "Yeah——Really!" he added.

"Did humans know there were diamonds here when they named it John Lennon?"

"No. *You* discovered that--five hundred years *later*. Funny, right?"

"You humans have a weird sense of humor. But then, I already knew that."

Just then, one of the hydraulic hoses in the cabin sprang a leak, spraying Gregory with black oil. MeBlii quickly clamped a patch around the hose and shut off pressure. "You OK?" she asked.

Gregory was coughing, spitting black out of his mouth, and rubbing oil out of his eyes. "Can't s-see——" he spluttered.

"Quick! Get back to the dorm!" MeBlii ordered. "Wash that stuff out of your eyes in the shower. I'll shut things down here and replace the hose. Get out! Clean up! Hurry!"

Gregory suited up with some help from MeBlii, and stumbled out the airlock door. *I hope he's OK to make it to the dorm. He's a mess but I don't think he's hurt,* MeBlii thought as she watched him go. Then she pulled out the tool kit and started cleaning up. She watched as Gregory hand-over-handed himself along the rope link pathway connecting the drilling rig to the dorm module. He seemed to be moving OK, but even if he had trouble seeing, he should be able to get there by touch——

At the other end of the asteroid, Rob and NaDii were in the comm cabin, where the q-entanglement communicator had failed. Without it, they had no contact with HQ at Vesta. Rob had found a broken connection to the B+ power bus. Apparently, siting the transceiver at the other end of the asteroid from where the blasting was going on wasn't good enough. The shaking had broken one of the power leads, anyway. The second had a crack in it, and looked like it was ready to go at any time.

"I'll need to reinforce both of these contacts by soldering down some small strips of copper, and I'll need to shock-mount the whole transceiver." Rob explained.

"Doesn't look like I can be much help." NaDii responded. HaChii tentacle-tips weren't much good with fine-detail surface-mount soldering techniques. Also, she had been distracted since she woke up this morning with--a certain condition she didn't want to talk to Rob about. Maybe this would be a good time to ask for an early break.

"Look, Rob," she began, "I haven't been feeling myself this morning, and I was wondering——"

"Sure." Rob answered. "There's not much you can do here, and it'll take me the rest of this shift, and then some, to shock-mount this puppy after I get the power connection rebuilt. Otherwise, this will be happening every time we blast. So--go back to the dorm. I'll see you this afternoon."

So NaDii suited up, climbed through the airlock, and headed across the terrain, pulling herself along the rope link connecting the comm cabin to the dorm module. At least, no one would be back to the dorm for the next three hours, she thought.

NaDii took a half hour to negotiate the rope link tied between poles across the landscape, before she got to Dorm Room L. *Every 12 weeks, HaChii females ovulate,* NaDii thought, *90% get cramps, 5% feel nothing at all--the rest get **incredibly** horny. **Me,** for instance.*

Well, she added to herself, *it's a good thing I've got a 'toy' back at the dorm that can help me out with that problem.*

She had told Rob that she wasn't feeling herself, and he let her go back to the dorm three hours early. Nobody else was due back off-shift for three more hours, so she had some time to herself.

The excuse wasn't, technically, a lie. Her ovipositor had been engorged and sticking out three centimeters since she woke up this morning. She wasn't feeling herself at the time she spoke to Rob, but now that she had gotten out of her coverall, she was planning to feel herself in the best way. Strapped to the sleep cushion, she reached for the

Brrop stick in the drawer by her bed. She rolled back her walking tentacles, grasped the stick in her right gripper, and inserted it into the gaping ovipositor, then began stroking the sensitive upper surface, and pushed the vibrate button. A feeble buzz was all that happened. "Ffurff!" she exclaimed. The nearest replacement batteries were more than 40 million clicks away. Well, if she worked at it, she would get where she wanted to, anyway; it was just going to take a lot longer——

She was already turning from her normal cyan to a light purple color when the door to the shower module popped open and the younger human male, Gregory, loosely wrapped in a towel, floated out, grasping the bedpost for support. He spotted her and froze. She froze, too, turning from purple to an embarrassed pink in a split-second.

"Are you doing what I--***think***--you're doing?" he said.

"Ummm." said NaDii, a human expression that seemed ideally suited for this situation.

Her tentacle had retracted and the Brrop stick was floating towards Gregory, who reached out for it, losing his grip on the towel. He kept his grip on the bedpost and captured the stick, turning it over and looking at it with interest. He thumbed the button and felt the feeble vibration.

"Looks like the batteries are running out." he said. "Yeah." NaDii agreed, "Now give it back."

"Our females use these too," he said. "They call them vibrators. But they're half again as big and long." The Brrop stick, she could see, only a little bit bigger and longer than Gregory's middle finger. *If this is true, that human middle-finger gesture would be a major understatement,* she thought.

"Pfuff Ka?" she said--a HaChii expression that meant, *"Is that so?"* but with overtones of *"C'mon! You can**not** be serious!"* He handed her back the Brrop stick and she stuck it to the grab strip on the bulkhead.

The reason for her skepticism was within easy grasp. She reached out the gripper that had held the Brrop stick and grasped the member that a 'vibrator' was supposed to replace.

"I don't believe you." she said, This," she continued, "is not even as long as a Brrop stick," she gave it a squeeze. "And not *nearly* as solid——"

But suddenly, it was bigger. She gave it another squeeze, and realized that as it was getting bigger, it was getting harder, too.

"How do you ***do*** that?" she asked. It wasn't at all how HaChii males worked. They were a lot different. A HaChii male had a -- what humans would call a bone -- in an organ that was basically the same size all the time.

"I -- don't think about it -- it just happens." he answered, lamely.

In addition to getting to pretty much the size he had described, what she was grasping was also ***hot***. Most of the time, one overlooked the fact about humans being warm-blooded, but this really made the difference obvious.

"I wonder——" she mused——

Gregory looked at her, thought a moment, and said, "You want to try?"

Considering what was already going on, she thought *this may be stupid,* but feigning a bravado she didn't really feel, she said, "Sure--why not?" and pulled Gregory away from the bedpost towards the sleeping cushion.

As he positioned himself above her, she wrapped her gripping arms around his shoulders, and he started to slide in, asking her "Where does it feel best to——?"

She was going to say slide up against the top, but he filled her so completely as he entered, that it didn't matter. She lunged up against him and he went in. Way in. When they started moving, he bottomed out. It felt like he was just scratching every itch she had ever had. He must be pushing against the end of her nerve cord. Then she stopped thinking and just moved. It just kept getting better and better for a timeless while——

Hot—— Why didn't anyone ever think of a ***heated*** Brrop stick? This is delicious——she thought. Then it became ***excruciatingly*** delicious.

The first convulsion spasmed her ovipositor. The next stroke convulsed her insides as well. The third--

Well, the third set off something else. She found herself flooded with a hot, wet sensation, deep inside, then she expelled his organ and another object out of her ovipositor in the biggest convulsion of all.

"I'm sorry." she said, an embarrassed pink again. And he said, "That's OK, I was pretty much finished anyway." Then she looked down at the bed. There was a slippery white egg, looking remarkably like a stubby bratwurst.

"That never happens when I masturbate." she said. "In fact, it never happens at all, unless the egg gets fertilized. And then, only after a couple of days." She picked up the egg and looked at it, puzzled. She stuck it up on the grab strip next to the Brrop stick.

"Don't worry." Gregory said. "Humans have DNA with four bases, and you HaChii have six. I'd be more likely to impregnate a tree by sticking it in a knothole, than fertilize a HaChii egg."

"I know that." She said. "But still, it was very odd. Also--by the way--it was very good. ***Thank you.*** I never thought being ***hot*** would make any difference, but that was about twice as fast as I ever——" she trailed off. She had probably said enough.

"You know," Gregory said. "You are probably about twenty degrees cooler than a human, but you made up for it with enthusiasm, and it didn't even—— matter——" and he ran out of breath. He had probably said enough, as well.

NaDii could see that Gregory was 'catching his breath,' as humans referred to oxygen debt. Bellows-breathers like humans were a bit of a puzzle to NaDii, but she had seen enough humans after hard exertion to know when he needed a few minutes to recover. "Gregory--after you catch your breath," she said, "would you like to do it again?"

"That could take a few minutes." Gregory said, "But OK. And call me Greg. I think we know each other well enough, now."

And a few minutes later, they did. It took Greg quite a bit longer this time, which was fine with NaDii. She didn't expel any more eggs, and was a light blue with oxygen debt herself when they were finally finished. Greg stuck an arm under the strap to hold himself in place, and his breathing slowed down, gradually, until he was breathing steadily and quietly. Her tentacles unwound and relaxed.

Probably asleep, NaDii thought, as she closed her eyes and fell asleep herself.

A while later, she was dreaming of repeating what she had just done, with every single human male she had ever known. This was a profoundly odd concept she would never have imagined, before today.

Suddenly, she was awakened by the clank of a hatch closing, and a loud squawk of outrage from just past the foot of the bed.

She blinked. There stood MeBlii, the other HaChii female, who must have just come in off-shift. She stared at the two of them, looked at the Brrop stick and egg on the grab strip, and her normal HaChii cyan color changed to a shade of chartreuse that was almost yellow. *Highly indignant,* NaDii thought.

"Eeeeww!" she said, a HaChii expression that meant "Eeeeww!"--

Her grey HaChii eyes bulged, pupils constricted. "You guys are ***disgusting!***" MeBlii shrieked, and she flounced off to her bunk, where she stripped off her coverall, put on pajamas, strapped-in, and turned her back to them.

Greg and NaDii looked at each other. She couldn't read human facial expressions terribly well, but his raised eyebrows must have mirrored what she felt. Both of them had turned bright pink. Somewhere in the back of NaDii's brain, she thought, *both pink--convergent evolution, how interesting*—— Then they hurriedly dressed.

CHAPTER 2 - In Business Together

Next day NaDii readied herself for the morning shift. While a few minutes were left, she started an inquiry on the net, searching the HaChii patent office to see if anyone held a patent on a heated Brrop stick. She had just clicked in the submission when MeBlii drifted past. She stopped and glowered at NaDii. "What have you got to say for yourself?" she asked.

"Well," NaDii said, "They always pair human males with HaChii females for mining teams. We are so much larger than our males, and human males are larger than most of their females, so mining is a business that throws us together. You don't think this is the first time this has happened, do you?"

MeBlii blanched. "Yes! I do! I never heard of anything like it, and I can think of at least *five* regulations in our contracts that expressly forbid--fraternization--on any level that *approaches* what we're talking about, here," she said, stridently.

NaDii's pupils swiveled from vertical to horizontal--the equivalent of a broad grin. "Fraternization? *That* wasn't the *least bit* fraternal, my dear."

MeBlii shuddered and turned bright yellow. "Eeeeww! And Ickkk, for good measure!" she added, slamming the airlock door for emphasis.

That gave NaDii another idea; she turned back to the console and added a second search--for "Brrop sticks longer than 4 parblecks." *For good measure, indeed,* she thought. She closed the screen and finished suiting up.

Rock face Lucy (*where did the humans get these names?* NaDii thought) was like a sheer cliff glittering with crystals. Some were red garnets, but among them were diamonds of various colors. In numerous star systems, HaChii-human teams worked rock faces like this with remarkable complementarity.

In addition to enhanced color vision sensitivity, HaChii brought advanced drilling equipment to their side of the team, while humans contributed efficient explosives plus outstanding electronic detonation technology. In the realm of dexterity, human hands and fingers (NaDii had never used computer keyboards; everything was done with joysticks) gave precision and nimbleness, while HaChii bonelessness, combined with great strength and traction, allowed their gripping tentacles to get into and pull apart things nothing with an internal skeleton could hope to negotiate.

MeBlii and NaDii were on opposite sides of a block that had been fractured by the explosive charges, but refused to move. With the two of them on either side, they could break loose the chunk of rock if it took anything less than five tons of force to budge.

"One, two, three--Now!" NaDii directed. Arms bulged, and a block the size of a bus *crunched*, and floated free. It appeared to be drifting slowly toward the loaders operated by the humans, but it would take as much force to stop it, as it had taken to break it free. "Coming at you, Greg!" NaDii shouted into her helmet mike.

"It's 'Greg' now, is it?" MeBlii sneered.

"Oh, please! Do I call you MeBlii or just May?" NaDii replied.

"May," she admitted, as the human-operated manipulator arm snared the block out of its trajectory and lowered it into an ore cart. "But--we've been working together longer."

"Seven months versus six?" NaDii answered.

"Fine," MeBlii huffed, "But I know that's all Ffurff anyway; you're turning bright pink!"

Damn HaChii skin, NaDii thought, *it's **just like a polygraph machine**——*

And so it went on for several hours, drilling, blasting, throwing, catching——fielding snide remarks with inadequate retorts——

The next shift would be MeBlii and Rob's. She could go back to Dorm Room L and check the communicator then.

Back at Dorm Room L, NaDii downloaded the patent search results, and found somebody else had already applied for a 5-parbleck design (moderate disappointment) but nobody had ever applied for a heated model (elated jubilation). She quickly began filling out an on-line application form.

"What's your body temperature, Greg?" she asked.

"37 Celsius." he answered, "Why do you ask?"

"Patent application." she answered, somewhat cryptically.

"Let me look." and Greg pulled himself over to the monitor. "Well, it sure looks like I'm out of business, as soon as *this* gets granted--and it will, I'm sure of it."

With sideways-pupils again, NaDii said, "No. You are definitely IN business; I've included your name on the application as co-inventor."

"Really?" Greg looked at the form, reading the HaChii characters he had overlooked before. "Gray-Go-Ree Fy-Ar-Stone. There I am. But what did *I* have to do with it?"

"Gave me the idea, silly." NaDii explained, "When would a HaChii ever run across a Brrop stick heated to 37 Celsius *normally*?"

"I guess that would be stretching *normal* pretty far!" Greg answered, as he worked his way through the remaining technical details of the application. "Well——umm——thanks," he said.

NaDii put a tentacle around his shoulders and said, "You know, it's not as though those are going to be rolling off the production line right now——" And Greg took the hint.

Afterwards, Greg looked up--with NaDii on top this time--and said, "Say, wasn't that egg thing on the wall white yesterday?"

Still slightly bluish, NaDii followed his gaze, turned white, and replied, "Oh, my——"

Greg turned white, too. "You don't mean——"

Both of us turned white--more convergent evolution, she thought, *maybe too much convergent evolution altogether.*

Just then, the hatch opened and the older human, Rob, floated in. "Hi, you two." he said cheerfully, looking at them.

"Eeep! You told him?!" NaDii asked, turning even paler than before.

"Well--yeah. It isn't every day someone runs out of batteries and uses me as a substitute, is it?" Greg explained. "Rob was a little startled at first. Then he thought about it and said it was bound to happen sooner or later."

"A *little* startled? Wait till we tell him about this." and NaDii gestured at the egg.

They took turns filling Rob in on the details. He already knew some of the story, but the egg had apparently been overlooked. He took down the mottled blue object and looked at it, open-mouthed, an expression of astonishment even NaDii could read. "How is that even possible?" he asked. Then his expression changed to one of concern. "Does it need to be in an incubator?"

The egg was moved to one of the drawers next to NaDii's sleep pad, cradled in a pillowcase. HaChii eggs didn't need to be warmed; the temperature in the Dorm was more than sufficient. But was that true if the DNA was part-human?

"I think we're going to need to call HQ." Rob said. "If it hatches--and it lives--" Rob argued, "it will have all kinds of implications. But I think you need medical advice if you want to get past the 'hatches and lives' part of the equation. There are both human and HaChii medical doctors up at HQ. Shouldn't we be getting them into the picture?"

"I'm not sure we can even tell May." NaDii responded.

And Greg shook his head in agreement. "I've gotten one of *those* looks from MeBlii, and even if I don't always grasp HaChii facial expressions, this one came through five by five. She's disgusted with both of us for what we did, and I'm afraid I wouldn't trust her alone with the egg, if she knew."

"Then you have to find some way to get it to HQ without tipping MeBlii off," Rob concluded, "so how do we do that?"

Greg caught the word *we* in that question, and said, "You shouldn't be involved, Rob. We're the ones that caused this problem——"

"Your problem is my problem, kids; don't you know that? We've got to figure out something that gets you up to medical on Vesta while I jolly MeBlii along with some story that has a plausible medical explanation." Rob furrowed his brow. "Now--where to start?"

CHAPTER 3 - Medical Emergency

And thus it was that two days later, Greg Firestone and NaDii Ix ChiiBii were operating one of the grab cranes that captured severed blocks of rock while Rob Harker and MeBlii Ix BaShii were operating the other. Explosive charges had been placed, and the grab-crane teams awaited detonation.

"Fire in the hole!" Rob cried, in the age-old warning. He pushed the button and a flash lit up the periphery around a rectangular block of facewall. The block defined by the flash slowly rose toward Rob and May's grab crane and May rotated the crane body attached to the ore carrier while Rob swung out the arm to intercept the chunk.

"Rock fragment impact! Loss of cabin pressure!" It was Greg's voice. "We have suit punctures!" was the call in NaDii's native language. "Patching cabin window puncture!" Greg's voice, but weaker.

Rob had just captured the rock slab. MeBlii keened. "They're hurt! What do we do?"

"Have you stabilized cabin pressure?" Rob called back to Greg and NaDii.

"Affirmative." NaDii's voice, "I am putting a tourniquet on Greg's right leg. Am trying to stop further blood loss."

"NaDii has a puncture in her back. It looks like it missed the dorsal nerve cord; there isn't much bleeding." Greg's voice.

"There wouldn't be," MeBlii whispered to Rob, in a worried voice. "HaChii skin is self-sealing, for small punctures. But she could be bleeding internally. An infection is possible."

"I've got the rock slab in the carrier." Rob said. "Can you shut down the crane while I go over? I can use their med scanner when I get there, if it isn't damaged by the rock fragments. I'll take over the first aid pack from here."

"Go! I'll shut things down here." MeBlii replied. "You can use the clamps, needles and sutures better than I can, anyway. Call me when you get over there. Good luck."

When Rob arrived, Greg and NaDii irised the airlock and let him in. A very workmanlike puncture in the left window panel was covered with a clear patch, and Greg's leg was wrapped in a piece of medkit bandage material. There were three patches on Greg's suit and two on NaDii's. Rob took out his utility knife and put a few realistic-looking, but functionally harmless, gouges in the control panel, and scattered some rock chips he took out of his pocket.

"All we need now is some blood." Rob said, as Greg grinned, and took what looked like a large hypodermic out of a pouch on his suit sleeve. It contained some two ounces of blood he had drawn from a vein the day before. "I'll spray some on the floor and let the rest drift around the cabin. It'll look like a lot more than it is."

They closed their helmets and Greg messed up the cabin floor and bulkheads enthusiastically. Finally, Rob lashed Greg and NaDii to stretcher frames and towed them out the airlock.

"I'm taking them in to the Vesta Infirmary in the runabout." he called back to MeBlii.

"They don't look too bad, but they'll need antibiotics, at the very least." he reported. He heard MeBlii make some incoherent sound in return, and made a big show of towing the stretcher frames to the runabout, pulling them in, and closing the hatch.

"See you in a few days," he called, as he fired up the thrusters.

MeBlii replied that she was sorry--sorry for a lot of things--and wished them good luck, mixed in with additional incoherent noises.

"Whew! We got away with that!" Rob said. "Next stop, Vesta Med." Greg and NaDii untied themselves from the frames and took off their helmets. Greg was grinning and NaDii had both pupils tilted as far sideways as they would go. She held up a box with the egg packed in cotton balls, taken out of Rob's first aid kit. The lid said "Bandages."

Two days later, at the half-way point, NaDii's communicator beeped. There was an incoming message from Placet, the HaChii home world. She read the screen and turned to Greg.

"My patent application has been granted!" she said. Her skin had paled down to a very pastel shade of cyan.

"And you're surprised?" Greg said, with a grin.

"What patent?" asked Rob, who was at the helm, as he turned around.

"It's not normal to even acknowledge receipt for a week or two. This is a HaChii bureaucracy we're dealing with, here." NaDii looked further down the message. "Oh! It has an industry sponsor! That makes a difference——"

"An industry sponsor?" said Greg. "How did anybody in industry find out about the patent application?"

"I suppose I *might* have told someone I know at the company that made my Brrop stick about the details of the patent application—— Wait! here's another message, from BrropCo——" She read for a few moments. Then she held out the message pad to Greg and pointed at the screen, making small, incoherent sounds.

Greg looked. "Rob, NaDii's--and my--patent application was for an oversized, heated vibrator running at my body temperature. She calls it a 'model 37'."

Rob grinned. "I wonder where she got *that* idea."

Greg continued, "It seems some of their employees built a prototype yesterday, and——This is a woman-owned company, right?"

NaDii was now shaking and making small, hysterical noises—— Greg took the message pad and continued his description to Rob.

"So--" Greg continued, "They tried out the prototype and were very pleased. Very, very pleased."

"I can imagine." Rob snickered.

"And then, they made another *twenty* prototypes."

NaDii was rolling on the cabin floor and pounding on it with one tentacle.

"And sent one to the Director of the HaChii Patent Office."

"Who is a HaChii female." Rob guessed astutely.

"And the Patent was granted the moment the Office opened this morning——"

"At the express order of the Director, no doubt."

"Right you are, Rob."

NaDii appeared to have passed out completely.

"I don't think you guys are going to be working for Federated Minerals much longer." Rob commented drily. "So where do I buy stock in BrropCo?"

"I'm sure NaDii knows somebody." Greg looked at NaDii lying on the floor. "But you may have to wait a little while to ask her, though."

The next day, NaDii received a contract from BrropCo, guaranteeing 10 percent royalties on every sale for the first 10,000 units, and 15 percent for all sales thereafter. It needed only her--and Greg's--electronic signatures.

Greg was asleep in the back section of the runabout. NaDii showed the message to Rob.

"How many females live on the HaChii home world?" Rob asked.

"About six billion." NaDii answered casually.

"And how many buy Brrop sticks?" He asked.

"Maybe one in twenty would admit it. Probably one in ten have them." she answered.

"And how many would replace theirs with this new model?" Rob was clicking at the communicator's keyboard rapidly. Then he handed the unit back.

"Pretty much all of them, once word gets out——I hope."

"I just bought 5,000 shares of BrropCo on the Interstellar Exchange."

"The Patent Office Director bought 80,000, Rob." NaDii noted, as she rolled through the financial reports on her communicator.

"Wow! Get 'em while they're hot!" Rob said. Then he grinned at his own *double entendre*. "So--Do we wake up Greg and tell him?"

"Let *me* do it, Rob--and give me a little time——"

Approaching Vesta: Vesta control had already received a report from MeBlii, that miners with injuries were arriving, and asked if the runabout needed escort to the surface. "Probably not," Rob replied at the helm, "but there are both human and HaChii patients. Could we be met by doctors from both species?"

"Will comply. Come in on landing pad 5. Vesta control out."

Rob began to initiate the docking procedure.

CHAPTER 4 - Doctor, Doctor, Give me the News

Day One:

Rob re-arranged the bandages on Greg and NaDii, and helped them into the wheelchairs the two orderlies had brought to the ship. NaDii carried the "Bandages" box on her lap. They were wheeled into an emergency room cubicle, helped up onto two beds, and the orderlies left. Rob stayed in the room with the two of them, and they waited for the doctors.

The human doctor, in green scrubs, arrived first. Rob looked up at the tall, thin, olive-skinned man whose name badge said **Dr. Subramanian O'Reilly**.

"Can I talk to you in confidence about these two patients?" he asked.

"Of course." the doctor replied in a calm, cultured tone.

"They're not really injured, but they have a medical problem that may be——very sensitive." He went over and took the "Bandages" box from NaDii, opened it, and showed it to the doctor.

"I'm no expert; that looks like a fertilized HaChii egg, but isn't its color a bit off?" the doctor said. "What's the problem?"

"Well," Rob said, "the only possible way it could have gotten fertilized, is that fellow over there." and he pointed at Greg.

The doctor shook his head. "No. That's not possible." he said. And then, "How could you believe such a thing?"

"I've lived in close quarters with her," (pointing at NaDii) "on a mining base, where there cannot have been any contact with HaChii males for at least the last seven months."

"And she had sex with *him*?" the doctor pointed.

Greg nodded his head, "That's what she told me."

"Give me a little while to think about this." Dr. O'Reilly said, and walked into a corner with his brow furrowed.

At that moment, the HaChii doctor walked in; he was a very short HaChii, also in green scrubs. A male, Rob guessed.

"Dr. Fii." Doctor O'Reilly said to him. "I think you should talk to that young lady." He gestured at NaDii.

"Doctor Fii Iz ChaDii." The HaChii doctor introduced himself, bowing to Rob and Greg. "Excuse me for not speaking to you first. I will speak to the lady and return." He walked over to NaDii and began speaking to her in the HaChii language.

They spoke for a while. Rob noticed that the cyan skin visible outside Dr. Fii's scrubs was becoming a shade of gray he had never seen on a HaChii.

Doctor Fii came back to Doctor O'Reilly and said to him, "This has to be a hoax. It cannot be true."

Doctor O'Reilly replied. "I'm inclined to agree with you, but there *is* a way to be sure. Why don't we scan the DNA? What can it hurt to be sure?"

"But it's ridiculous. There is no way the two forms of DNA are compatible. Fertilization processes aren't even remotely similar at the cellular level."

"Dr. Fii--How fast do the cells divide if it's a pure HaChii embryo?"

"If the egg was fertilized eight days ago, there would have been about twelve cell divisions for HaChii DNA, and there should be about 4,000 cells. If it's human DNA, the rate is slower, around eight divisions, and there would be about 300 cells. Even without looking at the DNA, we should be able to determine that." Doctor Fii answered. "Let's do an ultrasound cell count. It's non-invasive and won't harm the embryo. I don't want to take any DNA samples unless the count is lower than —— let's say 3,000 cells."

"OK. But we've got to get consent forms signed for both ultrasound and DNA."

"By both of them, Dr. O'Reilly?"

"I think we better. Just in case."

"How ridiculous! But OK. It's not like that's proof of paternity."

They stopped consulting and called the nursing desk. The nurse arrived with a datapad and a stylus.

"We want to have you sign here." Dr. Fii said to NaDii. She read and signed.

"Now you, Mr. Firestone." and Dr. Fii handed the datapad over to Greg with a slight shudder.

"Are you OK, Doctor?" Greg said, solicitously, as he signed. Dr. O'Reilly took the form and the egg with him and left the room.

"Just having a little trouble handling the whole idea." Dr. Fii replied.

"I couldn't help noticing you're Doctor Fii Iz ChaDii, not Ix ChaDii. You're a male, aren't you?"

"Yes. Couldn't you tell?" he looked down at his scrubs. "Well, maybe not. You *are* a human after all. But yes; this bothers me. A lot. For several reasons."

"Well, I hope we're wrong, and I just have some drastic misunderstanding of HaChii physiology, and this is a big mistake."

Dr. Fii was still very gray. "I hope so, too. It would be very, very complicated if you're not."

Dr. O'Reilly came back. "2,300." he said simply.

Dr. Fii turned white, and staggered against Rob, who held him up.

Greg looked about the same, but at least he was already sitting down.

Dr. Fii recovered somewhat. "Are you doing the DNA test now?"

"Oh, yes. It should be ready in a few minutes. If it's——uh——positive, I think we should put it in an incubator at some temperature between room temperature and human blood temperature." Dr. O'Reilly suggested.

A nurse came back carrying the "Bandages" box and a long strip of paper. Both doctors peered at the strip, following it down. Rob hurried over with two chairs; he didn't like the color of either doctor. They sat down, hard, and continued reading.

Greg and NaDii were looking over at each other. Rob knew that their wide-open eyes had the same significance in both physiologies. They were finally starting to believe it was really happening.

"Oh, Ffurff! 28 percent human DNA." Dr. Fii was the first to speak.

"Four-base DNA chromosomes amongst six-base DNA." Dr. O'Reilly said. "Is that even viable?"

"There have been more than 11 cell divisions." said Dr. Fii. "Q.E.D.--so far, so good?"

They looked at each other, and both seemed to become excited at the same moment. "We gotta write this up!" they both said in unison.

"We are going to be famous." Fii said to O'Reilly.

Then they both looked at Greg and NaDii. "No. ***They're*** going to be famous——" Dr. O'Reilly whispered.

Day Two:

"NaDii. I've got to learn something about being a HaChii father." Greg began, "Scratch that. I've got to learn *everything* about being a HaChii father."

"Well," NaDii started, "I was one of eight children. The oldest. So even if I was never a mother or a father, I took care of a lot of the younger kids. What do you want to know first?"

"I was an only child," Greg said, "so I've got nothing to go on. Although even if I had kids of my own, I don't think that would help me much. First thing I want to know: How long will it be before I'm a father?"

"Most eggs--in my family anyway--hatched in 3 or 4 Earth months. Maybe a little longer if there's human DNA, but it's going to be way small for a human baby, and I wouldn't guess more than 5 months, tops. About 200 HaChii days."

"Long for you; kinda rushed for me. Oh, Jeez, I gotta tell my Mom."

NaDii covered her eyes for a second. Then she said. "My parents. My brothers and sisters. They're——" she couldn't go on.

"We don't know if this is even going to work out——" Greg said.

"But I *want* it to work out." NaDii answered in a very small voice. "It's just——how do I explain?"

"My Mom is going to flip her wig." Greg said. "Your relatives, too?"

"We don't wear wigs, but if you mean, 'go out of their minds,' then yes." NaDii answered, "I think that's what's going to happen."

"We need to learn more. From the doctors." Greg said. Then he went looking for Doctor O'Reilly.

Everything had remained hush-hush and confidential, for about the first 20 hours. As the first doctors involved with the case, Fii and O'Reilly had to call in experts. The experts called in other experts. The chances of keeping a secret go down geometrically with the number of people who know it.

So it happened that in the middle of the second day, the news media arrived.

And so did somebody with an explanation.

A room full of reporters was interviewing Dr. O'Reilly and a HaChii doctor Greg had never seen before, when Gregory Firestone found him. Doctors O'Reilly, Fii, and the third person -- a HaChii female, it appeared--were all in white lab coats, rather than their usual green scrubs. The reporters all turned around and focused their cameras on Greg as he stepped in. He started to back out. *Oh, No!* was about as much as he could think as he turned to run.

"Come in, Greg. Come in." the reasonable, calm voice of Dr. O'Reilly said. It stopped him. "We've got someone here who has figured out something."

Against his better judgment, Greg returned. *At least Rob got out yesterday, when the getting was good,* he thought.

"Gregory Firestone, meet Dr. RuFii Ix ChaDii." O'Reilly said as he gestured Greg towards the new HaChii doctor.

"Ru——Fii?" Greg said. "As in 'Fii Iz ChaDii?'"

"Dr. Fii's sister." Dr. O'Reilly explained. Fii was standing right behind her. "She's an expert on HaChii reproduction and genetics."

"Oh. Pleased to meet you." She reached out a gripping tentacle. He grasped it gently, without shaking it, as NaDii had taught him.

"Hello, Brother," she replied, "I think I can tell you how this happened."

"How?" he said. "Well, I think I know *how* it happened——" he reddened, "But I suppose the question is: Why?"

Her pupils tilted slightly, in a shadow of that HaChii 'grin' he had come to know so well. "Did you know," she began, "when a HaChii female gets heat stroke--when her body temperature reaches dangerously high levels, sometimes she lays an egg that has started cell division without being fertilized?"

Something about this began to connect in Greg's brain. "How hot would her temperature have to be for this to happen?"

The news cameras were following them back and forth, like a ping-pong match.

"Oh, something extreme. Over 30 Celsius, I would think. But that usually kills a HaChii person." she answered.

"And if she lives and lays the egg, does the egg develop normally?" he asked.

"Oh, no. It is a haploid. It doesn't have all the chromosomes. The eggs never hatch." Dr. RuFii answered.

Greg had a feeling he was following a trail of crumbs, but decided to humor the doctor. "OK. What if the *egg itself* got heated. Would it still start to divide?"

Dr. RuFii's pupils swiveled all the way from vertical to horizontal. "Exactly. As long as it was in the last two hours of receptivity, just before the body starts to re-absorb it."

"So my--our--THE egg," he stammered, "is it one of these haploids, that will never hatch?"

"No. I mean yes. It probably WILL hatch. It seems that——*just* as it started to divide, and all its DNA unraveled, some *outside* DNA penetrated the egg, and got sort-of *tangled in* with the chromosomes that were unraveling. We think there was *just enough* of this *other DNA* that the embryo will probably develop. Although it may not be a normal HaChii——"

"And I'm going to be a father." he said.

"We think so--yes." and she continued to beam at him with her tilted gray eye-pupils.

And he began to grin, too.

Then Dr. RuFii turned to the press. "Did you get that? We think there is going to be a human-HaChii child hatched in about 5 Earth months, or 200 HaChii days!" Obviously, that announcement had been rehearsed, but Greg didn't care.

And the press members ran for the exits, each frantic to file the story before the others.

"Thank you, Dr. RuFii." Greg said to her, after they had left, and then again, "Thank you so much!"

She threw her gripping tentacles around him and hugged him. He hugged her back. "Congratulations!" she said. She had obviously studied human modes of expression.

She seems to like me, Greg thought. ***No sign of disgust at all—— how odd****.*

The rest of the day went by in a dazzle of press and euphoria. He managed to get the word to NaDii, despite the camera-and-mike-wielding mob in the room.

The press, ever fickle, eventually tired and went away.

Dr. Fii came into the room very timidly. Greg would have said "tiptoed in" except there were no toes involved. Greg and NaDii looked at him expectantly.

"What is it, doctor. Is there anything wrong?" NaDii asked.

"With the egg? No. But, Greg and NaDii, I've got to tell you something my sister didn't mention."

"What's that?" Greg recovered enough to ask first.

"Sometimes, those thermal-shock, haploid eggs *do* hatch," he said. "They are almost always retarded, and they don't live long. But sometimes they *do* hatch."

"How often is sometimes?" NaDii asked.

"Maybe once in 10,000 cases." Dr. Fii answered.

"Well, that's not very often." Greg said.

Then, NaDii and Greg looked at each other, his brown eyes and her gray ones (figuratively) picturing 600 million HaChii women using heated Brrop sticks.

"Uh, Oh."

CHAPTER 5 - Surgeon General's Warning

Day Three:

Vesta Infirmary had about as much transceiver equipment as any hospital that had to coordinate ambulances, emergency vehicles and the occasional private citizen bringing in a patient would suggest. NaDii and Dr. Fii had managed to get the use of one of the hospital's private three-way audiovisual channels with only a *slight* stretching of the rules. There was also a *slight* dent in the advance payment BrropCo had transferred into Greg and NaDii's bank accounts, but that was hardly enough to miss, and the infirmary--after evaluating the donation--was more than happy to give them twenty--even thirty--minutes' exclusive use of the comm center. The security level, consistent with transmission of medical data covered by the human HIPPAA protections, ensured that even the press would not overhear what was being discussed. After additional back-and-forth, in the middle of the third day at the Infirmary, Dr. Fii, Greg and NaDii made a secure call to the president of BrropCo, with RuFii Ix ChaDii in the third position as an interested party and medical consultant.

Two windows on the screen showed RuFii and a HaChii woman in a conservative purple pinstriped jumpsuit. NaDii addressed the businesswoman in HaChii: "Hi there FriiDa, you been busy?"

"Not too busy for an old college room-mate. Especially one who's going to make me rich." FriiDa replied.

"I have Dr. Fii Iz ChaDii and his sister RuFii on the line with us," NaDii continued, "along with my——mate——Mr. Gregory Firestone. Folks, this is FriiDa Ix KaaLo, President of BrropCo. You've probably guessed she was the one I copied the patent application to, right? FriiDa, we've been talking about something that might be a slight problem with our new product."

"Pfuff Ka?" the businesswoman said. "What could possibly be a problem with such a *wonderful* product?"

"Well," Dr. Fii began, "High temperatures affect germ cells in odd ways. If——ahhh..one uses the——er——product during just the right——or wrong——two hours, once every twelve weeks——" he seemed to be at a loss about how to continue.

His sister broke in, "You could possibly lay a self-fertilized egg."

FriiDa paled slightly. "Self-fertilized?"

"We call it a haploid." RuFii continued, "9,999 out of every 10,000 never hatch, but once in a while a short-lived child *does* hatch, one who has severe disabilities. They usually die within the first two weeks."

Taken aback, FriiDa thought a moment. "Is there anything we can do to prevent this?"

RuFii looked like she was thinking about an answer, but Greg broke in, speaking in his accented HaChii: "There is something my people do, if a product has some risk attached to it, but is also so useful that most of us would want to use it anyway, even despite the risk."

"That's a novel idea——acceptable risk——" FriiDa appeared interested. "What is this thing your people do?"

"It involves putting a label on the product with a warning, explaining what to do to avoid the risk, if that's possible," Greg explained.

"A warning? What kind of warning would make the risk any different?" FriiDa asked. "If something is risky, isn't it just as risky whether you warn people, or not?"

"Not really." Greg said. "For instance, we have a warning to human females that they should not drink beverages containing alcohol while they are pregnant. Ingesting small amounts of alcohol does not generally harm humans, but can harm the unborn child as it is developing inside the body."

"A good argument for letting the fetus develop outside the body," Dr. Fii interjected. "Not that humans have that choice."

"And not that HaChii have the other choice either," NaDii quipped.

"Back to the point, Mr. Firestone." FriiDa said, "Two questions occur to me. First: what would we have to tell women that would eliminate the risk. Second: Why should a customer trust any message from a company that--after all--is in business to sell the product?"

"I'd like to answer the first question," Dr. RuFii said. "The only time to avoid using the heated Brrop stick would be the second day after ovulation."

"Do HaChii women know when they're ovulating?" Greg whispered to NaDii. "Trust me, they do." NaDii whispered back. "Good" Greg whispered. "Not entirely." NaDii muttered.

"And then, I can answer the second question," Greg volunteered. "Our warning labels don't come from the company that makes the product. They are produced and certified by the Office of the 'Surgeon General' (for that phrase, Greg had to drop back into Terran English) of the United Nations organization. All the warning labels contain the seal of this 'Surgeon General.'"

"What is a 'Surgeon General' Mr. Firestone?" FriiDa inquired.

"A medical doctor. Usually one who is very highly regarded among human beings as being——umm——pretty smart——in all branches of health care. As long as people trust the 'Surgeon General,' they trust the message." Greg concluded.

FriiDa looked pensive. "When a danger warning has been added to something, hasn't that destroyed the market for the product?"

Greg thought. "You know, I can't think of a single case where it did. More often, sales actually go *up*. But that's for humans, I don't know how HaChii people would react to something that is a *little bit* dangerous."

NaDii interrupted. "Greg. When you get a chance, let me tell you about a HaChii activity that you humans call 'drag racing.'"

"This warning thing——it could be a stroke of marketing genius!" FriiDa exclaimed. "But the HaChii

Confederation doesn't have any such office as 'Surgeon General.' What do we do?"

"It would only have to be a highly respected medical doctor with a reputation in the area of——uh——sexual——" Dr. Fii stammered. "I nominate——my sister RuFii——as the obvious choice——to sponsor the warning label." he blurted out, and then turned very, very pink.

"That seems kind of nepotistic, to me." Greg whispered to NaDii "Does RuFii have any reputation with the general public?"

"Greg!" NaDii looked at him as if he had questioned the existence of gravity. "Haven't you ever heard of the net-cast show 'Good Sex with Dr. RuFii?'"

Blank stare.

More whispering. "No? Well--I guess not. You probably don't watch many HaChii net-casts anyway. Here's the deal--she has a viewership of over 18 *billion* on the 12 planets. Mostly *female*. BrropCo is one of her sponsors."

"Would you do this, RuFii?" FriiDa asked timidly.

"Would I!" RuFii exclaimed, "Have you ***tried*** one of those things? Oooo——"

Dr. Fii became a bright red and turned away from the audiovisual equipment.

FriiDa's pupils had rolled over into 'broad grin' mode.

FriiDa got one prototype. There were 20 other prototypes, Greg thought, *and* **now** *I know where* **one** *of the other ones went——* **No wonder** *Dr. RuFii likes me!*

"Mr. Firestone." FriiDa addressed him. "Can you give me your bank number? I'm not waiting. I'm sending you a bonus check right now——"

CHAPTER 6 - Meet the Folks

Day Four:

Greg's mother, Enya Firestone, NaDii's Mom and Dad, Chii Ix SiiFii and Bii Iz ChaaJii, plus six of her seven siblings, were arriving at Vestaport on the 100-meter space yacht *Good Vibrations*, guests of FriiDa Ix KaaLo, BrropCo owner and also the owner and pilot of the yacht.

That was fast, Greg thought. *It took us four days to get here from Lennon, and FriiDa's yacht gets from the HaChii homeworld to here in 5 hours. Must be nice to have money.*

Then he realized he *did* have money. And more to come.

Greg and NaDii awaited the party at the spaceport as they entered the small common area from the direction of Gate 3. Greg's mother moved over to the left side of the room and glowered at him and NaDii. NaDii's Mom and Dad and six HaChii youth of various genders, were on the right side. The parents were a mutt-'n-jeff combination of a large female and a small, but wiry male. Both of them were dressed modestly, had their gripping tentacles folded, and were only a shade more green than yellow. Four of the siblings were various shades of forest green and the two with folded limbs were a furious chartreuse, staring at Greg with undisguised loathing.

"I've seen you two on the news." Enya stated flatly.

"Hi Mom. Yeah," he tried to bluff his way through, "but you can never believe everything you see on the net."

"You." said Bii, "seduced my daughter?" Greg backed off a step, noticing that Bii wore a pocket protector full of pens, emblazoned with the logo of a well-known engineering society.

"Actually, Dad," NaDii ventured, "It was more my idea than his, really."

Wide eyes and pale gray coloring told Greg this was a surprise to Dad. He wasn't sure that his mother was buying the story either, from her appearance.

"You s-seduced my *son?*" Enya spluttered.

More like I ***used*** him, actually." NaDii stated, with a certain degree of bravado. "It was sort of a--more a matter of *convenience* than lust." she added, which didn't clarify anything.

Both of NaDii's parents were similar shades shade of blue-gray. Most of the siblings were, too.

"What does that color mean?" Greg whispered to NaDii. "I've never seen it before."

"Mortification." She answered. "I've shamed - is that the right word? - the family. They're embarrassed and humiliated by the way this reflects on my upbringing. But they're not indignant about you, anymore. You're off the hook."

Greg didn't think he was anything of the sort. But he had an idea that he might be able to appeal to a different side of NaDii's father.

"NaDii and I have just had a patent application granted," he told her father.

"Talk about changing the subject!" Enya exclaimed.

But it was working on Bii. "Is this true, NaDii?"

"Oh, yeah, Dad. Didn't FriiDa say anything about it?"

"FriiDa just gave us a really nice ride. I remember FriiDa from when you were in college, but I've never known much about FriiDa's business," Bii answered, "and she didn't say anything about it while she was piloting the ship. A patent, you say? Is it something FriiDa's company will be manufacturing? She seems to have the knack for making money, from what I can see."

Greg started to answer, but just then, NaDii's mom Chii spoke up for the first time. "Nevertheless, you are going to be parents. If you are responsible for the child, NaDii, then you have dragged Gregory into being a parent and his expenses are entirely due to your actions. Federated Minerals doesn't pay a lot of money. Even working together, can you support this child? From what I've heard, it may have special needs and may cost more than you can afford, just to support it."

"Don't worry about our supporting the child." Greg said. "We've signed a contract with FriiDa's company." and he held out the datapad for Chii to look at. Bii crowded in next to her.

Chii and Bii rolled through the lines. "Ten percent for the first 10,000 units; Fifteen percent for the rest. Projected sales for the first year——" and Chii turned white and dropped the datapad. *Uh, Oh. I know what that color means!* and Greg rushed to Chii's side just as she began to collapse to the floor. Realizing what was happening, Enya rushed in on the other side and together they helped to ease Chii to the floor. Bii had picked up the datapad and was staring at it transfixed, not noticing Chii's condition at all. "You're never going to have to work another day in your lives, are you?" Bii whispered to his daughter.

The siblings crowded in around their mother, concerned. Bii looked at them and said, "Look. It turns out you're not going to have to worry about needing to give money to your sister to help with her family. Quite the opposite——"

While Enya, who had picked up the datapad, and switched it from HaChii to Terran English, started to read it. "Go look after your Mother." NaDii said to Greg. "If she's anything like my Mom, I think she's going to need it."

And he walked her over to a chair, where Enya sat down and continued reading. In a few moments, she dropped the datapad with a clatter, looked up at Greg, and said, "Son. If this was a mistake, make the most of it!"

Chii seemed to be recovering, if a bit dazed. And Bii, who was obviously made of sterner stuff, even if he was half her size, walked over to Greg, held out a grasping tentacle, and as Greg took it, said "Mr. Firestone. If you ever want to change a subject like that again——go right ahead——"

There was still quite a bit of consternation. Greg caught one or another of NaDii's various siblings--they all seemed quite a bit younger than she was--looking askance at him. Greg's Mom looked at NaDii and the whole gaggle of her family members, and shuddered. She finally asked the question both families had probably been wondering about.

"So, what now? Are you going to live together? Who will bring up the child if you don't? Is it even possible to marry——one of——those?"

"I don't want to insult you humans," Chii broke in, "but I've been wondering the same thing. You have magistrates who perform bonding ceremonies, so do we, but I don't even know if any of them have any authority in this case. What authority do they have over humans, anyway? And there would probably be a public uproar if we tried to suggest a human bonding ceremony."

"Well, for now, we'll probably just live together and take care of the baby." NaDii said sensibly. "And let the rest sort itself out as time goes by."

Two big questions remained unspoken. NaDii's sister Brii asked the obvious one. "You know," she said, "you never told us what kind of invention you actually patented. What is it?"

NaDii took her sister a short distance away from the others and began whispering to her. ***Uh, Oh***. Greg thought for yet another time, prepared to see Brii turn white and collapse to the floor.

And at first it appeared that what he feared would happen, was happening. She collapsed. He started towards the two to see if help was needed.

But then he noticed she was rolling on the floor, making incoherent sounds, and pounding the carpet with a tentacle.

Oh, well--he had seen ***that*** reaction before, too——

And a bit later, Enya sidled up to NaDii, looked her up and down, and shook her head. "NaDii," she asked, "Do you love him?"

"I don't know." NaDii said miserably, "we're going to have a child together, and I never imagined having a child with——a human person, but it's going to need—— all our help."

"Well, then——" Enya asked with some concern, "——do you have *fun* with Greg?"

"Oh Furff, Yes, Mrs. Firestone!" she said. Then, thinking about who she was talking to, changed her statement to, "I mean, Oh Hell, Yes, Ma'am! I do!"

And remarkably, just at the same time, NaDii's father was asking Greg. "Do you love my daughter NaDii?" and Greg's answer was almost exactly what his mate had answered.

He said, "I don't know, sir. It's hard to say. Sometimes I can't tell what she wants--but then I don't know what human women want either. All I know is what I want *for* her."

"And what do you want *for* her?" Bii asked, curious.

"I want to take care of whatever she needs, so that she doesn't feel trapped or stuck. If that means being with me, I'll be very happy. If it means I take care of the baby so she can do something else, that's OK too. All I want to do is——to make sure that she is in control of her life. I never wanted to mess that up."

NaDii's Mom, Chii, who had been overhearing everything that was said, spoke quietly. "Gregory. I want to apologize for what I thought about you. At first I thought you were some kind of monster that had seduced——or even raped——my daughter. Then I thought——my daughter 'used' you——what your people call a 'one-night stand,' that the responsibility for the child was an unfair burden on you, and I was ashamed. But neither way did I suspect that you were a good enough 'person' to belong with my daughter, because you are so different. I was wrong. You *are* good enough for my daughter. You are *more* than good enough for my daughter. And you think you don't know what my daughter would want? You're wrong. What you want for her is *exactly* what she would want. And if that's not love, I don't know what it is——"

She 'walked' away, and Gregory watched her depart. "Son?"

Gregory had forgotten Bii was still there. He turned to look at him.

"The father of my grandchild is my son, even——even if he is a bonebag like you." Greg was wondering if he should be offended--but Bii was grinning at him with his eyes. "I'm proud of you, son. And I certainly hope you keep her. You're such odd creatures, I spent a lot of time thinking you weren't even persons, just a very bright sort of trained animal. But no--I can't imagine she would be better off with anyone else. I hope you stay together. not just for the baby--for her. There—— I never thought I'd say it——"

Chii approached Enya Firestone. Enya spotted the blue-green HaChii coming towards her, and recoiled slightly, but held her ground. Expecting vituperation, or at the very least a dressing-down, she braced herself.

"You have a winner, there." she heard Chii tell her. "Treasure him; he's amazing." And Chii gave her a hug. Astonished, Enya stood there with her mouth hanging open as Chii departed.

"My God, Greg." Enya asked her son shortly after, "What did you say to them?"

"I don't know, Ma. All I said was that I wanted to make sure NaDii was in control of her life. And that I would do the best I could for her and the baby to make sure that could happen."

She was silent for a few seconds. Tears silently ran down her cheeks. "In control of her life? That's all? That'll do, son. That'll do."

Moments later, each of NaDii's three brothers glided up to Greg, in turn, reached up and grasped his hand with a gripping tentacle, and gave his hand one shake--up and down. The girls hugged him. And the sister NaDii had been whispering with asked him *sotto voce*, "Are you really better than the stick thing, like NaDii says?"

"I certainly hope so," he answered, "or at least I hope *she* thinks so."

She left with grinning eyes.

CHAPTER 7 - Undermined

Denny Harris had begun his career as an asteroid miner when he came out of a year in the militia, and applied to Federated Minerals for a one-year hitch. Descended from a long line of West Virginia coal-mining people, he carried his Appalachian mountain background with him to his first job.

"Mah Daddy dun tol' me Ah'se got a mike mah own way fa ma sef." he said, when asked why he decided to apply for the Federated Minerals job.

"Ah'se got a be heppin' out, sen' some money home." he continued. "Mike big money inna mahnin bidnes. Better'n bein' a flahboy."

"What do you know about space flight and working in vacuum and microgravity?" he was asked.

"Ah tol ya. Ah's *bin* a flahboy. Ah's flone planes in tha Wes' Virginya Eer Nash'nl Gard." he answered. "Dun s'm *faincy* flahn. Mike lotta folks barf; no big deel ta me. Worn presha' soots, too, not much diffen' f'm spice soots, Ah rickon."

When asked about asteroid mining as a profession, he answered, "We's bin miners fa' hunnerds a years in ma fam'ly. It's in tha blood. Ah 'spect Ah be good ez innybody ilse."

"You'll be working with non-human crew. HaChii. You know about them?"

"Ah nose 'bout tha squids. Ah ain' got no bones ta pick with 'm. Do theer work, Ah do mahn, we git along fahn."

Mining was a dangerous job, and Federated was willing to accept quite a wide spectrum of types, as long as they were qualified. The recruiter worried a little bit about the tone of Denny's comments; it was not enough to disqualify him, but he added,

"OK. Just don't call them 'squids.' They don't like that much."

"Ah'll keep it in mind. Much obliged."

His first assignment was in the asteroid belt of HD82943, a system recently explored by HaChii probes. Asteroid (1931) DeVrii had been flagged for possible exotic metals, and prospectors had discovered a vein of zinc ore containing high concentrations of gallium.

Paired with Fred Gemsbok, BriiLaa Ix GiiDii and TuuRii Ix HaaBuu, Denny worked quietly for several months within the small group, somewhat of a loner even in close quarters. Off duty he seemed to confine his time to reading a Gideon Bible he had found in the chest of drawers by the bed. Apparently one of the earlier miners had picked it up in a hotel and left it in the Dorm Room module when he moved on. Denny appeared not to have any other off-duty interests. After a while, Fred began to notice Denny looking strangely at the HaChii workers, from time to time, but didn't think much of it. Denny never spoke much about it, but then, Denny never spoke much about anything.

One day, Fred and BriiLaa came in off-shift to find Denny engaged in a rather strenuous debate with TuuRii.

"Din' say ya gotta do nothin, jes' looka tha Good Book'!" Denny shouted.

He slapped his hand down on a book that rested lightly on chest of drawers by the bedstand. It bounced into the air and drifted across the room in the low gravity. Fred grabbed it as it floated by. It was Denny's Bible.

"Well I'm not interested in your Bible or reading it with you." TuuRii replied. "I've got better things to do than waste my time with your ridiculous Earth superstitions!"

TuuRii had turned quite red and had evidently been arguing with Denny about something for quite a while before the other two partners had come in.

"Ain no supastish'n!" Denny shot back. "Word a God!"

"Easy, guys." BriiLaa intervened. "What's the problem?"

"Denny wants me to read something called the *Book of Revelation*; he says it shows HaChii are some kind of creatures who prefigure the end of the world."

"Which world?" BriiLaa asked in a placating tone.

"Evverthin'!" Denny shouted. "World in tha Bible means all a Creation an' you HaChiis is the beast outa tha Revelation a Sain' John tha Divahn."

"They are not beasts, and you know that." Fred interposed. "They are people, maybe not like ourselves in every way, but certainly not beasts."

"They's opposed to God!" Denny shot back.

"Dennis. You know HaChii neither support nor oppose God." Fred tried to reason with him, "They simply don't have any worship practices at all."

"Matthew 12:30--If'n they ain' with God, they's agin' God!" Denny argued. "They won' read tha Bible." That seemed to settle it for him.

Fred and BriiLaa looked at each other for a moment, then shrugged, each in their own way.

Life returned to normal for a while. Denny continued to work with and back up both his human and HaChii partners in his day-to-day work. However, he became more distant with the HaChii; off-shift he simply wouldn't talk to either BriiLaa or TuuRii.

"Fred, wouldja ask TuuRii ta pass me tha salt?"

"She's right here, ask her yourself."

"Ah ain' fixin' ta talk ta her 'til she fess up Ah's right. Ah give 'er a Gideon Bible 'n she wouldn' even look at it."

"Jesus didn't come to her world, Denny. He was born a human and not a HaChii. Let it go."

Denny sulked, "They's heathens," he muttered under his breath.

And finally, the day came when, suited-up and on the job, Denny refused to help TuuRii with an electric jack-hammer she was using, when she asked him.

"I just need you to help hold this so I can use it to chop loose this block." she said.

Denny pretended he didn't hear her.

"You can hear me, Denny. Help me hold the jack-hammer."

No response. Finally, "You's a Heathen. I ***ain'*** gon' he'p you."

That was the final straw. TuuRii stuck the jackhammer up on a grab strip on the side of the crane, and walked back to where Fred and BriiLaa were working.

"I can't work with this guy. He's insane." she said simply. She explained in more detail, and Fred called HQ.

Denny was shipped off-site, back to the Federated Minerals main base on the dwarf planet GraaHii. Medical personnel offered to provide treatment, but Denny insisted there was nothing to treat. It was that stubborn Fred Gemsbok, who wouldn't listen to reason and back him up against HaChii heathenism, like he should, he complained.

Denny marched over to Human Resources, to complain of unfair treatment. He seemed startled when, instead of the staff there starting action against Fred Gemsbok, he was given a severance check and a ticket. The ticket directed him to the nearest starbase that could take him back home to Earth, namely, IffGraa Spaceport on the HaChii home world, Placet. Denny deposited his severance check into his credit account and packed his belongings for the trip to Placet.

A day later, standing in the crowd of passengers waiting to buy tickets at IffGraa, with his belongings in a bag in one hand and his credit card in the other, he felt a tug on the bag, and as he turned to look at the HaChii youth pulling on his bag, a second HaChii ripped the card out of his hand and ran.

Stranded. That was the moment the voices in his head began to talk to him.

You are in the belly of the Beast. You should have known this would happen. Get out of here! Find refuge! RUN!

He stumbled out into the sunlight with his bag clutched tightly, began wandering the streets of Placedon, and found a freeway overpass to sleep under when the darkness came and the temperature began to drop.

Days passed. Denny Harris despised the sight of every HaChii he could see, but, outside, they were the only people he could beg from, so he moved back into the spaceport. He took out his Bible and read it in the lobby. Mostly, he kept moving and slept in different parts of the spaceport every day.

Occasionally, he would do small odd jobs, especially for human passengers. In return, Denny would get coins for helping carry bags to and from the spaceport gates. He found himself cleaning up scattered food packaging and finding bits of uneaten meals that helped keep him going on days when cadging coins did not work terribly well. For a few days, he even had a job sweeping the floors around Gates 12 and 13, but that didn't last when his boss noticed he came to the job wearing the same clothes every day, and smelled like he had worn them for weeks, because, of course, he had.

One day muddled into the next. He lost track of time. The HaChii authorities, at least, didn't bother him, so life went on as it was. And then, one day, he realized that the human passenger whose bags he was carrying was Fred Gemsbok. Fred, as it happened, didn't recognize Denny Harris with his wild, untrimmed beard, hollow eyes and those thirty lost pounds. Gemsbok, however, sensed something about this bum who was assisting him, and shared the story of why he was leaving (1931) DeVrii with the scruffy vagrant who was helping him carry his bags.

"I was working a zinc and gallium strike in this system, here." Fred said, "The last of the ore vein played itself out. So, I'm on my way to the Sol system to work in *that* asteroid belt. But that's not all——"

Of course, Denny didn't ask about TuuRii or BriiLaa, but his ears pricked up when he heard what came next.

"Something happened to one of the mining teams in the Sol system." Fred whispered confidentially, "Looks like I'm replacing a human team member who got a HaChii woman knocked-up."

The voices in Denny's head, not very insistent of late, woke up and began to clamor more loudly, "Say again?" Harris said to Gemsbok.

"It's all over the news." Fred said, "Two miners at the Federated Minerals base on Vesta have an egg; looks like the human guy is the father and the HaChii is the mother. I'm headed to the Sol system to replace this guy."

It's a sign! all of Denny's voices screamed. Revelation 2. *These things saith the Son of God, who hath his eyes like unto a flame of fire ——thou sufferest that woman Jezebel, which calleth herself a prophetess, to teach and to seduce my servants to commit fornication—— And I gave her space to repent of her fornication; and she repented not—— And I will kill her children with death——*

Denny Harris dropped Fred's bags at the gate, and ran back to the nearest lounge, where there was a screen running a newsfeed continuously. He watched until the story was repeated, with mixed disbelief and awe. *These servants of the Devil were fornicating with the Sons of Man! Jezebel is a HaChii serpent and the Son of God will work through his servant, Denny Harris, to fight this evil.*

But Vesta Base was a long way away, and Denny had no way to buy a ride.

The Lord will provide. Denny thought. *If I can't get to Vesta, God will find a way to get Jezebel and her children to me here.*

And he went on with his life——such as it was.

CHAPTER 8 - On the Spot

Greg and NaDii traveled in disguise these days, even on Placet, the HaChii home world. A human-HaChii couple traveling anywhere attracted stares regardless, but their faces had been on the newsfeeds so often, that even the average HaChii on the street could recognize Greg, unfamiliar though they were with human appearance generally. The full beard Greg had grown in the past 18 weeks, plus shaving all the dark brown hair off his scalp, had altered his appearance enough for them to go out in public occasionally now.

This, however, had its drawbacks——

Bitter cold, stinging snow blew into Greg's face. For some reason, he had expected the HaChii home world to be tropical or at least temperate. NaDii and her people were not warm-blooded, but in whatever season this was, everyone went out wearing multi-layers of insulating, electrically-heated clothing, and looked like residents of Moscow in December. His eyebrows and beard were caking up with ice, melting water was running down into his eyes, his moustache was stiff with frost build-up from his breath and he dearly wished he hadn't shrugged off NaDii's suggestion that he take his warm, furry hat, as he walked NaDii towards the studio.

Once inside the dressing room, they shrugged out of the winter garb, NaDii took off the hat and sunglasses (in this weather, was that really camouflage?) and let the webfeed makeup people repair her appearance enough to go on camera looking like herself. Greg just dried himself off; he was here more for moral support than the interview.

He intended to stay in the wings, far, far in the background while the interview was going on.

The stage manager was warming up the audience for the opening scene; it was a big auditorium and there were at least a thousand people in the seats. Greg had seen this in webcast studios on Earth--probably another case of convergent evolution. Stage managers did the same things everywhere, whether they were human or not, it appeared.

This audience was a little different from others he had seen in the last few weeks; although there were few humans residing on Placet, four human females had managed to get tickets, and they were sitting together in the front row on stage left. He had never seen humans in a HaChii audience for this program before, but they seemed to be doing OK. He wondered what non-HaChii could get out of 'Good Sex with Dr. RuFii,' but figured it must be an 'outing,' maybe just for the novelty of the thing——

"——And let's hear it for——DR RUFII!" the manager thundered. From the stage right wings, RuFii walked out in her white lab coat, to uproarious audience cheering, waving a tentacle at Greg as she walked by.

"Hello, everyone," she began, "today we've got a **really big show**."

Even in HaChii, it sounded like a good opening line to Greg. She had used it at the start of every show he had brought NaDii to, and he mused, idly, that at some time in past history, it might have been the tagline of some other performer; he just didn't know who or when. Regardless, it worked for Dr. RuFii's audience really well. They all cheered.

"Today's guest," she continued, "is the inventor of good old number 37, and an adventurer in uncharted sexual territory, as we all know. Let's hear it for NaDii Ix ChiiBii!" Huge response from the audience. Amidst the hundreds of HaChii females, there were even a couple of HaChii males, apparently as much fans as their female counterparts. That was unusual too, Greg thought.

NaDii strolled out casually from stage left as though she had done this a hundred times before. Actually, Greg thought, that might almost be true. Greg had lost count over the weeks, but the number of appearances had to be in the dozens, at least. It was inevitable, given the public interest, that there would be invitations, as well as reporters just jumping in front of you on the street, but it was also good for business. And in the business they shared with FriiDa and her company, business had been very good, as Greg's bank account balance showed him every day.

"Hi, Dr. RuFii," NaDii greeted the host. They had become well acquainted over the past few months. "What would you like to talk about today?"

Suddenly, Greg found himself the center of attention from at least three of the makeup people, who were tidying up his appearance, powdering his face, and sliding a wig onto his carefully shaven pate. "Hey!" he reacted, a term which meant nothing in HaChii and bounced off the backstage crew with no effect. One held up a mirror as another fussed with the wig. *Remarkable,* Greg thought, *it actually looks like my regular hair——* ***used*** *to*——he thought wistfully. *Now why are they doing this to me?*

"You *and* Greg," RuFii picked up without missing a beat, "are the topic today."

NaDii appeared nonplussed. Greg wasn't part of the topic she expected.

The stagehands pushed Greg onto the stage, and he figured he had to go along with it, so he continued walking onstage until he was standing next to NaDii. Unlike appearances he had made on Earth, no chairs, tables or other stage furniture was present on RuFii's set, only a backdrop with the show's name.

"Well guys," RuFii continued as though she hadn't sandbagged them completely and they knew exactly what was coming, "are you having Good Sex?" Perfunctory audience reaction followed the oft-heard tagline.

"Ummm——I think so, yeah." Greg said noncommittally.

"Fabulous, as always!" NaDii responded with her characteristic bravado, "Why do you ask?"

"Greg!—— Greg!—— Greg!" the human girls on the front row began to chant. Now he knew what they were there for! And Greg blushed pink.

"Today's question," RuFii replied, "Was——I'm wondering if you've told us everything about you two." the doctor continued, "I've wondered whether——and in what way——Greg used those 'hands' (she used the Terran English word for them) of his——"

At this point the audience had become silent and most of them had acquired a pale orange hue (intense curiosity, Greg had learned from his interactions with NaDii's family).

NaDii reddened slightly. "My, my, the things you ask about—— Well, yes, he uses those, and there are—— other sources of pleasure, as well."

" Show the audience your 'hands' Greg. The humans also have an interesting organ called a 'tongue,'" Dr. RuFii explained to her audience, "as well as those 'hands'. " she continued. He turned from pink to red, more embarrassed at showing his hands than he ever had been in his life, and held them up.

A light began to dawn in NaDii's mind. "Aha," she said, "Have you been doing some——*research*——Dr RuFii?" she inquired, and this time it was RuFii's turn to flush bright pink.

"Hey! Look at that! I've actually managed to make Dr. RuFii blush!" NaDii exclaimed to the audience. For once, the doctor was speechless. The audience was not. They were pounding the arms of their chairs with their tentacles and making those hysterical noises Greg recognized as excessive HaChii mirth.

"Wow! That's a first——" he said. Greg, for once, had something to grin about. "Who's the lucky guy?" he asked. RuFii reddened even more.

"N-no. I mean—— OK, yes—— I-I-I—— I mean—— There's a human doctor I've been working with on your case——"

"Doctor O'Reilly?" NaDii shot back. "***Not*** Dr. O'Reilly?! Oh, My!"

RuFii only made an odd strangled noise and didn't reply.

"Well," Greg said, astonished, "and I always had the impression that he was a straight-laced sort of guy. Go figure!" Then he realized his remark had been in Terran English, so he translated it into his accented HaChii, groping for a phrase that denoted 'straight-laced,' and NaDii suggested the word for "timid--with overtones of prudishness."

"Obviously not," NaDii filled in. What had started out as Dr. RuFii's interview of NaDii had gotten completely out of hand, and NaDii took the initiative, gleeful at the opportunity to put RuFii on the spot for a change.

"So what was that like? I can't imagine that 'timid' (she used the HaChii word she had chosen for 'straight-laced' in an aside to the audience) had anything to do with it. Not if *you* were involved, RuFii——" The audience was eating it up, cheering her along.

Dr. RuFii managed to stammer a few words, "I-I-I——He wasn't 't-t-timid' at-at-at all!" she managed. More tentacle-pounding.

"Good to hear that Dr. RuFii knows the scientific method--confirm the other guy's experimental results--And——Always good to hear our Earth counterparts are willing to give a hand to the HaChii research community." Greg quipped..

RuFii was as wide-eyed as a Thorb caught in the headlights. Then she got the double meaning of 'give a hand'--only two beats behind her audience. Her eyes glazed over for a second. "I've got to learn how to use your Earth sense of humor." she whispered back to him. "It's ***killer*** with the audiences here."

Greg gestured at the audience, "MeBlii says my Earth sense of humor is weird. But you guys seem to get it anyway. I rest my case——"

The girls in the front row cheered. The rest waved gripping arms in the air.

RuFii recovered her composure for a minute, then spoke up, finally back at full voice. "So--Greg and NaDii, here, *confirm* (she winked at Greg) that there's more to human-HaChii--sexuality, than old number 37 would imply."

The stage manager signaled Dr. Rufii. Time to break for a message. "Back in a few——" she told her viewers, and the lights on the cameras went off.

RuFii signaled chagrin to Greg and NaDii with a shift from light pink to a buff-tan skin color. "Ffurff!" she said, "I thought I was going to put *you guys* on the spot, and have a little fun, but you were a million teka-parblecks ahead of me——"

Greg gave RuFii a grin. "Congratulations! And welcome to the club!"

The stage manager came at a trot, whispered something to RuFii, and departed stage left.

"Guys," she said, suddenly serious. "It looks like we'll have to cut this short. DaaNii--that's the stage manager--says he just got a message from my brother that the egg is starting to hatch. It usually takes six to eight hours, so you can get back to the Sol system on FriiDa's space yacht just in time, if you hurry. She's waiting in the SmallBall stadium next door. Go! Good Luck! Name it after me if it's a girl!" And off they went.

CHAPTER 9 - Enter Laughing

NaDii and Greg arrived at Vesta Infirmary about four-and-a-half hours later. FriiDa had not spared the trac drive. Of course, with ultrasound, everyone knew generally how the baby was going to look. As Greg and NaDii bent over the incubator, they saw cracks in the egg and a couple of chips on the bedding about fingernail size. Still, it was exciting to see the little blue hand reach out of the hole, grab an edge, and break another piece of shell off. Gradually, gradually, the baby enlarged the opening, first with one hand, and then with two at a time, finally levering himself (sorry, RuFii——can't name it after you) out of the opening, as the egg toppled over.

His face looked pure HaChii, except the brown eyes. The hands and forearms seemed to have a cartilage framework, and worked like human hands although the upper arms still seemed to have the boneless flexibility of HaChii tentacles. With his head, arms and chest out of the eggshell, he was getting more air and started to green up toward a normal HaChii color. He reached up his arms and gave a cry, flopping out of the egg as he reached towards NaDii.

"Can I pick him up?" She asked Dr. Fii.

"Sure. But keep him in the blankets. His body temperature's higher than yours or mine, and the room is pretty cold compared to the incubator. His temperature seems to stay regulated at a degree either side of 30 Celsius most of the time," Dr Fii said for Greg's benefit, "so that's where we've kept the incubator."

NaDii held the baby wrapped in a blanket the size of a large handkerchief. Like most HaChii babies, he weighed about three ounces at hatching. Experts had already synthesized a mix of HaChii formula and human breast milk they thought would be best for putting on weight. A HaChii nurse handed NaDii a pre-warmed bottle and she began to feed the baby.

Dr. O'Reilly stepped in. "Congratulations," he greeted them. Greg and NaDii looked at each other, and Greg broke into giggles. NaDii shivered helplessly and made small noises.

"Did I say something funny?" O'Reilly asked quizzically.

The nurse cracked up and leaned on Greg, trying to regain control of herself without success. "You weren't watching RuFii's webcast this morning, were you?" Greg said, pulling himself together. "But *she* did," he said, pointing at the nurse, who, by this time, had collapsed onto the floor.

Dr. Fii--who must *also* have seen the webcast, turned gray-blue and edged away from O'Reilly. O'Reilly turned slightly gray himself. "RuFii has been talking, hasn't she?" Dr. O'Reilly said to Greg.

"And you're surprised?"

Little Robert--'Rob' for short--put on weight a little more slowly than a HaChii baby would, but that was still phenomenally faster than a human. Having leased a house on Placet, NaDii and Greg brought the baby back to her home city, Placedon, five weeks after hatching. 'Rob' had reached five pounds--and at that weight--almost birth weight for a human baby--the doctors at Vesta Infirmary said they thought it was OK to go. Greg and NaDii had been getting by without Federated Minerals' health coverage (Both offered their resignations from Federated when it was clear their royalty checks would be more than Federated could ever offer them). Although their medical bills were 'out of pocket' while the infirmary team kept the egg--and the baby--under watch, their pockets were fairly deep, so they didn't really mind. Still, they were glad to be able to go home at the end of the five weeks.

By eight weeks, the baby weighed eight pounds, about like a human newborn. Greg tended to think of 'Rob' as though he *were* a newborn, until one morning that week, when NaDii picked him up to change a diaper, cooing to him that "Mommy loves Robbie." When he cooed back "Mommy. Love Mommy." and hugged her gripping arm with those hot little hands.

Greg almost dropped his coffee.

"Were those his first words?" Greg asked, astonished.

"Uh huh, and his first sentence as well." NaDii beamed, eyes akimbo.

"But——when do HaChii children *usually* start talking?" he asked.

"A little over one year of age," NaDii answered, "but that's a Placet year, about 493 Placet days."

Greg did a little mental math. Three hundred seventy some Earth days.

"Less than thirteen months, Earth reckoning," he said, "so Robbie's about eleven months early for talking?"

"But normal for a human, right?" Na Dii guessed.

"No. Humans develop at about the same rate as HaChii," Greg replied, "so we're in completely uncharted territory."

"Again?" Na Dii added.

"Again." Greg admitted.

CHAPTER 10 - Shore Leave

Four weeks after Robbie started talking, a knock on the door was answered by the house AI. Greg and NaDii had programmed it to let in a limited number of people, and these were not among the ones in its memory. The house beeped NaDii's message pad and showed her a picture of the two people at the door.

NaDii, feeding the baby, gave an inarticulate shriek when she saw the picture, and hollered for Greg. "Go get the door! Right away!"

Greg hurried to comply. He didn't know who was out there, but from NaDii's tone, he'd better not hang around asking for details. Opening the door, he found himself face-to-face with Rob and MeBlii. There they stood, holding arms full of gifts, and all Greg could do was gape. NaDii walked up behind him with the baby gripped tightly in one arm.

"Well? You going to invite us in, or do we have to set up camp out here?" Rob quipped.

Ushered in to the modest living room, MeBlii set her ribbon-wrapped packages on the table while Rob plunked his boxes on the floor. NaDii helped them both take off their coats, which she carried back to a bedroom. Little Rob, having been set on the floor, crawled over to one of the more brightly-colored of big Rob's boxes, and began to undo the ribbon.

"Wow! It's great to see you guys," Greg exclaimed. "I didn't know if I'd ever see you again."

"It was late; we had to break in a new crew, but we finally got shore leave last week," MeBlii explained, "and the Company decided we had earned an extra couple weeks of paid vacation, plus a bonus. Rob decided to spend it here, and invited me along."

"Rob! NaDii called as she walked in. Rob Harker turned toward her, and started to answer; at the same moment, the baby answered, "Yes, Mommy?"

MeBlii and Rob stared at the baby with undisguised astonishment. He had untied the ribbon, opened the box, and was holding up a pretty pink baby blanket that someone had knitted. "This for me, Mommy?" he asked innocently.

"I named him after you." Greg said to Rob. I don't know if he would be around without your help.

"O boy. We gotta talk," Rob said to Greg.

It turned out that when Rob had gotten back to (4147) Lennon, MeBlii had read him the riot act. She had seen the newsfeeds, and had been building up a head of steam for two days by the time Rob arrived.

He eventually smoothed things out with MeBlii and got her calmed down enough to start thinking about what was going to happen with the other half of their team. She didn't understand at first why they weren't coming back, egg or no egg, until he showed her the patent contract NaDii had let him copy from her message pad. Like Greg in an earlier situation, he had arranged the data to omit the nature of the product; only its patent number and the terms of the royalty agreement were there--along with projected sales.

Once Rob had convinced MeBlii that their partners weren't coming back, they started the procedures to get Federated to send some new workers to get the team back up to full strength. MeBlii was still stewing about the extra work, and the deception that Rob, Greg and NaDii had pulled on her. But she also remembered how bad she felt when she thought NaDii and Greg were hurt, and resolved that if she ever saw them again, she would forgive them.

The Company, having seen the newsfeeds themselves, agreed that the situation was unique. Greg and NaDii couldn't come back and keep working with a baby, and they had received resignations from both of them for reasons they didn't quite understand, but that clearly warranted sending new workers. However--they told MeBlii as the senior person present--the new workers weren't going to be able to hit the ground running and would need a certain amount of break-in and training. Everybody's contracts were extended an additional month. Two months' additional pay as bonus sweetened the deal, so MeBlii and Rob agreed to it.

And so, Fred Gemsbok and GiiDii Ix ChaaNii joined them at (4147) Lennon, some ten days after the news broke. Rob and MeBlii were then too busy for the next two weeks to get back in touch with Greg and NaDii, except for the occasional eMail, so their appearance on the doorstep had been a complete surprise.

"There is also the little factor that space-fare from the Sol System to Placet is more than your year's salary." NaDii pointed out to Rob. "How could you two afford to get here?"

Rob smiled. "You know those 5,000 shares of BrropCo I bought on the way out to Vesta? I sold 200 of them last week."

"Was that enough?" Greg asked. Rob looked askance at him and smirked.

Little Rob crawled over and listened to the story, still hugging the pink knit blanket.

"That looks hand-made." Greg remarked.

"That's because I made it with my hands." Rob answered. "MeBlii showed me how to knit when she was doing the blue one (he pointed to a box on the table) in *that* box. Neither of us knew whether it would be a boy or a girl."

"He finished it first." MeBlii added. "Human fingers knit *really fast."*

"You'd think we invented the stuff." Rob quipped.

Little Robbie crawled over to Big Rob, and looked up at him. "You Rob too?" he asked. When Rob answered in the affirmative, Robbie replied that Mommy and Daddy had told him there was a friend he was named after, and he was happy to meet the other Rob——

MeBlii was simply boggled. Rob seemed to take it in stride.

"And--they were worried about *developmental disabilities*?" Rob asked Greg.

"Obviously, not a problem," Greg replied, "but we're keeping it hush-hush for now. You can see why."

"I'll say."

NaDii and MeBlii were whispering in the corner, while Rob and Greg sat by little Robbie and watched him open presents.

"What scares me is the hate mail." NaDii said.

"I expected you might get some; I admit *my* reactions were--not very mature--myself," MeBlii said, "and I didn't even know about the baby at the time."

"I don't expect people to understand." NaDii replied. "There was no way I expected to become a parent. It wasn't even remotely possible, I thought. Now there are people who think 'monster' is too kind a word for Robbie, and I'm worried. Especially by the death threats."

One of the network photographers--what Greg called 'paparazzi'--had managed to get pictures with a long telephoto lens. Rob and NaDii had tried to stay in the house and out of sight, living a hermit's life for the first months after bringing the baby home. They had discreetly engaged the services of a security firm to establish a perimeter to try to keep news-hawks at a distance, but one day four weeks ago, NaDii and Robbie were just too close to a window. Polarizing filters and image processing beat security guards and intruder surveillance computers for privacy invasion. The next day, the more lurid HaChii newsfeeds posted the photos with headlines NaDii didn't even want to think about. The human media were no better.

"You can't stop people from being idiots." MeBlii said. "It took me a while to realize ***I*** was one. My fiancée had a long talk with me by q-link a couple of days after

Rob got back. Rob——was——worried about me. I was already furious at you for doing ——*that*—— with a human. And the newsfeeds about the egg were the last straw. Well, the last straw was really when I found out your medical emergency was a ruse to get out with the egg. He called his friend, ChuuRi, and told him about my rant. Chuu was able to open my eyes and help me see everything differently. Chuu told me how you guys and Rob were afraid I would destroy the egg if I knew. Rob might have been right, I wasn't thinking straight at all." MeBlii concluded, adding, "I'm so ashamed."

NaDii answered, "May, don't worry about that. I understand how you felt and I would agree with you about me being stupid, but if I hadn't found out how nice a person Greg is my life would be——Wait!——Did you say fiancée?"

"Oh——I forgot," MeBlii said, embarrassed, "part of the reason Rob cashed in his stocks is so I could get back here to pick up ChuuRii. Then we're going to Earth to get married. Rob's going to be Best Man at our wedding, and we wanted you to be Matron of Honor, and Greg part of the groom's party. Chuu has no brothers or sisters. Neither do I——"

"What's a Best Man and a Matron of Honor?" NaDii asked.

"Human wedding tradition. They stand alongside the couple when they are taking their vows. Sometimes the Best Man helps out in other ways, like handing the groom a ring. I don't know all the details. It was my Chuuie's idea. He said talking to Rob was why he called me. Rob was worried, and thought about Chuu. He introduced us when we went out on a double date with him and Sally. Chuu is that big guy who was the only HaChii male to ever get a job as a miner. That's how Rob met him. Anyway, Chuu made so much sense; he's so sweet and so reasonable, by the time we finished talking I realized how silly I had been, and——and I proposed to him. I guess he liked the idea, so anyway, he asked Rob what humans do when they get married."

"Well, the woman proposing to the man, that's *our* tradition," NaDii responded, "and the only reason I haven't asked Greg is that there isn't —— I don't think there is anyone, human or HaChii —— who could marry us legally. By the way, Greg thinks the *man* is supposed to ask the *woman*, but he figured it was the same impossible situation."

"I wonder——" MeBlii said, musing about something.

"Oops!" NaDii said. "Last time *I* said that, things got really crazy——"

"Well, here's the thing." MeBlii said. "While Chuu and I are taking our vows, you could repeat the words along with us -- *quietly* -- and substitute your names, and the 'clergyman' (she used a Terran English word that didn't have any equivalent in HaChii) might not be any the wiser. It might not be legal, but you *would* be married, at least in my opinion."

"If we marry each other, what do I care if it's on paper somewhere?" NaDii whispered. "Hang on a minute, I've got to go ask Greg a question——"

CHAPTER 11 - White Wedding

It was MeBlii's first visit to Earth, the human home world. Even though she had worked in the human solar system for over a year, there had never been an occasion to get this far in-system before. NaDii had been to Paris, but never Chicago. Now Rob and Greg took turns showing NaDii, MeBlii and ChuuRi the sights of Rob's home town.

"This little building has an interesting history." Rob said. It's not much to look at, with all the other architecture around here, but early in the first century after this city was built, it burned to the ground."

"This building?" MeBlii asked.

"No. The whole city." Rob explained. This had been the city's water tower and it was the only thing left for miles around. People took hope from it still standing, tall and proud, and they resolved the fire wouldn't bring them down. Out of the ashes, from the ground up, they rebuilt the city, bigger and better than before. It's a symbol of renewal"

"That's not all." Greg added. Even though he grew up in Baltimore, he knew the story.

"Two hundred years later, terrorists--who wanted to force their beliefs on everybody else in the world--blew up a nuclear bomb in a tall building in the downtown business district, two miles from here. It shattered, incinerated, and pulverized most of the buildings and what was left burned for days. But when the fallout settled and the smoke cleared, the people came up from the tunnels and the subways, and somehow, this building was still standing.

Once again, despite radioactivity, famine and pestilence, they looked up at the little water tower and said, 'We can do this.' And once again, they rolled up their sleeves and rebuilt the city from the ground up."

"But that's a long time ago——" NaDii interrupted.

"Yeah. But then, forty years ago," Rob picked up the story, "my father lived near here. He was a student with the astronomers working at the Yerkes Observatory in Williams Bay, Wisconsin, when they found comet Friedan-Maksimova. It was bigger than (4147) Lennon, on a collision course for Earth, and would have been an extinction-level event for the human race, if it couldn't be deflected or destroyed. The United Nations put together a plan that they hoped would shatter the comet to smithereens and scatter them so far apart, none would hit this world. Dad warned this wasn't a good idea, the bunch of fragments would still be heading the same way and some of them might hit the Earth, but they went ahead with the plan anyway. At the end, a kilometer-size fragment hit Lake Michigan, six miles east of the city."

"But it missed the city, right? That's good, isn't it?" said ChuuRii.

"Not good enough." Rob responded. "When the wave of water hit the shoreline, it was two kilometers high. At least this time, people knew that the disaster was coming. The whole city was evacuated, but for a few foolhardy souls. Buildings were flattened out all the way to Oak Park, but when the searchers flew into the downtown area, this building was still standing amidst the wreckage, and three survivors were waving from the windows."

"That was forty years ago?" ChuuRii asked. "Everything——(he waved at the buildings lining

Michigan Avenue)——was gone? You guys just don't give up, do you?"

"Rob, here, is a Cubs fan," Greg said, as if that explained everything.

The church MeBlii and ChuuRii had chosen was Holy Name cathedral. Rebuilt again and again, this structure was last reconstructed as a classic Gothic cathedral not far from the Water Tower. Although neither of them were members of, nor really understood, the Roman Catholic faith, they accepted Rob's judgment that this would be a good place for a traditional Earth-human style wedding ceremony. The fact that Rob was Catholic and his Mom's brother was the Cardinal might have had some influence on that choice.

His Eminence, John Cardinal Ryan, Archbishop of Chicago, welcomed Chuu and May to his office as they goggled around at the surroundings. "Rob told me about working with you, May, and about the words of tolerance and brotherhood that Chuu offered in regard to the case of Greg and NaDii." Greg and NaDii stood at the back of the room with Rob as his uncle spoke with the couple.

"You know, you're the first HaChii couple that has ever asked to be married by anyone on Earth? The Holy Father hinted to me that he's jealous. But, seriously, although I've talked to the magistrates in Placedon, and I can get the paperwork cleared up to marry you here, I was wondering, why?"

Chuu explained Rob's role in getting him and MeBlii together, and that he wanted to honor that by getting married in a human ceremony, with Rob as Best Man. The Cardinal looked at Rob, then Greg and NaDii.

"And these are your other colleagues from John Lennon's asteroid?" He turned toward NaDii and Greg. "I've certainly seen you two on the news lately. NaDii, how is the baby doing?"

"He's fine." she said, "He's staying with my parents on Placet."

"No," the Cardinal said, "I mean, how is he doing with all the publicity and notoriety. Does he get out much, have any friends his age to play with? Robert has told me about his--remarkable--development. What I've heard about his life sounds very confining for him."

"Your Eminence." NaDii answered, having been coached by Rob in the proper form of address, "I don't know if there are any friends his age that would actually be——his age; if you've spoken with Rob about his namesake, you know what I mean by that. He is with some of his cousins right now--my oldest brother's boys--so he has someone to play with. They are twice his age, but they're not talking yet, even though they're bigger than he is. At least, at that age, his odd appearance doesn't seem to bother them. I wish I could say the same for the adults on Placet."

The Cardinal nodded. "On Earth, too, I'm afraid. I'll say this: the Church has been watching your family with interest. Your courage is appreciated. The Holy Father is praying for you, as am I." Then he turned back to MeBlii and ChuuRi.

"I believe your wedding can be done quite simply, and with a minimum of fuss, which is what Robert tells me you want. However, I cannot guarantee the confidentiality of what we do here. If word leaks out, especially word that Greg and NaDii are here, we might get mobbed by news media people. If the latter happens, your wedding might turn into a bit of a circus. So, I'm going to propose something a little unusual." He paused for a beat to see what MeBlii and Chuu might say. They waited expectantly for him to speak.

"Okay. Here's what I think might work. Next Sunday is a Christian Holiday called Easter. We have a Vigil Mass the evening before, which is a religious service for Easter at the middle of the night. Afterwards, we usually clean up for the next hour or so, and then close until the next morning. Nobody would be expecting anything after Midnight Mass's closing. Suppose you and your wedding party were waiting somewhere else in the building, and we brought you down at -- let's say -- two in the morning?"

"An odd time of the day doesn't matter to us, does it?" MeBlii said, looking at ChuuRii, Greg, Rob and NaDii in turn. They huddled together, whispering, for a few moments, and then:

"We have all agreed. As long as it's OK with Your Eminence losing a little sleep, we're fine with the idea." ChuuRii said. They realized that it was, in fact, a *huge* imposition on the Cardinal, but agreed to pretend it was no big deal, at Rob's insistence.

"I don't think a choir is possible, but I've got an organist who may be able to stay behind," Cardinal Ryan added with a wink, "I think she'll be OK with this. It's my sister Mary, Robert's mother."

"We're very humbled by your generosity, your Eminence." MeBlii added, and she was. Humbled and impressed. Rob had been an amazing help for all of them, now he, and his family, had come through again. "We owe you a favor." she said, wondering how she could ever repay it——

A rented white wedding gown with a veil and a train, although designed for a human female, actually worked quite well with MeBlii's HaChii body type--the white men's suit rented for ChuuRii, not so much so. Each stood somewhat uncomfortably at the back of the nave. Rob and ChuuRi stood at the right of the altar. NaDii glided from the back to the altar, where the Archbishop was standing. When she arrived at the front she moved to Greg's right. The organist started playing Mendelssohn's Wedding March. Greg walked MeBlii down the aisle to the front, then stepped aside and moved next to NaDii. The wedding party was now complete.

There stood Cardinal Ryan, resplendent in his white Easter vestments. He opened the New Douay Bible to the beginning of Genesis.

"In the beginning, God created the Universe. The Universe was without form and void, and darkness was upon the deeps of space; the Spirit of God was moving over the face of the skies. And God said, 'Let there be light!' and there was light."

He continued, closing the book. "There may be differences in how we interpret our origins; some may say there was a conscious act of Creation; others may say it just happened. But the description in Genesis I, before telescopes and spaceflight, is essentially the same Big Bang vision that all scientists, human and HaChii, adhere to today. All of the stars and galaxies came from this, every atom and photon. All humans and HaChii began at this moment.

How did Moses, thousands of years ago, see so clearly how it began? In the Church, we believe that God gave him the vision to see things as they are.

Today we have two souls who wish to be united under our roof. They have not been raised in our Faith, but they have told me they are willing to accept that something happened to make the Universe start, and if we wish to call it God, that is acceptable with them. The Church, long years before humans ever encountered the HaChii, asked the question: 'How it would affect us if intelligent life were encountered elsewhere in the Universe?' and the doctrine of the Church is that, if all of this Universe was created at the same time, we are all part of that creation and it is hubris to put limits on what God can create. We must embrace our fellow-beings as works of the same Creator, as God gave us the vision to see things as they are.

So we embrace ChuuRi and MeBlii into the arms of our Church, and ask of them only that they take this Sacrament as seriously as anyone else who is married in this Church. May this be the start of a wonderful life together for both of them, in the name of the Father, and the Son, and the Holy Spirit."

"Amen." Rob and Greg said quietly.

With that, the vows began:

"ChuuRi Iz QuiiGaa and MeBlii Ix BaShii, do you come here freely and without reservation to give yourselves to each other in marriage?"

"We do." Chuu and May said. Next to them, Greg and NaDii looked at each other and whispered the same words.

"Will you honor each other as man and wife for the rest of your lives?"

"We will." Both couples said, with NaDii and Greg whispering.

"Will you accept children lovingly from God, and bring them up according to the law of Christ and his Church?"

(Chuu and May had discussed this--as far as they could tell, the law of Christ was to love one another. Details would have to be worked out later.)

"We will." Again spoken (or whispered) by both couples.

"Since it is your intention to enter into marriage, join your right hands, and declare your consent before God and his Church."

Surreptitiously, NaDii reached behind Greg, and he took her right gripping tentacle in his right hand.

ChuuRi spoke: "I, ChuuRii Iz QuiiGaa, take you, MeBlii Ix BaShii, for my wedded wife, to have and to hold, from this day forward, for better, for worse, for richer, for poorer, in sickness and in health, until death do us part." To the side, Greg whispered the same vow with his name and NaDii's.

MeBlii spoke: "I, MeBlii Ix BaShii, take you, ChuRii Iz QuiiGa, for my wedded husband, to have and to hold, from this day forward, for better, for worse, for richer, for poorer, in sickness and in health, until death do us part." And as quietly as possible, NaDii repeated this with her name and Greg's.

The Cardinal directed the bride and groom to exchange rings, which were actually something like bracelets for the left gripping tentacles, and said a prayer blessing the marriage. Greg let NaDii slip a ring on his finger, and slid a bracelet up onto her tentacle. *Excellent, h*e thought *we did that without being observed.*

Finally, Cardinal Ryan offered the Eucharist to Rob and Greg, the only actual Catholics present.

"Then, by the power vested in me," Cardinal Ryan intoned, "I declare you, ChuuRi and you, MeBlii, man and wife." At this point, everyone expected him to tell the groom he could kiss the bride or some similar, but gender-neutral wording, although the HaChii didn't have mouths that were designed for very effective kissing, but instead, he stated:

"Gregory Firestone and NaDii Ix ChiiBii, by authority of a higher power than anyone human or HaChii might vest in me, I also declare you man and wife."

MeBlii and ChuuRii threw their arms around each other, NaDii shrieked, and Greg kissed her soundly. "Sorry, guys," whispered Rob, "Not a whole lot gets by my Uncle. It's kind of hard to keep a secret from him."

CHAPTER 12 - The Lord Will Provide

The weeks rolled by. Denny Harris was still homeless, but he had a goal. Wait for the Lord to bring Jezebel and her child to him.

When the newsfeeds at the spaceport reported the hatching, and that the family decided to return to the mother's home city of Placedon, Denny knew the Lord was taking a hand in the fulfillment of prophecy.

Most days, Denny Harris 'worked' the crowds at the spaceport. Some days he stayed there all day, others, he wandered the streets of Placedon, looking to see what opportunity would present to him. Like all members of human-HaChii mining teams, he had not been sent into the field without a solid grounding in the HaChii language. To most HaChii, a homeless, derelict human wasn't very different from any other. The novelty of meeting one who spoke HaChii with reasonable fluency sometimes overcame the reticence that came with this one's shabby clothes and over-ripe odor.

He found a better place to stay at nights than the underpass. An old factory worker told him about a building that had been abandoned. It overlooked the Don river. Atop the building was a water tank, rusted and disused, and while exploring the rooftop, he found a breach in the tank just big enough to just crawl through. Inside its dark, cave-like interior, he was able to set up a hammock, hang his clothes on some pipes, even build a small fire, with smoke escaping through a rusted hole in the ceiling.

HaChii who thought of this strange human as an acquaintance had no idea he thought of them as 'informants' for his mission. One who had an interest in astronomy mentioned a store for hobbyists, from which Denny, that night, stole a pair of binoculars and a small telescope.

For Denny, the main attraction of the water tank atop the abandoned building was that the home Greg and NaDii had bought was near the river, and close enough to the factory that Harris could see into their windows from the roof. He was still most of a kilometer away, but with the binoculars and 'scope, he could make out Greg walking by the front room picture window, some nights.

Another 'informant' provided him with the address of a small museum specializing in exotic HaChii and off-world militaria. He took the tour one day, and broke in that night to steal an M1 Garand rifle. Finding ammunition for it took another two months. But he felt the Lord would provide, if his mission was destined to succeed.

He bided his time, and continued cadging coins and schlepping luggage at the spaceport by day, observing his quarry by night.

The next big break, as he saw it, occurred one day when a party of human military re-enactors appeared at the spaceport. He hustled their gear and luggage, and slipped one clip of .30-06 cal ammunition into his pocket. When he got to his night-time lair, he found, as he suspected, that the rounds were empty of powder, but the cartridge casings and bullets were authentic. Would the Lord provide what he needed to finish his task?

Cartridges require a primer. The cartridges in the 8-round clip had been emptied of powder, but the primers appeared to still be filled with fulminate. Would it work? A test with one of the empty cartridges in the rifle showed the primer was still active; the bullet popped out of the barrel and fell about 10 feet away, when the firing pin set off the primer in the empty cartridge. One round wasted, Harris knew, but his confidence in the others was now much higher.

Every year in West Virginia, deer hunting season is held in early October. Denny went out with his Dad, using hand-loaded cartridges and one of their two ancient hunting rifles, every year from the age of ten. He knew hunting and he knew hand-loading cartridges. What he didn't know was where to get gunpowder on Placet. Smokeless powder was more than he could hope for, and finding the ingredients to compound black powder could be possible, but might attract attention. What other options were possible?

Denny hoped again, that the Lord would provide. Some mornings, when he got up, he went to the small chapel by Gates 12 and 13, the area used for departures for human-space. He did not adhere to Church of Rome, but had very few Christian options in Placedon. This day, he saw the sacristan moving from place to place, lighting the candles for the morning Mass, as he had seen it done a hundred times before. Yet this time, he saw something he had not thought about before. Old-fashioned red phosphorus matches. The sacristan would strike them on the side of the box, and light two or three candles, then light another. For a moment Denny was afraid the man would take the matchbox back with him, but as he went into the back to get the altar cloths and the vestments, he left the match box unguarded. Denny moved swiftly and quietly.

Back at his warren that evening, Denny used his knife to shave red chips of match-head onto a piece of paper. Every time he pulled a new match from the box, he transferred the shavings from the paper to a plastic cup. He figured if he ignited one match while shaving it, he would just burn up the piece of paper. As the cup became more full, he slid the shavings off the paper very, very carefully. Even a single static spark could ruin all his work.

Finally, Denny had shaved all the matches in the box. He filled one .30-06 cartridge about two-thirds with the red chips, and cautiously forced the bullet into the throat of the cartridge. This was much 'touchier' stuff than smokeless powder, and a lot less powerful, but he had hope as eased the cartridge into the rifle and chambered it without mishap.

It was becoming dark. He could see the single picture window but not identify who was walking past it until the lights went on inside. Gradually, his eyes adjusted to the dark. He hoped that clamping the rifle barrel into the holder for the sighting 'scope on the side of the bigger telescope would ensure they were both pointed at the same target. Now, he had a shadow passing the window that might be the HaChii female. *Jezebel!* he thought.

With the magnification, the window filled the field of view of the powerful telescope. He centered on the middle of the window and pulled the trigger.

The report was more muffled and less sharp than he remembered from hunting, but it sounded as though it had worked. The recoil rocked the telescope on its tripod.

The view in the 'scope swung and bobbed crazily. Gradually, it settled down and he hunted around the window to see if the round had struck. At first he thought it had missed completely. Then he saw, far down and in the corner of the window, that a hole had been punched through the window glass and spidery cracks spread out from that corner. At that moment, someone shut the lights off and the field of view went black.

Patience, he thought, *The Lord will provide.*

CHAPTER 13 - As it Was in the Beginning——

At the age of nine months, little Rob asked his parents if they would teach him to read. He could speak clearly in both Terran English and HaChii, and while it was unlikely he could enroll in schools either on Placet or Earth, home-schooling was something Greg and NaDii had time for, if not much experience. The network programs that were available, for a price, were pretty good. Greg agreed to work with Robbie on the Latin alphabet half the week, and NaDii would help him practice HaChii lettering the other half. Since Rob had hands, Greg would teach him computer skills on a human keyboard, if for no other reason than--it was faster than HaChii input devices. Penmanship was another and different skill. Writing required different skills for human and HaChii lettering, but Robbie was equipped for both, and in the end, made good progress in English and even faster progress in HaChii.

As Greg found out, it was impossible to home-school someone in just one subject, without other ones coming up.

"Dad?" Robbie asked one day, when he was close to his first birthday, "Why is the sky dark at night?"

Rob hadn't given it a lot of thought, but he explained the best he could:

"The sun lights up the sky. When it's night, and the sun has set, that big, bright light isn't there, and the sky is dark without the sun making the sky light up." If Greg thought that would be satisfactory, he was in for a big surprise.

"You told me the stars in the night sky are suns, like our own, except really far away." Robbie responded.

"That's right." Greg said, "They are really far away, and really far apart."

"But--if they keep going on forever, and there are suns spread out everywhere, even if they're very far apart," Robbie argued, "then sooner or later, no matter which way you look, there should be a sun somewhere in the direction you're looking, and the whole sky should be as bright as the sun."

Uh, Oh. Greg thought. *How do I deal with that?* So he tried a reliable tactic he had learned from one of his Jesuit teachers in high school:

"Well, what do you think that might tell you?" he asked.

Robbie thought for a while. "Light takes time to get from one place to another, right?"

Greg said it did.

"So if we don't see stars filling the sky, it either means you run out of them as you get farther out, or else, they haven't been around forever."

Wow. Greg thought. Then he answered. "That's right. We don't think stars have been there forever. There is a time before which there weren't any stars. They started up about 14 billion years ago in something called the Big Bang."

"That makes sense——" Robbie continued. "If we can't see any stars older than -- that big number you told me -- we don't see any past -- where the earliest light could come from -- so they don't fill every space in the sky and the sky is dark at night——"

Jesus. Greg thought. *Good thing he figured that out for himself. I could have never explained it like that.* And that made him a little frightened—— *no*--he admitted to himself--it scared him silly.

"Why?" Robbie asked innocently.

"Why what, son?" Greg asked.

"Why did the stars start up then? Why weren't they always there?"

Oh, boy——

Greg spoke to NaDii about it that night.

"There are all sorts of stories about why the Universe got started. Do you suppose I should tell Robbie about all of them?"

"That can get into some pretty hairy physics." NaDii told him. "Robbie has just barely learned his numbers and I don't think M-theory and branes would make a whole lot of sense to him——"

"If I understood it myself——" Greg admitted.

"Yeah. Me too." NaDii said. "Tell me again about the part where he figured out the Universe hadn't always been there."

The next week, Greg found out he didn't need to search for explanations. There was Robbie, one morning, searching for them himself, on the web.

"Dad?" Greg saw Robbie surfing the web, and braced himself for another set of impossible 'why?' questions, as any toddler's father has to do sometime. "What do you think? A lot of this stuff (he waved a hand at diagrams illustrating M-theory) is 'way over my head,' but in a rational Universe, it just seems to me there should be something simpler."

"Like what, son?" More Jesuit logic——

"Well, I found this web page for your friend Rob's Uncle John." he clicked a link he had apparently saved a few minutes before.

Momentarily unable to connect the dots, Greg said, "Who?"

"Cardinal John J. Ryan," Robbie explained, "Archbishop of Chicago; see what it says here? He has a video series called *Life Is Worth Living.*" --another click-- "It covers a lot of the stuff I was wondering about."

Being a Catholic himself, Greg had a pretty good idea what that might be, but he browsed the web site Robbie had opened, for a few minutes. *Wow. Ryan is an unbelievable communicator,* he thought. *He makes everything so clear and sensible.*

"Dad?" that 'why?' look again.

"Uh, huh?" Greg answered, afraid of what might come next.

"Could this be what happened?"

"Ummm—— I believe everything has a logical, natural explanation. But the way I was brought up, this is one of those explanations you have to consider possible.

I'd say——I'm not sure——but this idea——that the Universe was created intentionally——it's not impossible."

Over the next three months, Robbie's vocabulary grew by leaps and bounds, aided by his browsing on the web. He had learned some number skills. Not yet two, he could add, subtract, multiply and divide. At least he had the concepts down, although long division was a tough slog for Greg and NaDii to teach him. "A lot of steps." he would say, then soldier on, practicing until he could remember all the pieces in this game, and the moves each one made.

Two days before Robbie's second birthday, a rifle bullet punched into one corner of that front room window through which the photographer had taken the picture in the previous year. NaDii did not recognize what had happened, but Greg, realizing the danger immediately, screamed "Kill the lights!"

Nobody was hurt, but a terrified NaDii cashed in a part of her BrropCo savings, bought steel shutters that covered all the windows, and increased the perimeter the security guard was supposed to cover by half. HaChii detectives searched the neighborhood but were unable to identify where the shot had come from. The bullet was analyzed and found to be of a style used in ancient Earth rifles, over 500 years old.

Everybody felt a little more mortal that day——

Just after his second birthday, out of the blue, Robbie came into the bedroom one morning, and said, "Dad?"

"Hmmm?" Greg mumbled non-committally. It was rather ***early*** in the morning--

"I wrote to Rob's Uncle John this morning." he said.

Greg sat up abruptly. "What did you write?"

"Oh--just that I was interested in what Catholics thought about things, and I wondered if I could learn more."

"Did he answer?"

"Oh, sure. He said he had been thinking about me and was glad to hear from me--do you think that's really true?"

"I'm sure of it, son. He told me about that just before our wedding--I mean MeBlii and ChuuRii's wedding," he corrected himself.

"Good. I ***wanted*** to trust him after watching his video entries, but you never know if the person on the screen is for real—— Anyway, he sent me a file called a Catechism, and said if I could read as well as he ***guessed*** I could, I should go ahead and look at it."

"I don't think it can hurt anything, son. Just talk to me and your Mom if you have questions. Do you have the com open now, with that file?"

"Uh, huh." Now it was Robbie's turn to be non-committal.

"Maybe you should go read it while I talk to your Mother."

And Robbie left for the front room, where the com panel was.

"NaDii, honey," he reached out and shook her "Wake up. We've got to talk."

"Hmmm?" she rolled over; more non-committivity——

"Robbie's starting to explore religion."

"Religion? What religion?" NaDii was more awake now.

"Mine. Mine and Rob's, I mean. He's been talking on the q-net with Cardinal Ryan." Greg sounded worried.

"That wonderful, nice man in Chicago?" she answered with a distinct look of amusement. "That wonderful, wise, *brave* person in Chicago who married us?"

"Mmmm, yeah, *that* one——"

"Oh, *sure.*" She said sarcastically, "I'm *really worried* about Robbie talking with *him,*" and with that comment, she rolled over and went back to sleep.

*Wow. She's **really** figured out how this Earth-sense-of-humor thing works.* Greg thought, chuckling to himself. Then he went back to sleep, too.

Next morning, Greg found NaDii at the her com screen in the bedroom, reading a download of Robbie's Catechism file. Next thing he knew, she was browsing Aquinas' *Summa Theologica.* She stayed with the screen for the next four hours, without saying a word. At the end, she shut down the com, closed her eyes for a second, and said one word. "Deep."

Then she asked. "You think that gunman got him thinking?"

"Sure made *me* think." he answered.

Greg was glad that she had done some homework. He was sure Robbie wouldn't just ask Dad questions; he was sure to ask Mom, too, and now she was at least a little bit prepared.

"Maybe there's some comfort in this——religion stuff——" NaDii mused out loud. "But I'm still scared."

CHAPTER 14 - Music Hath Charms

As if to underscore the point of inheriting different skills from different parts of his family, two-and-a-half year old Robbie, who looked HaChii in many respects, but had human-like hands, asked one day for a new keyboard.

"What's wrong with the com keyboard you've got?" his mother asked. Money wasn't a drawback, but she didn't want to be indulgent, and end up with a spoiled, selfish child, even if there was very little opportunity for him to be selfish with anyone else.

"It doesn't play music very well, at all." Robbie answered. That set her back. She knew humans made keyboards with musical notes on them; she just hadn't associated that with her son, whom she visualized as HaChii most of the time, even when faced with evidence to the contrary.

"Do you know any music that you would like to play?" She asked.

He said, "Well I've tried this——" He started an app on the com panel, then began tapping keys widely spaced on the text keypad of the console. Out of the speakers came a reasonably synthesized set of organ notes, albeit with some mistakes, for a tune NaDii had heard before, Mendelssohn's *Wedding March.* It sounded good, at least *close* to the way it had sounded in Holy Name Cathedral, but there was something wooden about it——almost rigid——in its precision.

"I can't bridge the chords very easily, mommy——" he said, "it messes up putting any expression into the music."

Holy Ffurff, she thought, *he's taught himself to play with an alphabetic keyboard--which was never intended for anything like this--and he's* ***worried that he can't get expression into his music?***

"Look, Mom," he said, clicking a link on the com panel, "Here is a used keyboard for auction on the ePlay web market. It wouldn't cost much more than——" and he named a toy she had gotten him for his last birthday.

The next morning, delivery men rolled in a shiny black synthesizer/organ unit with a full 88-key keyboard. Greg, having only heard about the whole business second-hand, watched as NaDii plugged it in and wired it to the com system.

"Let's see if the boy can figure out how this works." he said, "After all, it isn't much like an alphanumeric keyboard. I played a little when I was young. I can give him some lessons if he——"

And he stopped talking, for at that moment, Robbie had spotted the keyboard and came running toward it with a squeal. He ran his hands across the keyboard. *Noise.* Greg thought, then realized, *music-noise, not chaos-noise*—— And then, a step at a time, Robbie tried a run of notes going up the sharps and flats from left to right, a few chords, flipped a few levers to hear the different effects that they produced on the basic organ sound, and then——

And then, Robbie found the setting that corresponded to a large pipe organ. And he began to play Bach's Wedge Fugue in E minor, a bit faster than Greg remembered it, but with feeling and power. Greg fell apart, sobbing. The organist had played this at his father's funeral, when he was ten.

NaDii rushed to his side, uncertain what was wrong. Robbie turned around and stopped playing. "Daddy!" he ran over. "I'm sorry——I *know* it's not as good without the foot pedals, but——"

"Foot pedals?" Greg managed to splutter through his tears. "I'll get you foot pedals if you want them. It wasn't about foot pedals."

And both NaDii and Rob looked at him with the same quizzical HaChii expression.

"It was just so beautiful——and so sad——" and he couldn't talk for a minute. Finally, he choked out, "It's what they played at my Dad's funeral when he got killed in the mining accident on (3834) Zappafrank."

"Your Dad was a miner?" they both said in unison.

"And his Dad, and his, too." Greg said.

"Dad's family has a strange history with asteroids named after musicians." Robbie said to his mother, strangely thoughtful, "Maybe I'm going to be a miner—— or a musician——"

Shortly after his third birthday. Robbie wrote a Sonata. Using the com system for multichannel overlays, he synthesized a violin part and recorded it to compete and work in counterpoint with a piano part. The piano felt like pure J. S. Bach, with elements of the *Third Brandenburg Concerto,* the violin part pure Lennon-McCartney, with elements of *Sergeant Pepper's Lonely Hearts Club Band*, yet both and neither, and the whole was at the same time a single composition, with the same themes, weaving in and out between the instruments. NaDii and Greg loved it, but they just didn't know enough about classical music to know if anyone else would think it was any good. As a test, they posted it on the web as a performance by an anonymous artist.

Reaction to the performance was unprecedented. Music critics demanded to know which musicians had recorded it. DiiRaa, the *Daily Vibe*'s HaChii music critic wanted to know why it was recorded as a Sonata rather than having a larger string section; he felt it was by nature a Concerto.

Keeping their son's anonymity, but to allow him to play further with the music, they suspended his other home-schooling, while he elaborated the violin part into a string quartet, expanded the piano piece, and re-released it on the web as a Concerto the next day.

DiiRaa, who had made the Sonata-Concerto comment, exclaimed that the master who made the changes had humbled him by calling his bluff in a single day; there was never anything wrong with the original composition, he added, but he had wanted to see if the composer could adapt. The adaptation, he concluded, had so far exceeded his expectations, that it *had* to be--he then named a prominent classical composer whom he thought *must* be the author of the piece--concluding with a substantial wager that this was who wrote it.

"Prove me wrong!" he said.

Greg looked at the amount of the wager. It wouldn't make a *big* bump in their already substantial bank balance, but it would be nice to have that little extra 'cushion' in there, and besides, skewering the critic would make it almost worth the headaches he expected if he brought little Robbie out of the 'closet' and let people see what he really could do——

He asked Robbie if he would be OK with going public.

"I thought you'd never ask." Robbie responded. "It's time. I think it's more than time—— I've felt really cooped-up in here. I'd like to see Placedon."

So they contacted the critic, and arranged to meet them at Symphony Hall in Placedon, in four days. DiiRaa said he would be ready with a piano, a string quartet of his choosing, and——"Would they bring the composer and his sheet music..?"

"Sure." Rob agreed. They would even post a copy of the sheet music for the violin parts on the network for the quartet to practice with.

Three days passed. DiiRaa had found four violinists who would practice the music posted on the net. There weren't many pianos on Placet, but the Symphony Hall had an ancient Steinway, and the critic had found a HaChii tuner with perfect pitch who could tune it. One more day, he said.

The fourth day came. In the evening, terrified and exhilarated, Greg and NaDii hired an armored car to take them to the Hall. They were relieved at getting into the vehicle without incident, and delighted when an escort into the Hall ushered them in without recognizing them. Robbie wore a cape over his robe, that kept his hands covered as he walked/glided toward the stage with his parents. There was

DiiRaa, the music critic, wearing black robes. A half-dozen HaChii colleagues of his, some presumably having challenged his wager, wore robes of various colors. There were a quartet of human violinists, in formal attire. And to the side stood one human, in a gray business suit, who was the composer DiiRaa had named, apparently present either to show that he was *not* performing the music, or out of curiosity to see who would show up to claim credit for the composition.

Greg handed copies of the sheet music to the violinists and DiiRaa, knowing that, of the people present, the piano must be for a human performer, asked, "Are you the composer, or just an artist who will be performing his work?"

"Neither." Greg answered, as Robbie slipped off his cape. "I'm his Dad."

Climbing the piano stool with some difficulty, for it was much higher than he was used to, he placed his hands onto the keyboard. Just right. The keys were spaced exactly like his keyboard at home. He set his sheet music on the piano, not that he needed it.

DiiRaa goggled. "The Monster child!" slipped out, before he could cover his own mouth. Robbie shrugged. He flexed his fingers, "Let's see what I can deMONSTRate for you, today, shall we?" he quipped.

The quartet began the opening, some of them having a hard time looking at the sheet music and not the player. Robbie began with a simple theme that built to a crescendo, then the two groups began their counterpoint, and the composition rolled into the first movement. The critic, and nearly everyone else present, closed their eyes for a moment and stopped seeing performers, only concentrating on the music. The human composer beamed with a joy that might have escaped the HaChii present, but was not lost on the humans.

At the end of the performance, the humans applauded, the HaChii cheered, and the human composer held his hand out towards DiiRaa.

"Fifty large, I think you said." He grinned broadly at Robbie.

Several other hands were held out, and similar quantities of valuta crossed their palms or grippers.

Finally, Greg made a show of giving his portion of the wager to his son. "You can get that set of pipe-organ foot pedals now, if you want to."

The chagrined, but bemused, DiiRaa held up a tentacle.

"Does the young Robbie (for he knew the name from the newsfeeds) have an encore he would like to present?"

"I suppose I could play the Sonata you criticized originally," he thought out loud, "but I've got a new piece for piano that doesn't require any violins, and it wouldn't sound like a rehash of the piece we just did. Is that OK?"

Everybody agreed and he began to play.

In the back of the auditorium, Denny Harris, garbed in his tattered clothes, waited in the shadows. *Here is the child.* The voices in his head whispered and cajoled. *All of this careful waiting has paid off.* He had finally been able to track his prey, when, for the first time in three years, Jezebel and the child had ***actually left the house***. Harris had entered the building, past guards and metal detectors, working by depending on people seeing what he wanted them to see: *I have no metal. I am just a vagrant. I am harmless.*

Bide your time. the voices said to Denny. *You will get him alone. That is foretold. He is yours.*

Robbie concluded his new composition. More of a Fugue than a Sonata, everyone was delighted with it regardless of what it might be called. Oblivious to the extra spectator in the auditorium, DiiRaa offered to take them all back to his special viewing box, where there were snacks and refreshments. Some of them were not appropriate for someone of Robbie's age, of course--everybody had expected the composer to be an adult--but there would be GiiFaa juice, and that was OK for kids.

The adults crowded into the tight staircase leading up to DiiRaa's box, unaware of having been preceded by a spectral figure moments earlier. As they entered the modest viewing room at the third level, Robbie offered to take their coats to the cloak room just to the left of the entrance. Everybody gratefully handed their coats to the little boy, and as they popped open the champagne, handed around the sandwiches, and passed the bottle of GiiFaa juice, Robbie toddled off towards the cloak room, bearing a bundle of garments almost his own size.

He entered the darkened room. *Now, where is the light switch?*

At that moment, the door closed. Robbie, startled, dropped the clothes onto the floor in a pile, and fumbled for the switch. The light came on, and there was a scruffy-looking man in a torn coat holding up a glittering glass knife in one hand.

"Spawn a Satan! Child a tha Divil! Antichrist!" Harris hissed as he raised the weapon.

Robbie fell to his knees in mortal fear, putting his hands together.

"Are you going to beg, boy?" Harris said. The voices in his head were urging him to strike now, not talk, but he felt a need to taunt his victim.

And the boy, shaking, spoke:

"Our Father, who art in Heaven——"

Nooo! the voices screamed. *Nooo! This can't be happening!"* Denny hesitated.

"——thy will be done on Earth as it is in Heaven——"

Kill him! voices screamed, but others said, *Nooo!! That cannot be the Antichrist!! How could he beg for God's help!! He would not call the Lord!!*

"——but deliver us from Evil——"

Who is the evil one here, if you kill him?! screamed the loudest voice in Denny Harris's mind. And his nerveless fingers dropped the glass knife, which fell, sticking into the carpeting point first.

Denny whirled and crashed out the door. The revelers in the other room, hearing the noise and the incoherent scream of the man fleeing down the stairs, rushed to see what had happened. There, in the middle of the room beside a pile of cloaks and coats, the little human-HaChii boy was still kneeling on the carpet, staring at a large glass knife embedded in the floor less than half a meter in front of him.

"——Amen," he concluded.

CHAPTER 15 - Going to the Chapel

DiiRaa and his guests surrounded Greg and NaDii as they took in the tableau.

"Mommy! That man wanted to kill me." Robbie said. "But he changed his mind."

NaDii had turned very white and Greg was holding her up. "What did he say to you?" Greg asked.

"Something about Satan and the Antichrist. But he ran away after I started to pray."

"Pray?" NaDii asked.

"Talk to the Lord. The Catechism has a prayer in it that I remembered. It asks the Lord to deliver us from evil." he said simply.

"That he certainly did, son." Greg answered. He looked at the glass knife embedded in the carpeting. Then he started to reach for it.

"Wait a minute." DiiRaa cautioned. He went back to the viewing box and came back with a napkin. Wrapping the knife in the napkin, he picked it up.

DiiRaa looked at the glass blade. "This should never have happened. I'll call the police." he said simply.

Celebration forgotten, Greg and the other guests stepped into the hallway and talked for a while as they waited for the authorities. NaDii simply clung onto her son.

Two HaChii detectives arrived in matching tan robes. The shorter one, Grii, showed her credentials while the other pulled out a recorder to take their depositions. After NaDii, Greg and the other guests described what had happened, they turned to Robbie, who was wearing his cape again. They didn't expect much, because Robbie looked almost like any other HaChii 3-year-old.

They were surprised how detailed and sophisticated his powers of observation were. Once they finished speaking to him, Jii, the larger detective, turned to NaDii and said, "Your son's eyes look very unusual. Was he injured by the assailant in some way that affected his vision?"

NaDii thought for a moment. "No. His vision is fine. He has his father's eyes, and that makes him a little unusual, but there's nothing wrong with his vision."

The detectives both struck a pose that indicated curiosity, but when NaDii was not forthcoming, decided not to pursue it.

DiiRaa brought out the knife. He presented it, still wrapped in the napkin, and explained, "I thought there might be prints from the gripper-ridges." he said.

Jii looked at him quizzically. "I thought this was a human we were talking about, not a HaChii." he said.

"Ah—— Of course," DiiRaa replied, "But they have something called fingerprints, which are just like our gripper ridges, only a little different. You see, I read mystery stories, both human and HaChii--actually something of an addict, I'm afraid."

Detective Grii shrugged, took the blade with her, carefully cradled in the napkin, and headed down the stairs.

After speaking to the detectives, NaDii called the armored car back, and they left the Symphony hall.

Late that evening, NaDii opened her q-net connection, and checked what time it was in Chicago. 2:30PM--not an unreasonable time. Once assured that it was not an outrageous time of the night (although the Cardinal was still pretty sharp at 2:30AM, she recalled) she searched for the *Life is Worth Living* screen.

Within a few moments she had the link to messaging for Cardinal Ryan. Should she try to reach him? *Yes, I should.* she thought. She composed a blind query bearing her name and waited to see if it would be answered. *Probably such a busy man wouldn't have time for messaging. I'll probably get a response from some assistant in a day or two.* Gripping the joystick, she steered the marker to the submit button and squeezed.

A few seconds passed and then a picture box popped up in one corner. There was the clergyman, wearing a red cassock and a red *biretta.*

"Hello, NaDii," he addressed her, as though they spoke every day.

"Hello, Your Emin--" NaDii started.

"Never mind that Eminence stuff. Just call me Jack." said the Cardinal.

"--Jack, then. I wanted to call you to thank you for saving my son's life."

"How did I do that?" Ryan said with a raised eyebrow.

"A fanatic stalked him and was going to stab him with a glass knife——"

"Glass?"

"Must've thought it would get by the metal detectors. He guessed right."

"Anyway, the bad guy with the knife called Robbie a Spawn (is that the right word?) of Satan, a Demon and Antichrist, and he raised the knife."

"Sounds bad. Then what happened?"

"Robbie kneeled down and said the 'Our Father,' I think you call it. The bad guy dropped the knife and ran away," she added, "and I don't know why."

"Sounds right." said Ryan. If this guy believes in Satan and Demons and an Antichrist in a literal way--and I'm certain that he does--the Lord's Prayer would mess with his head, because no Satan or Demon would--or could--invoke the Lord when threatened. So I'm glad Robbie thought to do that."

"Ffurff, So am I—— Thanks! If you hadn't sent him that Catechism, I don't think he'd be here today."

"Is he awake now? Could I talk to him?" Ryan inquired.

"No. He's in bed now. It's pretty late here." she said. "Do you want me to get him up?"

"No. Let him sleep. He's only three." Ryan replied.

"We owe you big time." NaDii used a human expression she had learned from Greg. "What could we possibly do?" she asked rhetorically.

"I'll tell you what. Take Robbie to Mass this weekend. You and Greg. Talk to a priest in Placedon and tell him your story."

"A priest in Placedon?" NaDii said, puzzled. "Are there any churches in Placedon?"

"Father Boyle. At the airport. There's a little chapel there for the human travelers."

"Thanks. We'll go tomorrow. First thing."

"Say Hi for me to Father Boyle; he was a student of mine once."

"Will Do."

"Goodbye."

"Bye."

Sunrise. NaDii had checked when the chapel opened and the first mass was at 4 on the 16-number HaChii clock, halfway between midnight and midday. Greg had figured the armored car was more useful as a decoy than a protection, had it arrive at half past three, then head towards the Symphony Hall, while he, NaDii and Robbie slipped out the back and walked towards the airport in the dark. It was only a few minutes' walk from their house.

Once inside, they asked at the information desk where the Catholic chapel was, and were directed to a doorway between Gates 12 and 13. Slipping inside, they saw an elderly human moving from candle to candle, lighting them with old-fashioned wooden matches. There was one person in the front pew at the right, kneeling, and nobody else yet in the room. NaDii walked Robbie up towards the front, and Greg walked over towards the person lighting the candles.

"Are you Father Boyle?" Greg asked.

"Heavens, no." said the sacristan. "I just prepare everything for him. He'll be here any minute now."

As Greg waited by the altar, NaDii and Robbie arrived at the front, and seated themselves at the left end of the bench from the human who was already there. Robbie knelt, and his mother imitated him. He folded his hands and looked at the gentleman to his right. He blanched, then edged toward his mother, who was trying to imitate the pose she had seen Robbie take.

"Mom!" he whispered, "That's the man. At the end of the row. The one that threatened me."

She saw the shabby clothes and ragged beard. Although she had only caught a glimpse of the man disappearing down the staircase, these details matched what she had seen from behind.

"Are you sure?" she whispered back.

"Dead sure, Mom." Robbie used an Earth idiom that seemed all too appropriate.

NaDii and Robbie began to edge out of the row, back toward the aisle they had come from. Greg, standing by the altar, noticed their sudden turnabout and strange faded coloration. At that moment the priest came in and almost bumped into Greg.

"Can I help you, Sir?"

"Yes. Greg said, still distracted by his family's retreat in the other direction. "Are you Father Boyle."

"I am. And who do I have the pleasure of addressing?"

"Greg Firestone. Cardinal Ryan suggested I come here to talk to you about something involving my son——"

And just at that moment, Denny Harris stood up and walked towards the altar.

"Dad! Watch out!" Robbie shouted. "That's the guy!"

Greg had a moment's hesitation as to whether Robbie meant the priest or the vagrant, but reacted quickly enough to tackle Denny before he took another step. They ended up on the floor, struggling, but Greg's superior weight and condition quickly decided the outcome.

He lashed Denny's hands behind him with his belt, and the priest, dumbstruck by this behavior in his chapel, stood stock still for a moment longer, then assisted Greg in holding the man down while at the same time asking, "What in Heaven is going on here?"

Denny saw NaDii and Robbie draw closer.

"Are you the man that tried to hurt me yesterday?" Robbie asked.

"What a ***yew*** doin' 'n this chapel?!" was Denny's retort. He looked at Robbie and NaDii as though he were seeing ghosts. His voices were screaming at him that this was impossible, that it couldn't be happening.

"I believe in God the Father Almighty, Creator of Heaven and Earth." Robbie said in answer.

Denny wailed and pounded his head against the wooden pews.

The priest gaped in stunned incomprehension. Greg called the police on his message pad.

Three plainclothesmen in tan robes arrived. Two led Denny away, one stopped and spoke to Greg.

"We meet again." It was detective Jii. "I didn't expect to get a fingerprint match so quickly, but the scanner confirms it. His prints are the same as the ones that were on the knife."

Greg was relieved. He was hoping he hadn't just grabbed a stranger that his son had mis-identified. Now he was sure that he hadn't.

"Do you still want to press charges?" the detective asked.

"I believe so." Greg replied. "Why do you ask?"

"I may be a poor judge of human fitness," Jii replied, "but this fellow appears to be--mentally unfit--to stand trial. At least from what I can see, any defense lawyer is going to use the insanity defense."

Probably true. Greg thought. "What happens if he proves to be insane?"

"They'll probably send him to Earth, where they will re-program his brain." Jii said, "If you press charges, that is——"

Greg thought about the ugly results of brain re-programming he'd heard about. It was a creepy procedure, and the person who came out was never the person who went in, but—— Then he said, "I have few illusions about what might happen the next time this man decides somebody's child is a demon."

"Yes. We will press charges." NaDii agreed. Robbie just stared at the man.

The priest, who knew Denny only as a harmless derelict who muttered strange imprecations about HaaChii devils and Jezebel between his prayers, began to suspect that he had much to discuss with Greg and NaDii.

"So Archbishop Ryan sent you, did he?" he began. "Tell me more."

And Robbie, NaDii and Greg began telling Father Boyle the story. It took quite a while——

CHAPTER 16 - Road Trip

Greg and NaDii worked on home-schooling Robbie, and in the course of studying Earth history they discovered they weren't the first parents with a three-year old who wrote concert music. But Robbie's father wasn't a Kapellmeister, and couldn't teach him to read and write music. Robbie had done that for himself. Then he taught his Dad.

So, while Greg and Robbie worked on music, NaDii sharpened up her mathematics, preparing to teach Robbie how arithmetic worked. In the process, she got ideas for several improvements in household items, and kept the Patent Office in Placedon busy. To everybody's surprise, especially her own, she found out that she was not as much of a one-trick pony as she had thought. If not for her project with FriiDaa's company, she might not have been able to open the doors to other manufacturing outfits that made more prosaic products, but those doors were open to her now, she found.

The police had searched Denny Harris's hideout shortly after his arrest, and found the rifle, which they returned to the museum. When they reported back to NaDii, they thought she would be relieved that the threat was eliminated, but although Denny no longer remained in his sniper's nest, she could not relax. The hate letters and death threats had not stopped. In fact, as word of Robbie's musical talent spread, they became more numerous and vituperative.

DiiRaa had offered to become Robbie's Brian Epstein and Ed Sullivan rolled into one. Reluctant at first, NaDii allowed a few public performances at Symphony

Hall, with the highest possible level of security, and was pleasantly surprised that there was no heckling or disruption from any members of the audience. Classical concerts apparently did not attract the people that wrote the threats; perhaps they did not connect the dots the way other people did. In the end, NaDii did not care; she was nervous, regardless, and kept the steel shutters over the picture windows at home, Denny or no Denny.

At age five, Robbie wrote his first Symphony. It was well received and offers to perform throughout the HaChii system came in. There was also an offer to have him conduct it at the Chicago Symphony Orchestra. It had been a while since Greg and NaDii had seen Rob and his uncle Jack, so NaDii decided to call up MeBlii and ChuuRii, and see if they'd like to make a group road-trip of it for their wedding anniversary.

Robbie had thought, in addition to his Symphony, that he should bring another composition, possibly one for the Church in Chicago. Other composers had done so much with the *Missa Solemnis* form that he didn't want to venture in that direction. In the end, he composed a Gregorian Chant version of the Lord's Prayer, to be sung in Latin. He felt that he owed the Cardinal at least that much, but wondered if the clergyman would be able--or even want--to fit it into a service while Robbie was there. He sent the sheet music via q-link to Mary Ryan Harker, Rob's mother and the church organist at Holy Name cathedral. She reported back that the Cardinal would be delighted and would have the choir perform it at the Mass where ChuuRii and MeBlii planned to renew their vows, if Robbie and his parents would attend.

Preparations for the trip took quite a bit of organization. DiiRaa wanted to come along, May and

Chuu had to get there from Cluret, Placet's second-biggest city. Greg's mother would meet them at O'Hare spaceport when they arrived. Greg, Robbie, NaDii, MeBlii and ChuuRii would meet Robert and his mother at the Church, and Cardinal Ryan had invited all of them out to a Cubs game after they arrived and had a chance to settle in at the hotel a while.

With all the hustle and bustle, NaDii had not been paying strict attention to the calendar, so one week before they were scheduled to depart, she and Greg found themselves looking at another egg lying on the bedsheets.

"Oh, my." Nadii said softly, "Dr. RuFii said it was a million-to-one shot last time. Do you suppose this one is fertilized too?"

"Time will tell," Greg said, then wrapped it in a warm towel and placed it in an empty fish tank with an aquarium heater.

"What temperature did Dr. RuFii say it should be kept at?" he asked NaDii.

"Thirty Celsius." she replied. "At least I think that's close. I'll call RuFii and check."

When she got back, she told Greg that was right. "I guess we'll know in a day or so whether it is developing. And RuFii agreed to come over with one of the new scanners that can do a DNA check right in the shell, non-invasively. She can come by and check tomorrow, she said."

"I'll program the house AI to recognize her." Greg said.

"Oh. Something else." NaDii added. "There was a message from Chuu and May. They're expecting. Hatching in three months."

"They've been trying for a while." She added

"Wow. Big things usually come in threes. I wonder what's next." Greg replied.

NaDii went back to the monitor to send a congratulation message to Chuu and May, and there was a second message link waiting for attention. Click——

"I hear you're going to the Sol System." FriiDa's voice said out of the q-link monitor. "I've got some business in-system at Marsport. Want a ride?"

"It's a big group, FriiDa, you sure you're OK with that?"

"It's a big yacht, NaDii," FriiDa replied, "and I don't get to take it out-system nearly as much as I'd like."

"Let me go cancel some tickets." NaDii concluded.

"FriiDa's coming too?" Greg asked.

"Well," NaDii said, "she's saying she has business at Marsport, but I saw her monitor reflected in a mirror. There was another window beside ours and she had just ordered Cubs tickets for that game on Tuesday."

"FriiDa's got a big heart." Greg said.

"Three of them, actually, same as me." NaDii replied brightly.

Next day the egg was the same shade of mottled blue that had grabbed their attention on (4147) Lennon.

They didn't want to tell Robbie anything until RuFii arrived with the scanner.

Early in the afternoon, 9 on the HaChii clock, RuFii arrived.

"Hi kids." RuFii greeted them. "Where's the patient?" she kidded.

""Over here." NaDii led her to the bedroom. "We haven't told Robbie; wanted to be sure we knew what to tell him first——"

"He's playing on the keyboard. Won't be likely to notice you're here for another hour." Greg said.

"OK." the HaChii doctor said, as she extracted an object from her shoulder bag. "Electronics. Human-made. Can scan the DNA and get a sequence from outside the shell. Fabulous stuff." she concluded.

She pointed the object at the egg NaDii had taken from the aquarium tank. Ran it down the length of the egg, and looked at the readout.

"I'll be screedged," she exclaimed, "32% human DNA, more than Robbie, even. And -- yep. It's going to be a female. Wow. *Never* thought that would happen again."

"You think it'll be OK?" Greg asked.

"Pretty sure. With that much additional DNA, she'll be even more robust than Robbie, and he's 'way big for a male his age."

"I've got to go tell Robbie." Greg said.

"And I've got to call May. "NaDii concluded.

"Will you come with me, RuFii?" Greg said, "Robbie's bound to have a million questions, and I don't know the answers to most of them."

"You bet." RuFii answered. "How much have you told him about reproduction?"

"A lot. Probably not enough. But he finds stuff on the q-net that probably gets into it deeper than I can manage, anyway."

"I'll keep that in mind."

The day of the trip, FriiDa's space yacht appeared over the river, turned, and hovered about 50 meters above the house. Robbie, Greg and NaDii walked out into the back yard, accompanied by DiiRa, ChuuRii and MeBlii. The 100-meter space yacht *Good Vibrations* couldn't come down any lower without smashing half-a-dozen houses in the neighborhood to smithereens. And they looked up, curious as to what kind of staircase or ladder would be let down to get them into the ship.

A section of the craft's bottom slid open. A beam illuminated the six persons and some sort of scanning process seemed to be taking place. Then they all felt the sensation of a solid flat surface under their feet suddenly beginning to lift them up. A few clumps of dirt and vegetation, apparently clipped off just below the soles of their feet, began to rise with them. The very solid, but completely invisible, surface continued to rise until they were inside the ship. The open section of flooring slid back into place and they were lowered a few inches until they were settled down onto the floor. Then the beam shut off and they all dropped a tiny fraction of an inch into solid contact with the real floor surface.

FriiDa stood off to the side of the room they now found themselves in.

"New toy." she said. "What do you think of it?"

"Wow! Whoever thought of that," Greg said, "must have read a ***lot*** of UFO abduction stories——"

It was Robbie's first trip to anyplace off-planet, and he was endlessly effusive about the sights as the ship lifted out past the atmosphere, and then the gravity well, of Placet. FriDaa invited them all up to the ship's bridge, to get a better look at the view. When FriiDa engaged the trac drive, HaChii and humans covered their eyes or looked away from the windows. Seeing the Universe contracted into a cosmic washboard, with the ship tunneling through the waves, caused vertigo in most people. Not Robbie.

"Space is all scrunched." he said to FriiDa.

"That's right." FriiDa replied. "Right now, it's compressed about 300,000 to 1 compared to when we see flat space.

"How fast are we going, really?" Robbie asked.

"About 90 percent of light-speed. Have your folks explained percentages yet?"

"Sure. Ninety percent means almost all, but not quite; that would be 100 percent."

"Good." That's the part that gets us through. We go through contracted-space at *not quite* the speed of light, but the space is compressed a lot, so we get there fast."

Robbie did some mental arithmetic. "So, the 160 light-years from Placet to Earth would take a little over 5 hours?"

FriiDa looked sideways at Robbie. "You did that in your head?"

"Just an estimate. How close did I get?"

Estimate? FriiDa thought after checking the flight screen. "Five hours and twelve minutes——" she answered.

Arrival at Chicago involved making arrangements to land at O'Hare. Might as well meet Enya where everybody was expecting her, after all.

FriiDa landed, pulled up to one of the gates, and everybody disembarked.

Greg's mother, Enya Firestone, greeted them. She had her blond hair bobbed short and was wearing a green dress. By sheer coincidence, NaDii had chosen a green robe to wear herself. They compared colors for a moment. Same color.

"Matches your eyes." NaDii told Enya.

Robbie stepped up to his mother and grandmother. He looked into their eyes closely for a few moments, first one, and then the other. Then, his color changed from ordinary HaChii cyan to alternating bands of green and gray, with the bands rolling down his arms to his fingertips. Then he reversed the motion of the color-bands so they flowed from his fingertips back up his arms to where they disappeared into his jacket.

"There! Now I match both your eyes——" he said.

Enya stared at him, astounded, turned to NaDii, and asked. "Can all HaChii children do that?"

"I didn't know that ***any*** HaChii could do that!" NaDii replied. "Robbie? How long have you been able to do that, and where did you get the idea?"

"Since yesterday." Robbie answered, innocently. "I was looking at some videos of places in Chicago on FriiDa's monitor, and there were these pictures from a place called Shedd Aquarium. There was a creature called a cuttlefish, doing that, and I figured it would be neat to try. Took a while to figure it out, but now I can do pretty much anything." He flashed red with white Coca-Cola logos on every visible surface of his body, then turned back to his normal blue-green color.

"Show-off!" his mother said. But her pupils were tilted sideways, and Robbie knew she wasn't really annoyed at him. Greg, May and Chuu all stared with the same wide-eyed expression of astonishment.

DiiRaa came over and asked Robbie. "Could you do that again?"

Robbie obliged and turned into bright blue with logos from half a dozen HaChii soft-drink companies.

"I don't think you should do that while you're playing music at concerts." he said, "At least, not until we get the ***endorsement contracts*** signed——"

Greg could imagine the cash-register wheels turning over in DiiRaa's head. He couldn't blame him, really. The same wheels were turning in his own head——

And they all walked towards the baggage claim area.

Later, at the Cubs game, as Robbie and his family ate popcorn in the bleachers and Cardinal Ryan explained the principles of baseball to those who had never seen the game played before, Robbie held up a finger for a moment. "Your Eminence?"

"Call me Father Jack."

"Very well, Father Jack." Robbie whispered as the Cardinal bent over to listen to him. "There is a question I wanted to ask."

"Fire away. Was it the part about stolen bases or the rules about how a player is tagged out?"

"None of those." Robbie replied. "It's about the church ceremony tomorrow."

"Hmmm?" the Cardinal said, in a curious tone.

"After I play the music, and Uncle Chuu and Aunt May take their vows," he continued, "could you manage to work in something for me?"

"Depends. What would that be?"

"Well, I've never been Baptized. And that guy with the knife really made me think. Maybe I should be——"

"My pleasure, Robbie, I'll do it formally after the wedding. But this is a serious business, I know your life has been threatened more than once."

Ryan took a piece of ice out of the soda he had been drinking.

He held the piece of ice against Robbie's forehead, just above his eyes. A little trickle of water began to drip down his face as the ice melted.

"Robert Firestone, I baptize thee in the Name of the Father, the Son, and the Holy Spirit." and then for good measure, "Ego te baptizo in nomine Patris, et Filii, et Spiritu Sanctii," he concluded.

"That's it?" Robbie asked.

"That's all that's really needed." Cardinal Ryan answered. "There's a lot more in the formal ceremony, but right now, you're baptized. I'll talk to your parents about the formal Baptism later. You don't think they'll mind, do you?"

"Dad was baptized when he was a lot smaller than I am now. And grandma Enya's Catholic," Robbie replied, "but it's Mom I'm not sure about. HaChii people don't have any worship practices at all, and I don't know what she'll think."

"I'll talk to her after the game." the Cardinal said.

The leadoff man, Frank Chance, was a namesake of a Cubs player from centuries earlier--he may even have been related. He kept popping up foul balls into the stands until the pitcher was getting exhausted and MeBlii had actually caught a ball, then blasted the next pitch into the right field stands.

Twelve hits and three double-plays later, the game ended, Cubs 10, Giants 4.

As they walked out of New Wrigley Field, May asked the Cardinal, "Do I have to return the ball to the player?"

"Nope." the Cardinal stated simply. "Even though it is technically the property of Major League Baseball, there is a 'finders keepers' rule that says if you catch it, you can keep it. The only fans who throw the ball back are the ones you saw in these bleachers, who caught a ball from the ***opposing*** team. They always throw ***those*** back." he concluded.

"Interesting tradition." MeBlii remarked, then she tucked the ball into a pocket of her robe.

As they walked out to the monorail platform, the Cardinal asked NaDii for a moment of her time.

"Robbie told me he wants to be Baptized into the Catholic Church." Ryan told her, simply.

"I've been reading his Catechism, and other things related to the Church." NaDii said.

"I've been watching what he is -- interested in -- and I was actually expecting this," she concluded.

"Well, what do you think about it?" Ryan inquired.

"It's -- complicated. Like I've said, if he's interested in something, I try to follow up on it as much as I can——although I won't pretend that I can understand how he writes music, or everything about what's written in all the Church doctrine and dogma I've read in the past few months." She paused for a moment. "At first, I thought--this Church thing--there's no harm in it. Lately, though——"

And the Cardinal began to look worried.

"I think God has intervened in his life. I never believed in a God; never even thought about such an idea most of my life. But there's only so much coincidence I can take before I start to think there's something there."

She paused for a few more beats, and the Cardinal remained silent, but looked at her quizzically.

"I guess what I'm saying is——Yes——and could you baptize me too?"

Wide-eyed, the Cardinal nodded. "You bet. I guess you've been doing more reading than I thought. Robbie wanted to do the ceremony after May and Chuu renew their vows. There is a little -- paperwork -- and some more stuff to read, but if it's OK with you, we do Baptisms as part of the Easter Vigil Mass, and instead of doing it after the wedding anniversary tomorrow night, why don't you just come in tonight, the day before Easter, at Easter Vigil, and I'll baptize both of you with the others——"

"Is there anything special we should wear, any special preparations to make?"

"What you've got on is fine. Stop at a store and buy candles for everyone who is going to be baptized. Bring Greg. I understand from Father Boyle that he has been to Mass several times since we spoke. Oh! And I understand congratulations are in order; Robbie is going to have a little sister, is that right?"

"Yes it is. We expect the egg to hatch in July." NaDii added distractedly, as she put a note into her message pad to 'buy candles.'

NaDii had studied on the q-net and came in with Greg, Robbie and Enya knowing what to expect for an Easter Vigil service. Cardinal Ryan smiled at them as they came in to the church, then his eyebrows raised as his nephew Rob walked in with MeBlii and ChuuRii.

Knowing Robbie's musical talent and ability to quick-study almost anything, the priests were not surprised that he was able to sing the *Exsultet.* That the rest of the HaChii present were also able to do so flawlessly was a bigger surprise. *I'll bet Robbie has been coaching the others,* the Archbishop thought to himself.

By the end of the service, all three (or three-and-a-half, counting Robbie) of the HaChii present had been Baptized, taken Communion, and were congratulated collectively and individually by a great many members of the congregation.

MeBlii and ChuuRii's wedding vows were renewed that night after the Vigil Mass, everybody having expected the same small party to attend who had been present two years earlier, with only the addition of Greg's mother. Word seemed to have slipped out and spread around the congregation, however, and many stayed behind to attend the wedding vows, as well.

During the ceremony, parishioners with cameras at several locations around the church had been busy. By the next morning, a still photograph of the Hachii, their heads bowed along with the rest of the congregation, fronted almost every q-net newsfeed website. The photographer who had first submitted the picture to the newsfeeds had added the caption "Brothers in Christ" to the bottom of the picture and -- politically incorrect or not -- almost nobody had found the nerve to take that caption off the picture on Easter morning. The video from the renewal service with young Robbie singing his Gregorian chant version of the *Pater Noster* went 'viral' within hours.

Jack Ryan expected to take some flak, and have the Archdiocese's messaging equipment swamped by incoming messages. He wasn't disappointed there; messages crashed the system early that morning. Nonetheless, one message ***did*** manage to get through, when a courier walked in with a diplomatic pouch. Inside was a single sheet of paper.

" Good work." it said. "Now I really ***am*** jealous. How did you ***do*** that?"

--Signed, His Holiness, Pope Clement XXV.

Monday evening young Robbie was to conduct the Chicago Symphony Orchestra, who would be playing his First Symphony.

People started to line up outside Symphony Hall at six in the morning. By mid-day, when the size of the crowd began to approach 100,000, city officials came in to confer with the administrators. Large viewing screens were prepared and placed outside the building, and at various locations to stream live video to those who would not fit into the hall. Additional screens were placed in the band-shell at Grant Park for those who were willing to relocate there for the concert.

By concert time, 500,000 people were located throughout the downtown area to see the performance on the screens. At the Symphony Hall, entrance was granted to Ticket-holders only, with the exception of a few celebrities and politicians. All were screened very rigorously by security, even the politicians——

After the performance, and everybody's standing ovation, the Mayor presented Robbie and his family with certificates giving them the status of honorary citizens of the City of Chicago, each plaque having a small gold key attached to the plaque below the printing.

"What is that for, your honor?" Robbie pointed at the key.

"It's symbolic." the Mayor replied. "Cities don't have walls and city gates anymore, but these keys open the City of Chicago to you symbolically. They mean you are welcome here any time."

"Well, thank you, your Honor." was all Robbie could say. He didn't know if this was just an amusing piece of political theatrics, or something sincere on behalf of all the people. *I suppose it could be both,* he thought.

He asked his father later, and Greg popped up a screen on his message pad. "They ran your Symphony on live newsfeeds from several links." he pointed out. "They polled the public throughout Chicago afterwards, asking if they felt we should be offered honorary citizenship. Two million responded; the vote was 98.5 percent in favor, 1.5 percent opposed."

"I guess that ***was*** sincere, after all." Robbie surmised.

"Not that everything isn't politics, too. This is Chicago, after all." his Dad concluded.

CHAPTER 17 - Just a Lucky Guess

The return trip to Placedon was uneventful. Robbie practiced the new skill he had discovered. A trip to the Shedd Aquarium as a guest of one of their zoologists allowed him to get a close-up look at how those cuttlefish used the chromatophores in their skin as a traveling-light display. In return, Robbie showed Shedd zoologists the 'Coca-Cola' effect, and explained how he was able to use visualization to modify his own chromatophores' appearance. Never having had the ability to ask the cuttlefish how they did it, they were delighted in having someone with the same ability, who was able to describe how it *feels* to do that——

On the way back, FriiDa told NaDii she should think about moving ahead a little differently on Robbie's math training.

"Find out how he estimates numbers," she said, "and decide if there's something you need to be doing instead of ordinary arithmetic."

"Estimates numbers?" NaDii had never observed this.

"I told him the trip through contracted-space was compressed 300,000 to 1, and we were going 90% of the speed of light. He thought about it for a few seconds and said the 160 light years would take a little more than 5 hours."

"Was that very close, FriiDa?" asked NaDii.

"Within about 96% accuracy. Maybe closer depending on how much 'a little' is." FriiDa stated. "It could be a lucky guess, but I know folks out there who do 'lucky' like this all the time. When they do it, they have techniques that only a genius could come up with. Try him out on some math problems like this, and if he's as good as I think, then ask him how he does it. The answers may be enlightening."

"Okay. I'll try that out."

Robbie was looking at the video of a cuttlefish with the moving bands running down his tentacles, and matching the pattern. NaDii asked Robbie how long it would take him to go to Earth if he could find a trac drive that compressed space 500,000 to 1. He answered with a question: "Does it move through the compressed space at 0.9c like FriiDa's ship?"

"Let's suppose it does." NaDii answered.

"Three hours and seven minutes, then." Robbie answered.

NaDii had memorized the result FriiDa gave her earlier from the ship console. It was three hours and a little over 7 minutes.

"How did you do it?" she asked him.

"Easy, Mom," He said, "I already knew it was 5 hours and a little less than 12 minutes at 300,000 to 1. At 500,000 to 1 everything would take 3/5 as long, and 3/5 of 5 is 3. Then I figured 3/5 of 12 minutes is .6 times 12 and that's 7.2. But 12 is a little big so 7.2 is a little big, and I just rounded it down to 7. So 3 hours 7 minutes should be pretty close."

"Mmmm hmmm." NaDii said, non-committally.

"All right. How close to 7 minutes was it?" he asked.

"It was 7.004." she said softly.

"Less than a quarter of a second off. That'll do." Robbie said.

"Tell me how you got the quarter-second part."

"Sure. 6 times 4 is 24. I pull the decimal point one place because there are 60 seconds in a minute instead of 6. Then I pull it back three the other way because there's a .004 instead of a 4. And the 24 ends up at .24, and .25 is a quarter, so of course, it's less than a quarter."

"Of course." NaDii said.

"You know what squares are?" she tried next.

Robbie drew a shape in the air.

"No, I mean square numbers, like 10 times 10."

"Oh, that. A special case of multiplication." Robbie answered.

"So what's the square of 48?" she asked

"It would be close to 2300." Robbie answered.

"How'd you get that?" she asked.

"Well--48 is close to 50. I know 5 times 5 is 25. So 50 times 50 is 2500. 48 is 2 less than 50 so you take 2 rows of 50 off the top and side. That's 200, so I took 200 from 2500 and got 2300."

"Suppose you wanted to get closer?" NaDii asked.

"Hmm. Well the two 48s end in 8, so when you multiply 8s you get 64, and the last digit has to be a 4. So I suppose I would guess that instead of 2300 I should guess 2304."

NaDii entered numbers into her comm pad, then clicked. 48 times 48 was 2304.

"Close enough." *Damn——*

"There's another way to look at it." Robbie added. "48 is 4 percent less than 50. So you double that and the square should be 8 percent less than 2500. Eight 25s are 200. So you take away 200 and get 2300."

"Why would you double the 4 percent?" NaDii asked.

"It's a square. You're taking 4 percent off the height, and 4 percent off the width. Just made sense. If I were doing a cube, I'd triple it, wouldn't I? Right, Mom?"

"I have no idea. Might be interesting to try."

"Okay. Let's try 10.1 cubed." Robbie said. "That's one percent higher than 10, and 10 cubed is a thousand. So add ***three*** percent of 1000——"

"Thirty." NaDii said.

"Yeah, thirty. That gives 1030."

"Let me try this." NaDii said. "The end digits are 1s and 1 times 1 is 1. So I guess it's 1031 instead of 1030. Now let's try it with the machine." NaDii fiddled with her message pad. "Nope. It's 1030.301."

"But Mom," Robbie said, "the ones are one place ***past*** the decimal point, so the 1 at the end of the cube ends up ***three*** places past the decimal point. It wouldn't come out in the ones place no matter what."

Ouch. NaDii thought.

"I could multiply it all out, like I could multiply 48 times 48. But it's a lot quicker to just roll the two rows off the sides of the square. And in the case of 10.1 cubed, there's a lot of carrying and summing and keeping track of places in that. Lots of places to make a mistake. The answer is going to be closer than 48 times 48, because 10.1 is closer to 10 than 48 is to 50, so you can just use the answer, without even looking for the last digit."

"I suppose so." *Interesting,* she thought, *accepting tolerable levels of inaccuracy lets you do things faster, as long as you know how much you can tolerate.*

"Try another, Mom. 5.1 cubed."

"OK. 5 times 5 times 5 is 125."

"Good."

"5.1 is two percent higher than 5"

"Right."

"So I add 3 times 2 = 6 percent of 5. That's 0.3"

"Nope. Try again."

"***Oh.*** I add 6 percent of **125**, which is——7.5."

"That's it, Mom."

"And that gives me 132.5"

"So now let's check it out."

"The message pad says 132.651; is that close enough?"

"About 99.9% accuracy. How do you feel about that?"

Pretty good. NaDii thought. *Wait a minute. Who's doing the home schooling here?*

CHAPTER 18 - Playmates

Dr. RuFii came to visit; she was intending to do a health check on the egg, and had brought Greg and NaDii an incubator unit that would be considerably better than a tank with an aquarium heater in it. Robbie came in to look as the egg was transferred into its new housing.

"Development looks good at this stage. It appears that she will have many of Robbie's characteristics." RuFii reported.

"Hybrid vigor?" Robbie asked.

"What?" RuFii answered, non-plussed by the question.

"Heterozygote advantage." Robbie clarified. To his parents, of course, this clarified nothing, but to RuFii, it meant she could guess what he already knew, and tailor an answer that wasn't limited to what a 5-year-old was ***expected*** to be able to grasp.

"Probably." she said. "I imagine you know that you're the ultimate outcross. Compared to you, every living thing on Earth and Placedon is massively inbred."

"Except my sister." Robbie pointed at the egg.

"Except her." RuFii walked over into the corner and spoke with Robbie privately for about ten minutes. Then she walked over to where NaDii and Greg were, and asked them a question that had been on her mind for a while. "Have you ever had intelligence testing done on Robbie?"

"Nope." Greg answered, "But I think it's obvious what the result would be."

"No. I mean there might be others--human and HaChii--that are as bright or brighter. Don't take this the wrong way, but it would be great if he could interact with some others who--operate at the same level he does."

"I'm not insulted." NaDii said. "I figured out he's brighter than I was a long time ago."

Greg chimed in. "I didn't go into mining because I was the valedictorian of my class. Anybody can see that Robbie runs rings around us. But how would we find other kids his age that are as bright?"

"I didn't say ***kids***. I just spent ten minutes talking with him about the implications of heterozygotic inheritance and he knows more than ***I*** do. He has some conjectures——" She trailed off. "Well, I don't think it's just music. He appears to be gifted in all areas of thinking."

"Where do we get him tested?" Greg asked.

"I'll bring him in some standard tests tomorrow." RuFii said. "If he blows the roof off of them——as I expect he will——then I'll take him over to the DeVrii Institute for some further testing. OK?"

RuFii brought in a standard test, and Robbie didn't miss any questions, so all she could say was "somewhere in the stratosphere." She then took Robbie, with his parents, to the DeVrii Institute, where the researchers undertook more extensive testing.

Robbie's testing took longer than NaDii and Greg expected. About four hours into the morning, a researcher, who introduced herself as TiiChaa, stepped out of the testing room and asked to talk with Greg and NaDii. They asked if anything was wrong.

"We've gotten into the test questions they normally do with 15-year olds. He's still answering them," she explained simply.

"What does that mean?" Greg said.

"You humans have a standard of measure you call IQ." TiiChaa answered, "It's often misused and misinterpreted, but basically it compares mental age to physical age."

"I didn't know that," Greg said. "I thought it was just some standard where the average guy on the street was 100 and they went up and down from there."

"Well, for adults, it is." TiiChaa replied, "But with children, if, for instance, a four-year-old can answer questions as well as an average four-year-old, that is 100% of what's expected, and the IQ is 100. If she can answer questions as well as a six-year-old, the IQ is 6 ÷ 4 or 150%, of what's expected, and the IQ is 150."

"So if Robbie is answering questions at the 15-year-old level, and he's 5, that means an IQ of 300?"

"At least. Remember, I said he was ***still answering*** questions that would be normal for a 15-year-old. I didn't say we had reached his limit yet."

After a couple more hours, TiiChaa finally came out with a tired-looking Robbie. "You get some rest now." she told him.

"He topped out," TiiChaa said, "where an average 18-or-19-year old human or HaChii would reach her limit."

"Or ***his*** limit," Greg corrected.

"Oops! Yes--***his*** limit," TiiChaa agreed. "Which your people would relate to an IQ of 360 or thereabouts."

NaDii, having no familiarity with human testing concepts, said, "Is that unusual?"

"It varies with age, what it means. For five-year-olds, apparently, there are three others known in the 25 planets of the HaChii-Human domain who are within 70 points. None are over 300.

You should know--this tends to move towards the average as kids get older. Kids like this are called ***precocious***. But they don't always stay that precocious as they grow up.

But right now, he's the brightest five-year old anywhere. If he were an eight-year old, he would still be the brightest 8-year-old on the 12 planets of the HaChii system. But there are a couple on Gracet--identical twins--who would match his test scores." TiiChaa concluded.

"Are there any others under eight years old?" NaDii asked, because at this point, Robbie was already the size of a seven-year-old HaChii male child.

"Two humans. One on Mars, one on Earth." TiiChaa answered after some searching. "***Oh.*** Is it OK for me to add Robbie to that database?"

Gracet, Earth, Mars--a long way to go to find playmates. NaDii thought.

"Greg?" NaDii said, and Greg had a feeling it was going to be one of those offers he couldn't refuse, "FriiDa saved us a bunch of money on that last road trip. Do you suppose we could use some of it to visit one of those kids and get Robbie together with someone his own age that he could actually relate to?"

Robbie had, of course, played with his HaChii cousins on NaDii's side of the family, but although they were a bit older, and although he tried to please them, the kind of playing they wanted to do 'bored him to death,' he later told his mother.

"Robbie needs friends his own age. I think--first we have to see if any of these kids would like to meet him. And I guess he should be on that database so the others can find him on the q-net," Greg said. "As for the kids, if their parents say it's OK, who am I to disagree?"

"We could start by setting up a meeting on the q-net." NaDii suggested.

It turned out the parents of the girls on Gracet--the twins--would be delighted to find somebody their daughters could talk to. Like Robbie, they didn't have a lot of friends their age they could relate to.

"Hello, RaBii," said Vrii, the more outgoing of the two. "I am Vrii Ix DriiBo This is my sister Chii."

"Hi. It's just Robbie. Robbie Firestone." Robbie said, pronouncing 'Robbie' with the emphasis on the first syllable instead of the last.

"Oh. What an unusual name. Is it Earther?" Vrii asked.

"It's a pure Earth name. My Dad's human. I suppose if my name were constructed according to HaChii rules, I would be RaBii Iz GreNaa or RaBii Iz GreNaDii. But in Terran English, that sounds like the name of an explosive device." He could not grin with his eyes like HaChii, but he decorated his skin with grinning eyes using his chromatophores.

"Oh, look at that!" the reticent Chii exclaimed.

"Can you do that again?" Vrii asked.

Robbie ran red-and-white stripes up his tentacles, flowing up from under his shirt, and disappearing at the top of his head, as more stripes continued to flow upward.

The girls were stunned into silence. Then Vrii said:

"I have the recording from your concert in Chicago. Your First Symphony. Have you written another?"

"Wait right here." he slid across to the keyboard, and rolled it in front of the screen. "It's no Symphony, but here's something new."

And he started to play.

"Oh! Look" Chii exclaimed again.

And they noticed that bands of color, and other geometric shapes, were moving up his arms from his fingertips, in time with the music.

"How odd that looks!" said the less-than-tactful Vrii.

"What part?" Robbie asked.

"I don't know what's odder, those 'hand' things on the end of your arms, or the--thing you do--with your skin color. When you put them together, it's quite a show." Vrii added.

Vrii had the nerve to ask. "Do you play anything besides Classical Music?"

Robbie thought for a second, then he flipped a few controls on the keyboard and started playing the lead guitar part from Van Halen's *Panama.*

The girls just froze and watched him march his hands back and forth across the keyboard. They both turned violet, then shuddered a little and turned pink. ***What was that all about?*** he wondered.

He finished, and then he said. "You know about me from the recordings, but I don't know anything about you. What do you like to do?"

The two girls' images on the viewscreen looked at each other. Their eyes tilted out in a big grin. "This is a *polyadok* board." Vrii said. "It's sort of like the Earth game, chess."

"But more complicated." Chii added. "Vrii's the expert."

Two hours later, Robbie understood the rules, but still lost every game to Vrii. ***Strategy*** had never been of any importance to him; now he began to appreciate its use. "Let's see. In that last game, where I moved the Lord's Serf from B4 to E5, I should have moved it to E7 instead and let you capture the Judge. Then I could have positioned my Princess to take the Lord's Guard and put him in Exile."

"You remember the whole game?" Chii asked.

"The last five games, too. Could I play game three over from the board position where the Serf had the Judge in thrall?"

Vrii clicked back to that game, and reversed the movements of the pieces to the point he described. "That spot?"

"Yes." And he began at that point with Vrii playing the twins' side. She was the stronger player, but in ten moves she could see where he was going.

"Oh, dear." she said, "I concede. I will lose this game in another three moves at best."

"Really?" Robbie said.

Chii looked at him, looked at her sister, and grinned. "That's the first time she's lost this year."

"Who does she play?" he asked.

"Everybody." Chii answered, "She's the planetary champion for the 8-to-12 age group on Gracet.

"Can I play that game back from five moves ago?" Vrii asked, timid for once.

"Sure." Robbie answered.

But she lost again. Robbie had gotten the feel of the game, and he had thought of something clever he could do using a Serf and a Merchant to distract the opponent from his attack on the Lord using the Lancer, a minor player.

"That's a HuuSill gambit!" Chii exclaimed, a bit too late for her sister Vrii, "Where did you learn that!"

"Oh. It's got a name?" he answered. "Well, I reasoned that——"

And as he explained his reasoning, Vrii paled. "You worked that out for yourself?"

"Sorry." he said, "Was it something I'm not allowed to do?"

"Oh, no." Vrii responded, "But--you're not in the 8-to-12 age group, are you?"

"I'm sorry. No, I'm not really your age." Chii tilted her head sideways while Vrii looked somewhat relieved.

"I'm only five." Robbie concluded.

Vrii went white again, Chii had fallen down on the floor and was pounding on it with her tentacles.

I've seen that before, Robbie thought. ***Having hysterics, I think it's called.***

Vrii went somewhere, leaving her sister.

After Chii settled down, Robbie told her, "You know. I have a grandmother named Chii. My Mom is NaDii Ix ChiiBii."

"Of course she is. Everybody knows about you." Chii elaborated.

"They do?" Robbie said, "Oh, yeah. I guess they do. I just forget about that sometimes. So what kind of things do you like besides ***polyadok***?"

"That's hard. Do you know much about fractal mathematics?"

"I've heard of it. There are some really interesting image-generating programs on the q-net. The one that tosses random dots into space and they end up building a complete HaChii person is particularly interesting."

"I wrote that one," Chii said.

"How did you find the right coefficients?" Robbie asked.

"Well, that's interesting. I started with one of Ramanujan's unproven theorems——"

"Hold on. Ramanujan, the number-theory guy?" Robbie asked.

"Yeah. That's him." Chii replied.

"Remember, I'm only five. I'm not up on number theory past simple summation," he apologized.

"Cool." Chii said, "Then you haven't got as much to un-learn as the average mathematician. Look, it's simple——"

And it was simple for the next four hours. At the end, Robbie was starting to understand things he had been thinking about for a while, but had never had anybody to bounce the ideas off of.

"Have you ever thought about how protein-folding from DNA could use the DNA as coefficients in a base-six fractal number system? Or base four—— Me, I've got a little of both——"

"That's interesting." Chii said. If I put the coefficients I found into base-six (for HaChii DNA) and ran the protein-folding program that I've got with my graphics package in reverse, do you suppose the generating-function it forms would match the code of HaChii DNA?"

"Let's try." And half-way through the test, NaDii called Robbie and told him it was time for bed.

"'Bye, Chii." he said. Call me in the morning and let me know how it works out."

"You bet."

Next morning, ***early***, Chii called Robbie back. She looked as though she hadn't slept all night.

"It ***worked!"*** she exulted. "There was a 95 percent match from my coefficients back to the DNA. I started with HaChii DNA and ran it forward, and only three of my coefficients had to be changed, and then only a small amount each."

"So, you can prove that DNA contains the coefficients of a fractal iterated function set that constructs the structure of a HaChii person?" Robbie asked.

"Better than that, I can prove that DNA for ***anything*** generates the structure of the creature from a set of coefficients written in the DNA. I did it for the base-four human genome, as well. Here is a genome that was on the q-net for an individual. First I run the transform that maps it into a set of coefficients——" She started a merge program she had written——

The points on the screen built a nervous system and blood vessels, then tissue began to fill in the structure. It gradually built into a ball of cells, then began to change shape.

"I'm varying one of the parameters that shows the way the shape of the organism varies with time." she said.

It began to look like a human baby with black hair and brown eyes.

"Now we run the numbers forward into adulthood." she said.

And the computer image refreshed every second into a child, then a young man, and then——

"Hey! That's my Dad!" Robbie exclaimed. "Where did you get that DNA map?"

"Your q-net account." Chii said, very softly

"But it's encrypted, behind the security, and——"

"That prime-number thing?" she said, "I figured out how to crack the one you're using ***months*** ago." she said.

"I'll--keep that in mind." Robbie said.

"I didn't mean any harm by doing it," Chii said contritely.

"Ffurff. I might have done it myself, if I had your chops at math." Robbie replied.

"Well, I'm sending it off to ***Annalen der Biomathematische Wissenschaft.***" she said.

"What's that?" he asked.

"German Science magazine on the human homeworld."

"Sounds pretty obscure."

"Isn't. It's the primary publication on the q-net for mathematical biology. It's available in all languages and anything that's anything gets published there first."

"Well, good. I'm pleased for you. This ***is*** a breakthrough——"

"Be pleased for yourself, too. I listed you as co-author. You were the one who had the idea, I just supplied some number-crunching."

Some number-crunching, he thought. "Well, thanks. That reminds me of something my Dad said, when his name was included on a patent application——"

"Hmmm???"

"I'll explain it to you when you're a little older." Even his parents didn't know he'd downloaded the patent application from the HaChii Patent Office files. Nobody had ever thought to put a child-lock on the access for that part of the network, and he wasn't going to tell them that they should——

CHAPTER 19 - Friends in High Places

Robbie, Greg and NaDii went to Sunday Mass at the spaceport Chapel most weekends. The only other 'parishioners' were the sacristan, human tourists passing through, and occasionally ChuuRii and MeBlii, when they were in town.

This Sunday, Father Boyle asked everybody to pray for the Holy Father, because Pope Clement XXV was very, very ill. They all bowed their heads, because the current pontiff had done a lot of good works, and everybody hoped against hope that he could recover and continue his ministry.

Human religions did not get much coverage on the newsfeeds most HaChii households received; for the most part, HaChii did not take that aspect of humans' lives very seriously. Robbie, however, was able to link through to the Vatican Terran English broadcasts over the q-net, and checked from time to time to follow the progress of the pontiff's medical treatment. Thus it was that on Wednesday, he learned that Clement XXV had died, and Robbie went to the Chapel that evening, with his parents, to say a prayer for the repose of his soul.

"What happens now that the Holy Father has died?" Robbie asked Father Boyle.

Boyle, having lived through the transitions of five popes by now, explained to Robbie that a meeting of the Cardinals, called a Conclave, would meet in Rome to elect a new pope, and even now, the College of Cardinals was gathering far-flung members from around the Earth and throughout human-space.

Robbie wondered if his friend, Cardinal Ryan of Chicago, was already in Rome.

"No." Father Boyle said. "There are nine days of mourning. Then the Cardinal Camerlengo in Rome arranges the funeral and burial of the pope. Then, after another 10 to 15 days of 'General Congregations' following the funeral--***then*** the Camerlengo calls the Conclave, and ***that*** is when the Cardinals gather together to begin selection of a new pope."

"That's quite a while for the Church to go without a leader." Robbie said.

"The Catholic Church is never hurried about anything, son, and this is no exception." the priest explained. And then he added, "In the interim, the Cardinal Camerlengo is acting head of the Church. Even so, it can still be days and days before the Cardinals finally choose a pope and one of their own membership walks out as the new Holy Father."

"Well then," Robbie said, "I will say a prayer for Cardinal Ryan, that he will have a safe trip and find the wisdom to choose a worthy successor for Pope Clement."

"I will certainly say that prayer with you." Father Boyle agreed.

And they both knelt at the altar for a few minutes.

Several weeks later, Robbie browsed the Vatican English-language coverage of the Conclave, periodically checking if the smoke from the burning of the ballots was black or white. Over and over, black smoke would issue from the small chimney that the newsfeed cameras kept watch on.

Finally, on the third day after three more ballots, white smoke finally burst forth from the smokestack, and the cameras turned to the central balcony of Saint Peter's Basilica.

"Annuntio vobis gaudium magnum."

"Habemus Papam!" the Cardinal Deacon announced.

Robbie struggled with the Latin. ***Announced with great (something)? We have a pope***, that much was clear.

Eminentissimum ac reverendissimum Dominum, ***Eminence——reverend——Lord, a title of his Eminence, so it's a Cardinal. No surprise there——***

Dominum Ioannem, ***John——***

Sanctæ Romanæ Ecclesiæ Cardinalem, ***(of the) Holy Roman College of Cardinals,***

Ryan. ***RYAN!***

Qui sibi nomen imposuit, ***Who has chosen the name,***

Patricius Primus. ***Patrick the First.***

Oh, My God—— It began to sink in——

Robbie yelled for his father. "Dad! Come Quick!"

And his father rushed into the room, just in time to see the new Pope walk out onto the balcony.

Pope Patrick the First was Cardinal Jack Ryan of Chicago.

"Holy shit!" his father said.

"Language, Dad," Robbie reminded him. "And by the way, I happen to agree——"

The next day, Chii left a message to pop up when Robbie opened his q-net browser for the first time. ***CALL ME*** it said with no further explanation.

Robbie called.

"Robbie. Our paper has been published in ***Annalen der Biomathematische Wissenschaft.***"

Our *paper*. He had almost forgotten about it. "It was cleared by the referees and is in the issue that was posted this morning," she said.

"Wow. Well, that is very nice." Robbie said. "I don't know if I really contributed that much to it——" he said. "But it's nice to have something besides music with my name on it, I guess. Thanks, again, for including me."

"You keep saying that. But without your idea, I would have never been able to do the rest. ***Congratulations to you***, do you hear me. Go look at it. Here's the link to the magazine."

So he opened another window. ***Über DNA und dem IFS der Fraktalische Mathematik***

He thought he had been struggling with Latin yesterday! Then, recognizing DNA, IFS (Barnsley's Iterated Function Set for fractal generation)and of course, Fractal Mathematics, he at least recognized that he had found the right article, perhaps not in the right language.

Then he rolled down the page and saw that the rest of the article was in Terran English. That, at least, was a language he knew.

There was the idea he remembered talking with Chii about. Most of it was still a fog of mathematical symbols that made no more sense to him than had it been in German or Latin, but the description, the diagrams, and the conclusion, he could follow.

"How about that——" He looked back at the screen and there were Chii and Vrii. They were clearly identical twins. There were, he knew, very few of those among HaChii children.

"You know, I never asked before, who was hatched first and who was hatched second——" he asked.

"We were in the same egg, silly!" Vrii answered. So we both hatched out together."

He had never heard of that before. Clearly, they didn't have the arrangement humans had, where they could be born separately, one after another. No wonder it was such a rarity.

Vrii said to him. "I wish I had stayed with you when you started working with my sister on that Math thing. I was a bad loser. Would you like another game of *polyadok?*"

"No, thanks; not right now." he said, "Maybe later."

"Well, Robbie, I'm a little surprised that article got published so quickly."

"I am, too. a little." Chii said. "By the way, the editor contacted me and seemed to think he needed to see my Mommy. I explained I was the author and my Mom didn't know anything about number theory or fractals. It took me the longest time to convince him."

"Ageism." Robbie pronounced. "I wonder what they would have thought if they saw me——"

"I told him how old you were, when he guessed my collaborator 'Robert Firestone' must be an adult human, who really did all the work." she said, "I had to convince him all over again——until I showed him your recording with the Symphony. He said something I couldn't translate into HaChii. Then he said the two of us together would have to double our combined ages to equal the age of their next youngest author."

"Somehow, I can believe that——" Robbie said.

"And——" Chii continued, "He said something about your picture in Church."

"Oh, That——" Robbie said.

"He asked if you knew somebody called the Pope. Sounded like a big deal to him. What was that about?"

"Oh, sure." Robbie said, "We go way back. I suppose it is a big deal to some humans. But he's just Father Jack to me."

"I thought his name was Patrick." Vrii said, somewhat confused.

"It is now, the Pope takes a new name when he is elected."

"Oh, now you're putting us on." Vrii said, "And you're only five; what do you mean, 'We go way back?'"

"He married my parents when I was two. That's pretty far back, for me."

"I ***guess***——" Vrii still looked skeptical.

"Well--now what?" Robbie asked.

"What do you mean, 'Now what?'" Chii asked.

"I guess I should show my parents. They're not going to understand one word in ten, but——like I said, then what?"

"I don't know. We might get offers to teach mathematics somewhere, I suppose, or maybe biology, in your case."

"Where? In first grade?" he asked, joking with one of the terms he had learned from his Dad.

"I've looked at the Earth educational system," Chii answered. "I don't think you're old enough for first grade."

"Now that I remember," he said, "My Dad didn't start first grade until he was six. I guess you're right."

Eventually, Robbie called his parents over to look at the paper. As he had expected, they couldn't make heads or tails of it.

"Show it to RuFii," his mother said.

Robbie forwarded the link. Then he didn't think any more about it. Until RuFii called back.

"That's impressive." she said, "I don't know whether it's up my alley. I showed it to a mathematician and he said it was Fields Medal or Abel Prize stuff. To me, it looked like a Nobel Prize for Physiology or Medicine candidate. Does any of this make sense to you?"

Robbie was taken aback. "Nobel Prize, even I've heard of that. The other one, that Abel prize, I don't know about. But I'm too young. Nobody will give me any kind of prize for my part in it. Still, it's nice to see my name at the top."

"Robbie, you are too modest." Dr RuFii answered, "This is groundbreaking stuff. You talked to me about it as a speculation last month. This month, here it is, all worked out. Don't kid yourself. This is as big as the music thing, even bigger if I'm any judge."

"Well, thanks. Glad there's somebody who can understand it——"

"Not a chance. I only know that it works from the pictures——" RuFii answered. Then she congratulated him again, and said goodbye.

It's over <u>her</u> head? he thought, ***Sometimes, I even impress myself.***

And then he didn't think any more about it.

He did, however, remember to send congratulations to Father Jack.

Are you supposed to congratulate a Pope? I don't know——Do I call you Father Pat now? I guess it's Holy Father Pat. Oh, well, Congratulations. I'll pray for you at Mass this Sunday. -- Robbie

CHAPTER 20 - Winners

Three years had passed. Robbie asked his Mom, at age 6, that she please call him Bobby, instead. His little sister had been named TiiNa, after her great-grandmother and mother. He had learned to feed her with a bottle, and found, to his surprise, that at the age of 8 weeks, when she found her first word, it was 'Bobby.' She couldn't say 'Robbie,' and he decided he liked it——

Every time somebody contacted Bobby about 'the paper' in the ***Annalen*** he felt like *such a fraud.* Chii said she would coach him, and he worked with her every day to learn to use the tools she had used to prove his conjecture. By the second year, he actually understood what he was working with. He even understood some of the math well enough to go back and look at the m-theory and branes, which he had earlier dismissed as too complicated. Surprisingly, it didn't look too complicated any more. And he started working with Chii to apply some of the implications of what he knew, now.

He spoke with Father Boyle one Sunday after Mass. "Father, I wonder if I could talk to you about something that's bothering me." he said.

"I heard your confession yesterday; what is bothering you that we couldn't talk about then?" the priest asked.

"Well, Father, it's the mathematics. I used to think the Big Bang--the origin of the universe--was a lot simpler to explain as an act of creation than it would be to explain by some rational physical process. But just now, I'm working with someone on math--and it looks a lot less complicated than it did when I was younger. I think I could come up with a perfectly logical, rational way for the Universe to begin, without any Creator being necessary. And that worries me. If I pursue this line of reasoning, am I questioning the existence of God?"

Father Boyle thought about this for a few moments. "How sure are you of this mathematical work?"

"It's rock solid, Father." Bobby said. "I've double-checked it with Chii, and she's the most advanced mathematician I know."

"Well, if it follows logical rules, and is a consequence of laws of nature that can be described, it's just as possible that God did the reasoning and He is responsible for the fact that these rules can be applied to make the Big Bang possible. He said 'Let there be light,' the Bible doesn't say how He decided to do it—— So, No, I think if you can shed some light (he winked) on that process, nobody who takes rational thinking seriously will say you are questioning the existence of God, just revealing a deeper insight into how the Universe he created works."

"So——You know the Holy Father better than I do——Do you think he would object to a paper that describes the Universe originating without a conscious act of will?"

"I think you know him pretty well. He wouldn't object to anything that expands the knowledge we have of the Universe. And he knows you. Believe me, he wouldn't object. Go ahead and publish the paper, if you're really sure. And if it makes you feel better, I have a private message-link I can call him on, and I'll talk to him about this tonight."

"Thanks, Father."

Bobby called Chii and she posted up on his q-net page almost immediately.

"I know that something was bothering you, Bobby," she said, "but you look a little more relaxed. Have you decided if it's time to publish this paper?"

"It still worries me that this might be controversial in--certain circles--but I think I've got a friend in the Vatican who might help smooth things out for me." Bobby said. "I really don't think there is going to be any trouble from that direction. There are others who interpret the Bible more literally. They don't always listen to the Holy Father. But I don't think there is much I can do about them. Thank God there aren't many HaChii Christians who don't know me, and the rest wouldn't have any objection I can imagine."

"Other HaChii Christians you don't know?" Chii asked, "I think you could count them on the tentacles of one hand." she kidded.

He looked at one hand. Not a lot of tentacles there. "Right——" he said.

"So we publish?" Chii asked softly.

"Yes. We publish." Bobby answered. ***And may God have mercy on my soul.***

Chii left the field of view, and then her sister, Vrii, slid into view.

"OK Hotshot. You ready for a game of ***polyadok?***"

"Yeah. It would take my mind off this other stuff," he answered.

He could still win about every third game. Vrii hadn't stood still. She bore down on improving her ***polyadok*** game, while Bobby only played 'off the cuff' as it were. ***Still, he would rank near the top on Gracet, Placet, or any other world of the HaChii Confederation,*** Vrii thought, ***if only he would compete.***

The next year, Bobbie finished his Third and Fourth Symphonies. The Chicago Symphony Orchestra had right of first refusal, and they hadn't refused, yet. So he had a steady flow of fan mail, most of which he ignored, from Earth.

He continued to work with Chii. They had become very close while working on mathematical concepts together. ***Too bad that she's so far away on Gracet, in the Draff system,*** he thought. ***Well, maybe I can talk Mom and Dad into making that Road Trip they promised, three years ago.***

TiiNa was certainly old enough to travel now. They had been playing duets since she was two, and her musical talents were already apparent.

He had written a 'two players' piano part for his Fourth Symphony, and hoped the CSO would invite him to Earth again, so the two of them could perform that part together. But there was just not enough of an excuse, if the CSO did ***not*** invite him. And that wouldn't get him to Gracet, at any rate.

So he opened this morning's mail without much in the way of expectations——

Fan mail from Earthers—— He started to dump the lot into the oubliette, but one piece caught his eye. 'King of Norway' was the title line in the message list. ***What the heck,*** he thought, ***this might be good for a laugh."***

From Oscar VI, King of Norway, To Robert Firestone, Greetings. it began.

The Norwegian Academy of Science and Letters has decided to award the

Abel Prize for 2588 to Robert Firestone of Placedon, Placet, HaChii Confederation and Chii Ix DriiBo, of Gracet, Draff System, HaChii Confederation. Firestone and DriiBo receive the Abel Prize "for their profound achievements in fractal geometry and in particular for its application to identification of DNA function in biological structure".

The Abel Award ceremony will take place in Oslo on Tuesday, the 20th of May.

HM King Oscar VI will present the Abel Prize.

This didn't look like a hoax. If it was legitimate, he would be able to find reference to it on the q-net. He looked up ***Abel Prize***. There were the names of the winners for the past hundred years, all except for this year. As he was watching, the entry for 2588 popped up. Somebody must have just updated the listing. And there——Robert Firestone and Chii Ix DriiBo.

He read further down. The award consisted of a 'diploma' and some sort of plaque or certificate. The pictures he saw looked like a clear plastic or glass plaque, decorated with a pattern that appeared to be an abstract version of a human head. He wondered whether it would look like that this year. ***That would be ironic, given who the recipients are,*** he thought.

But that wasn't the entirety of the award. The recipients were expected to give a lecture on the topic of their work. ***We could do that,*** he thought.

And there was a monetary stipend. Bobby looked at the figure. Then he looked at it again. ***Then*** he decided whether to scream and wake his parents, or call Chii and ***then*** scream and wake everybody.

He called first. Added an alarm, which was very rude, but would wake up the q-link and would create enough noise that it probably would also wake up anyone in the house the q-link was in——

"Bobby?" A sleepy-looking Chii appeared in a window centered on his screen.

"What are you calling about at this time of the morning?" she said, politely, but you could hear in her voice a slight undertone of ***and this had better be pretty good——***

"Have you looked at your message list this morning?" he said, a little ***too*** sweetly and innocently.

"Not yet——" Chii said.

"Look at the one that says 'King of Norway' right now." he urged.

She looked. "What's the Abel Prize?" she asked.

"It's a plaque -- and a diploma -- awarded by the King of Norway to mathematicians. In Oslo, Norway.

And there is a cash prize of twenty million credits that goes with it."

She screamed, and stole his thunder completely.

Greg, NaDii and TiiNa ran into the room. "What's wrong?" they all asked together, and looked at Chii screaming on the monitor.

Bobby pointed at the window with the message, and the window with the description of the prize. Greg put a finger on the financial part of the screen and began counting zeroes. He looked up at Bobby with very wide eyes.

NaDii fainted.

In the third window, Chii was still screaming, and pointing toward Bobby, which really meant she was pointing her parents towards the screen, and all the other things it contained.

Chii's father and mother, and her sister Vrii threw their arms around her and each other and they jumped up and down for a while. Not an easy thing for HaChii to do, but they managed it fine.

NaDii had recovered, and threw her arms around Bobby, as did Greg and TiiNa.

They jumped up and down for a while, too.

King Oscar VI of Norway absent-mindedly pulled on his handlebar moustache. He had encountered a dilemma. When he contacted the Oslo Philharmonic, which always sent some outstanding musicians to entertain the guests of honor for the Nobel Peace Prize and Abel Prize presentations, this time, they refused.

"Why?" the King asked the Philharmonic Director. ***Was there prejudice against HaChii, or did Robert's mixed parentage offend them so much they could not find musicians who would entertain the night of May 20th?*** He wondered what possible reason there could be for such a refusal, and the Philharmonic Director told him what the musicians had said.

"We're not worthy." he told the King.

"What?" Oscar could not believe his ears.

"We're not worthy. Do you know who this Robert Firestone ***is***?" the Director asked the King. Oscar shook his head. He knew very little about contemporary mathematicians.

"Here." the Director said simply, and pushed a few keys on his message-pad.

Music filled the room. "That is beautiful music." the King commented.

"Listen to the piano piece." the Director said, and as Firestone's Third Symphony moved into its second movement, the Director stood there with tears streaming down his face, not saying a word. After a while, the King looked up wide-eyed.

"I don't think I've ever heard a piano played so beautifully," he said. And now the King had a tear in his eye, himself, "but what does this have to do with the prize in Mathematics?"

"Your Highness." the Director finally said in a shaking voice. The music you heard was composed by Robert Firestone. The pianist you were listening to was Robert Firestone. And one of the two persons you are giving the Abel Prize for Mathematics to next month is the very same Robert Firestone."

"The Mathematician and the Composer are the same person?" Oscar said, aghast.

"The Mathematician, the Pianist, and the Composer are one and the same person, and ***he is an eight-year-old boy***." the Director sobbed. "We are not worthy to shine his shoes! None of us are. It would be like crows strutting before a peacock at a fashion show."

"Then what are we to do?" the King inquired.

"We would be delighted to play ***with*** Robert Firestone, if he would agree to play the piano while our players support him with a string quartet and some violins. But to play ***for*** him, to have such talent in the room without being used. That would be a travesty."

"Well, it is highly unusual, but I will ask Robert Firestone if he would play ***with*** your musicians, instead of just sitting there and listening. Would that be acceptable?"

It turned out it would be ***very*** acceptable to Bobby. He spoke with the King. Then he spoke with the Oslo Philharmonic Director.

"If you would like me to play the piano part from the Third Symphony, I would be very happy to do so. But there is one thing I would ask you to do for me, one piece of music you could perform ***without me***, please. Because I would very much like to have one dance with my partner,

Chii. And I could not perform the music and dance with her at the same time. Could you make an exception for me in that one little thing?"

"Anything, Master," the Director said, reflecting in his mind that he was speaking to an ***eight-year-old child***, and yet the title 'Master' was entirely right and fitting.

"Play the ***Blue Danube Waltz*** for me?" Bobby asked.

"Of course."

"Oh. My sister can play the piano for you if you'd like. She is small, so put a cushion on the bench to let her reach the keys. She's very, very good."

FriiDa, of course, offered to give them the ride to Earth. "I think we could afford our own space yacht, if we wanted one," NaDii said to her friend, "but of course we would love to go with you, if you promise to be our guest at the award ceremony."

As a citizen born in the United States of America, Greg was informed that Haakon Kristiansen, USA ambassador to Norway, would be present.

As citizens of Placet, Bobby and NaDii were informed that GriiYaa Ix NaBii, the HaChii ambassador to the Planet Earth, would be present. He was a distant cousin of NaDii's father, Bii, they were told.

And as the Firestone family contained more than half of the known Catholics in the HaChii Confederation, all of them were informed that a representative of the Vatican would be present.

Various forms of protocol were described in messages from each one. They agreed in general details, but the only one that concerned Bobby was the one from the Norwegian government. When in Oslo, do as the -- Osloborger -- do.

Gardermoen Spaceport was similar to the spaceport in Placedon, or pretty much any other spaceport Bobby had seen (which would be O'Hare, and that was pretty much the list). His party arrived on Monday, May 19th, 2588, by the calendar used on Earth, and proceeded to the Radisson Blu Scandinavia Hotel, which was very close to the Royal Palace.

Bobby checked to see if Chii and her family had arrived. and found that they were in room 307. He and his family were in 304, across the hall, so after getting settled into the room, Bobby, TiiNa and their parents walked across the hall and knocked on the door. He wasn't sure that would be understood, as HaChii couldn't knock on doors, but Chii's father, BoTii, opened the door and welcomed them in.

Chii looked at Bobby very strangely. ***Hasn't she seen me almost every day on the q-net?*** he thought. ***I couldn't look that different from what she would expect, could I?*** he wondered.

Then she said, "Bobby?" as though she wasn't sure.

"Of course I'm Bobby!" he answered, held up his hands and wiggled his fingers, which would be distinctive enough among HaChii, in any event.

"But you are only eight years old!" she said softly, "How come you're so ***big?***"

Bobby had forgotten that he had been growing faster than a HaChii child of his age, and was now as large as a twelve-or-thirteen year old HaChii male would be. In fact, as he stepped forward towards Chii, he was looking slightly ***down*** into her eyes. She was eleven, boys were always much shorter and less mature than girls at this age. It was the same for humans, he knew.

It must be startling to Chii to be looking ***up*** at a boy who was three years her junior. But he was not really HaChii, and there lay the difference.

He reached out and grasped the shoulders of her gripping-arms. She threw her arms around him and hugged him. "You really ***are*** Bobby. I have wanted to meet you in person for ***so*** long!" she lay her head against his chest and hugged him as though she would never let him go.

Bobby was standing in room 307. holding Chii, and she seemed totally oblivious of her parents, Robbie's family, or anything in the room.

"Harrumph!" her father, BoTii, ***harrumphed***.

They broke apart. Then Bobby looked, really ***looked*** at Chii. She was only eleven years old, but her parents had wealth, it appeared, (or at least they ***anticipated*** wealth, perhaps) for they had spared no expense in dressing their young daughter in the finest HaChii fashion. She was to be presented with the highest Honor the planet Earth had to bestow on a mathematician, and they had prepared her accordingly. He had seen her in the monitor in the morning. He had seen her in her pajamas before breakfast. He had never seen her wearing makeup, and, let's put it frankly, ***dressed to kill***. And he was an impressionable young boy.

"You know something, Chii," he said to her, "You--are ***beautiful***."

"Harrumph!" BoTii added for emphasis, and after further introductions, the families went back to their respective rooms.

"You know." Greg said, "That's not what she is going to be wearing tomorrow."

"It's not?"

"I doubt it." Greg winked. "Tomorrow, look for her to be wearing something ***really spectacular.***"

And the next evening, she wasn't just beautiful. She was ***stunning***.

Ambassadors were announced. Most just bowed and entered the room with their companions. The Vatican representative, mysteriously cowled in a hooded robe, had no companion, of course. FriiDa and the members of the Firestone and DriiBo families were announced.

There were speeches. Then the King announced the names of the award recipients and Bobby walked up from his family's table, then Chii walked up from hers.

The King presented them each with a trophy. The design had been altered this time, to make the abstract-art human head look more like a HaChii head. ***Good.*** Bobby thought.

Then, they presented the lecture based on their paper. Polite applause completed the presentation; Bobby was sure the diplomats hadn't understood every fiftieth word that was said, but they knew it merited appreciation.

Finally, Chii walked back to her parents' table, and Bobby, instead of returning to his, went to a grand piano and sat down, just as the violinists-plus-string quartet walked in from off-stage. They began the second movement of Firestone's Third Symphony. When it was completed, much louder applause and cheering saluted the performance. ***That, they understood,*** Bobby thought.

He bowed, and everybody expected him to return to his table, but his parents were already 'in' on the surprise. Bobby walked toward the DriiBo table as his sister TiiNa, climbed up onto the piano bench and seated herself on the cushion one of the violinists had placed there.

Bobby walked to the place where Chii was seated, and she looked up at him, completely puzzled. The musicians began the prelude to the ***Blue Danube Waltz***, and Bobby held out his hand towards Chii.

"May I have this dance?" he asked simply.

He had one hand holding her gripper, while the other was around her waist, and he spun her around the room while some guests stared in astonishment, and others applauded. Then a few other couples joined them, and soon the platform set up to present the award became a miniature ballroom.

"Where did you learn to dance?" Chii said, surprise in her voice.

"My Dad taught me. He's pretty good." Just then Greg and NaDii swept by.

My goodness, he moves well, she thought, ***and does he have any idea how romantic all this is? He planned all this, so he must have had it in mind.***

As they danced. Bobby noticed Chii looking up at him from time to time, very strangely. Her skin had turned a pale lavender color instead of the common blue-green color normal for HaChii. ***Now what does that mean?*** he wondered.

Of course, Bobby, with precision control over his skin coloration, could camouflage his feelings perfectly and stayed a neutral HaChii cyan instead of turning a curious orange.

After the dance, he walked her back to the DriiBo table, then headed back towards his own. As he left, Chii followed him with her eyes.

"Harrumph!" her father said, then added, "That Harrumph was for you, not him, young lady. Size does not matter. He is only an ***eight-year-old child***, and don't forget it! You must remember that you are only eleven, and he is even younger, so get those stars out of your eyes, no matter how--romantic--things may ***appear,*** he is really just a child. He is just trying to be nice to you, nothing more."

My father is certainly a gentleman of the old school, Chii reflected. ***So I must give him a reply that fits his frame of mind right now.***

"Father," she said, "I understand exactly what you mean, and I promise not to have any romantic thoughts about him until much later, when it is more appropriate."

"All right, then." Her father, hearing what he ***wanted*** to hear, seemed mollified.

But deep in her soul, she said to herself, ***and much later will be as soon as I can possibly arrange it to be.***

Meanwhile, at the Firestone table, FriiDa whispered to Bobby. "That girl really likes you. If she liked you before, that little gambit has her really hooked."

"You're kidding!" he whispered back, "Uh, uh." FriiDa said, "I watched her turn violet," she said.

"But--what does that ***mean***?" he asked.

"No, no, no--too young," she said, "but you ***do*** know how to look things up on the q-net, don't you? 'Bye." and she turned to NaDii to talk to her.

Periodically during the evening, guests would walk up to the table and congratulate Bobby. Late in the evening, the Vatican representative in his hooded robe, edged up to the table, pulled aside the fold of cowling that had covered his face most of the night, and said, "Congratulations, Robbie——"

It was Father Jack -- or rather, Pope Patrick the First.

"Holy——ummm——Holy Father!" Bobby exclaimed, *sotto* voce, "how the --heck-- did you manage to pull this off? Did anybody recognize you yet?"

"Not a soul," the pontiff wisecracked.

Just then, Greg turned around and got a glimpse of who was inside the hooded robe. "Oh, my," he whispered, "You actually did it. You made it all the way through the evening without being recognized."

"It isn't every day a friend of mine gets elected the top mathematician on the planet." Jack explained.

"It isn't every day a friend of mine gets elected the top priest on the planet, either." Bobby whispered back.

He stood up and hugged the pontiff.

NaDii noticed the visitor, got up and walked around the table and bent down to see who her son and husband were talking to. The cowled visitor looked up and gave her a peek at his face, and she reached out and hugged him.

"Ffurff, it's good to see you. Now get out of here. Before you get spotted. I don't know that many popes. I don't want anything to happen to the one I do."

He left.

After that, everything else was an anticlimax. They went back to their rooms early. After all, the guests of honor were both less than twelve years old; the rest of the guests could stay up late, but taking the kids back because it was past their bedtime seemed a good excuse.

CHAPTER 21 - True Confessions

Next morning, the two families had planned a shopping trip together. They took in the sights and shopped for fabric at a place called Grønland. Turns out Chii's mother DriiLa was a seamstress. She had made all those delightful outfits Bobby had seen Chii wearing over the last three days.

Little TiiNa asked DriiLa if she could teach her how to sew. She wanted to make a dress ***just like*** the one she had seen Chii wearing last night.

"Isn't that a little——grown up——for you to wear?" DriiLa tried to discourage her a bit.

"Not if I alter the pattern." she fired back.

"Well, I suppose I could teach you how to do that, too," DriiLa said, "How much math do you know?"

"Only through algebra and trigonometry," three-year-old TiiNa said, "but I suppose Chii could give me some help on that. Do I need analytic geometry for the pattern redesign?"

DriiLa looked back at Greg and NaDii with a slightly stricken expression on her face that said, ***Are they all like this?*** "No. No analytic——geometry—— Not at all——"

After a morning of productive shopping, the group went to lunch at a restaurant called Klosteret. Bobby ordered grilled tunafish. So did Chii. He caught her stealing glances at him as he ate, so he used his knife and fork very precisely as his father had taught him. His mother, of course, did not have hands, and could not use a knife and fork in the same way, but she, Vrii and Chii all did fine with the human utensils. Using knives and forks with grippers did not seem to pose any difficulty at all.

After lunch, TiiNa said she wanted to go to the Zoological museum and the Botanical Garden. Vrii said that she did too, and Chii said she wasn't interested but would anybody mind if she went back to the hotel and worked on the final details of a paper she and Bobby had written about crystallography and group theory, before she was ready to submit it to the ***Annalen***? Her parents agreed. The Firestone family would go to the hotel with Bobby while the DriiBo family would take Vrii and TiiNa to the botanic garden and Zoological Museum. And Chii would go back to room 307 to work on the paper.

Bobby listened to this with some puzzlement. He took Chii aside when she had finished talking to her parents.

"What was that about?" he whispered, "We don't have any paper on crystallography."

"That was a diversion. I want to have some time without the whole bunch of them around, and I never seem to get any privacy."

The DriiBo family headed out the door, while Greg, NaDii, Bobby and Chii waited for an elevator.

"OK, then," he said, still a little puzzled, "If you need me for anything, I'll be right across the hall with Mom and Dad. You can page me on the message pad. You have my code."

And he caught her looking askance at him with that strange expression again, as she opened the door to her room, while he and his parents went into the room across the hall.

NaDii lay down on the bed while Greg started the q-net monitor in the room. In a few minutes, NaDii had fallen asleep, Greg was watching a newsfeed about last night's award ceremony, and Bobby went into the bathroom.

Just as he was finishing up and had flushed the toilet, his message pad beeped. He took it out of his pocket. There was Chii.

"Can you make some excuse to come over here?" she said.

"You're being very mysterious today." he said, "But OK——"

Then he called her back. "Is this a short-time excuse. like a few minutes, or a longer one, like an hour or two?"

"Let's make it an hour or two, OK?"

"OK. Here goes." and he put his message pad back in his pocket.

He stepped out of the bathroom. "Dad?" he asked.

"Yeah, Bobby?" he was semi-distracted by a story on the newsfeed.

Bobby was rummaging through one of the pieces of luggage. ***Aha! there it is***——he took out **a *polyadok*** board and a bag of pieces.

"Chii just called me on the message pad." ***Always easier to start a tall tale with an element of truth——***

"She would like me to go over and give her some ***polyadok*** lessons. She always loses to her sister, Vrii, and I'm the only one that's been able to beat Vrii in the last two years. She wants me to teach her the HuuSill gambit. That's one that worked really well a while ago.

She called me to see if I could coach her while Vrii wasn't there. She'd like to surprise her the next time they play."

"Ha!" Greg said. "That'd serve her right. I've heard Vrii brag about her ***polyadok*** game and she thinks she's hot stuff. She needs to be brought down a notch. Help Chii out. I'd love to see Vrii's face the day she loses a game to her sister."

"OK. Back in an hour or two. 'Bye."

He stepped out the door with his ***polyadok*** board and bag of pieces, crossed the hall, and knocked on the door.

That was easy. Now what? he wondered.

Chii opened the door and he stepped in. She was wearing a simple bathrobe, probably one of the hotel ones. She closed the door and asked him, "What did you tell them?"

"Mom's asleep. I told Dad," he said as he held up the board and bag of pieces, "that I was coming over to give you ***polyadok*** lessons so you could surprise your sister and beat her at a game for once."

"Wow. That's not a bad idea. You're the only one that's beaten her in the last two years, and you're hardly trying. I bet you ***could*** teach me. Maybe I'll take you up on it sometime."

"So what's up?" he said, as he set up the board on a table.

She looked at him with that strange look, again. Wordlessly, she took his right hand in her two grippers as he put down the last ***polyadok*** piece with his left, and lifted his hand to her mouth. Then she put his fingers into her mouth and closed the two ridges that serve HaChii for teeth on his fingers gently. The inside of her mouth was soft and wet, but had no tongue like a human mouth. Then she released his hand and held it tightly in her grippers. She looked up at him again.

It was a poignant and strangely moving gesture. He had absolutely no idea what it meant, but it was very intimate, and a complete surprise to him.

"Wha..?"

"I love you, Bobby Firestone." she said, simply.

This was the first time they'd been alone together and face-to-face. They had always worked through the q-net. but that wasn't the same. On the net, she couldn't even guess that he wasn't a pint-size kid, like the HaChii boys in her classes at school. He had wanted to be with her and looked forward to meeting her. But love? That idea took a little getting used to.

Was this what HaChii people did instead of kissing? Surely not. They didn't have hands and fingers. Was it something she thought of herself?

He took her right gripper in his two hands, brought it up to his mouth, bit gently on the gripper and then released it, like she had done with his hand.

"I love you too, Chii Ix DriiBo." he replied.

She threw her arms around him and hugged him. Then she looked up at him with that same strange look, her eyes smiling, took his hand, and led him into the spacious bathroom. She kicked the door shut and turned the lock, ***click,*** with one gripper while she held his hand with the other.

"You told me," she said, "that you would explain something to me when I was older."

He was a bit disconcerted by what was going on, and groping in his mind for what she could possibly be talking about. "Hmmm?" he said, quizzically.

"When I added your name to the DNA paper, you said it reminded you of when your Dad's name was added to a patent application."

"Oh. That. That was three years ago." He didn't want to avoid the subject, but he wasn't sure how he could talk to her about it.

"Well, I'm older now," she reminded him.

"I guess you are. If you ***really*** want to know, OK. It's a pretty adult subject, and I shouldn't even know about it myself, except the Patent Office wasn't expecting five-year-olds to be doing patent searches so they never put child locks on the patent files. This is ***really*** awkward to talk about——"

"Oh, Ffurff!" She didn't want to see him squirm. "I already know what it is."

"How do you know that?" again, trying to figure out after three years, what had transpired in the past.

"When I broke the security of your q-net files, and got that file of your Dad's DNA, That patent application was ***also*** in that bunch of files."

"So you've known all this time what the Model 37 was?"

She had her chin on her chest and looked up at him with wide eyes. It was very appealing. "Am I forgiven for breaking into your files? I never did it again."

"Of course." he said, and held her in his arms, because she looked so vulnerable and contrite. After a few moments, he let go of her and she stepped back.

She pulled the sash on the robe and dropped it to the floor.

"Chii——" he said——his breath caught for a minute—— "You were beautiful in those fine clothes last night. But you are ***even more*** beautiful right now."

She reached for the buttons on his jacket. "I want to see you, too."

And he undressed. She kicked the pile of clothes into the corner, he kicked his shoes and socks into the pile, then she picked up the robe and dropped it over the pile of clothes, covering it up. She threw some towels down on the floor. Then she stepped into his arms.

"Your eyes are like your father's," she said, as she stroked his back with her grippers. "and your hands." Then she looked down. "And your feet." and finally, "If that patent thing is to be believed, you have inherited the other thing I'm looking at from your father too."

Slowly, gently, clumsily, but with infinite tenderness, they began to do something that, at their ages, they shouldn't have known how to do. Something that, at their ages, shouldn't have even been possible.

And it was patient.
And it was serene.
And it was loving.
And it was amazing.
And it was beautiful.
And it was complete.
And then it was over.

They lay afterward, side by side on the floor, on the towels. There was a ***tremendous*** afterglow. Life would never be the same again.

Then a shout at the door. "Chii, can you get finished in there so I can come in and use the toilet?" ***It was her father!***

He saw panic in her eyes. But Bobby knew what to do. He stepped into the tub. pressed himself into the back wall, and disappeared.

Chii gaped for half a beat. He was still there, if she reached out and touched him, she could feel his warm skin. But there was a perfect ***trompe l'oeil*** effect. Where he had been, there were now a few extra folds of shower curtain. His eyes opened. He checked himself in the mirror.

Startling! eyes in the middle of a shower curtain! Then he closed them again, the pattern on his lids returned and it completed the illusion. "Let him in," he whispered.

Chii wrapped herself in a towel, let her Dad in, walked out, and he did his business, without any special attention to the tub and the shower curtain.

Bobby was very still and very quiet. BoTii washed his grippers and was out. He could hear Chii asking him whether the rest of the family was coming back from the botanical garden and museum, and he said no, he had just come back because they needed his credit card and he had left it in the room. He was heading back to them while they walked around the botanical garden, and then he would use his credit card to get them into the Museum. He said good-bye and left.

Bobby quickly gathered his clothes from under the robe and dressed. He was putting on his shoes when Chii came back into the bathroom.

"I guess I should have known you could do ***that***," she said, "but what a spot to be in——"

He looked at her, "That wasn't a perfect escape." he said.

"How so?" she asked.

"Right now, my Dad knows I am over here, playing ***polyadok*** with you. But your Dad knows there was no one here, and you were either just coming out of the shower, or just about to take one. If they talk to each other, something will not look right, unless I go back to my Dad right now and say you decided not to practice ***polyadok*** and decided to take a shower instead, so I came back. The chances are neither of them will check the times these things are happening. Both our Dads will just figure that BoTii came in after I left and went back to my place. But it means I can't stay here with you. I've got to leave now."

And he picked up his ***polyadok*** set and left.

She was disappointed he couldn't stay, but impressed that he had thought out the scenario most plausible to work as a cover-up.

Well, she thought, ***I might as well take a shower. It's not like I don't need one after doing that——***

And she went into the bathroom, wrapped in her towel.

Bobby walked into room 304, his Dad still viewing newsfeed stories and his Mom still sound asleep. "Hi," he addressed Greg, "Chii decided she wasn't up for learning ***polyadok*** strategy after all. She decided to take a shower and then take a nap. So I came back."

"Mmm hmmm." his father said, with all the attention Bobby had expected.

But he was still troubled. Using a few tricks he had discovered while surfing the hotel web, he pulled up a listing of guests in the hotel, and noticed that the Vatican representative in room 312 had not checked out.

He grabbed the ice bucket and told his Dad, "Going out for some ice. Be back in a few minutes."

He knocked on the door to room 312. The door opened a crack and John Ryan, AKA Patrick the First, looked out. "Robbie! come in, come in. Let me see you!" and he let him in, closing the door.

"It's 'Bobby' now, Holy Father," he said. "Changed it after the new sister started calling me that."

"I'll call you Bobby if you call me Jack," the pontiff replied.

Bobby put his hands over his eyes for a moment, gathering his thoughts.

"Jack, could you hear my confession right now?"

"As long as it doesn't last more than an hour. I've got to catch a sub-orbital hop back to Rome at the spaceport, and it leaves in three hours."

"Fair enough. This won't take long."

"Bless me Father, for I have sinned. My last confession was last Saturday."

"It has been about an hour since I sinned. I think the name of the sin is fornication. It didn't feel like a sin at the time, but now I'm not so sure, and I think I better get it off my chest."

"At your age? Are you sure that's right? Tell me what happened."

——..

A while later, the pope blessed Bobby and was trying to think of a penance that was reasonably within his capacity to do.

"Sometimes I'm not sure why a beautiful, loving act like that is a sin."

"In your case, you certainly couldn't have been married, at this age. It will still be many, many years before you would be old enough to marry, and there is still that whole 'cross-species' thing. And besides, it's not as though either of you are old enough to have children. I'm sure Chii's too young to lay eggs." He poked a few keys on his message pad. "Average menarche at 12½—— No. I don't think so. At least I hope not."

"So——I'd have to say what you did is more of a Mistake than a Mortal Sin."

"Say five Our Fathers and five Hail Marys, then tell the young lady that she really ought to think about waiting until you are both old enough to marry before planning such a thing again. And if you still love her, marry her first."

"Oh. Say another five Our Fathers for deceiving Chii's father. Covering up misbehavior is as bad as the misbehavior itself. Although, frankly, I'm glad you didn't get caught, because I don't know ***what*** I would have done to you if I'd been her father. It probably wouldn't have been pretty."

Properly chastised, Bobby returned to his room, having remembered to fill the ice bucket at the last moment.

"That was a long run for ice." Greg remarked.

"Ran into someone I knew down the hallway." Bobbie said.

"Who?"

"The Pope." ***At least that part is true.***

Greg looked nonplussed. "Is he still here?"

"Nope." Bobby said truthfully. "He had to go to the spaceport."

The next day, everybody said goodbye at the Gardermoen spaceport. FriiDa was going to take the Firestone contingent back to Placet, and the DriiBo family was preparing to depart on a commercial vessel bound for Gracet.

Chii stood with her parents and Vrii. Bobby walked over and grasped her grippers in his hands.

"I'm sorry we couldn't be together more. I'm going to miss you a lot." There were things he wanted to say, but couldn't with her parents present.

"Bobby." she stopped and seemed unable to talk for a minute. "I wish we were both ten years older——"

And Bobby, hoping her parents wouldn't be offended, but feeling that it had to be said, added, "If that were the case, I would marry you in a minute."

Surprisingly, BoTii, who would have normally ***harrumphed*** at this point, said, "I hope you still feel that way in ten years. Really. I do."

His wife, DriiLa, who didn't speak much normally, added, "Maybe we could arrange to visit Placet next time I get a vacation from work. We can certainly afford the trip now." She looked at BoTii, who conveyed agreement.

They left a miserable-looking Chii and her parents standing in the concourse as they walked back towards the gate where FriiDa's yacht was waiting. Unlike commercial passengers, they could leave any time. As soon as FriiDa got clearance from the control tower, they left.

Bobby had been invited onto the ship's bridge, where FriiDa was conning the flight. Normally, he would have had his nose pressed up against the windows watching the planet dwindle into a tiny dot in space. Not this time. He was sitting in a seat on the bridge, his chin resting on his hands, looking at nothing in particular.

"You got it bad, don't you?" FriiDa asked.

"Hmmm?" Bobby said, only marginally aware that anyone was talking to him.

"That little girl got under your skin, didn't she?"

Bobby looked at FriiDa, thinking ***I wonder if she would understand about this.***

"Actually, I got under hers." he answered, waiting to see if FriiDa would get the implication.

FriiDa's eyes widened. "Figuratively, or physically?" she asked.

Yeah, I think she got that**——** he thought.

"Both," he answered, and her eyes widened even further.

"Do you mean what I think you're saying? You're not old enough——"

"Sorry——don't bet on that; you'd lose." he said.

FriiDa was aghast. "You're kidding! What gave you the idea you could——"

"She--It wasn't really my idea. I think 'she jumped my bones' would be the Earth expression. Not that I fought her off. I was a little surprised that it worked, actually, at my age. But it worked pretty well. Amazingly well, in fact. But that might have made it worse. I'm pretty sure it was a mistake."

"Why?" FriiDa was curious.

"You told me, the night of the award, that I had her -- 'hooked' is the phrase I think you used. And I did what you suggested when I got back to the room. I looked up what the HaChii violet skin color implied in terms of emotional or physical reaction."

"Well yes. I expected you would, but you're a bright boy; I expect you would have looked it up even if I hadn't suggested it."

"Yeah. That's what bothers me. I knew what it meant. I should have figured out something when she told me she wanted to get me alone, but I was blindsided. I didn't see it coming."

"You are ***eight years old***!" FriiDa said. "I would be surprised if you ***could*** put yourself in somebody else's mind and imagine that they would think that way. Frankly, I'm surprised that Chii ***could*** think that way, but being eleven years old and female is a lot different from being eight and male. I could see the signs. Maybe I should have spoken to you more honestly, but your parents were present, and I didn't think——"

"Ffurff, no. Don't blame yourself. You handled that as adroitly as you could, given the -- inhibiting conditions -- at the table. The shortcoming was mine. Everything tells me I shouldn't have let this happen."

"Damn. Bobby, you are without a doubt the ***oldest*** eight-year-old I have ever met. You have problems a 25-year-old should be worrying about."

He thought about that for a second. "With an IQ over 300," he explained, "I ***am*** a 25-year-old, in every way but physically. And I'm at least four years ahead of my age group in growth. For a HaChii, anyway. Maybe two years for a human——but I'm more HaChii than human."

"So?"

"So I've got adult problems. Worse, I love Chii—— I love her something awful, FriiDa, to tell the truth."

"How is that worse?" FriiDa seemed puzzled.

"Because I gave her what she wanted, but I can't give her what she ***deserves*** and -- to expand on that phrase you coined at the dinner table -- she is ***really, really hooked*** now. That's not fair, with me being only eight years old. That 'only eight years old' phrase keeps coming back to haunt me——"

"You said you can't give her what she ***deserves***. What did you mean by that?"

"I can't marry her." Bobby said simply. "Not for at least ten years."

"Wow——" FriiDa said, as she made the jump to contracted-space.

That evening, back on Placet, FriiDa had dinner with Greg, Bobby and NaDii They had finished the meal and were having drinks.

Bobby had gone to his room and was playing ***polyadok*** with Vrii on the q-net.

"Your son has a problem." FriDaa said, very directly.

"What kind of a problem?" Greg asked.

"Chii is in love with him." FriiDa continued.

NaDii grinned at her. "That's kind of cute, at that age." she said.

FriiDa looked at her with disbelief. "Cute?"

"Oh yeah. Childhood crush and all that——" NaDii explained.

"I think you're missing the point," FriiDa continued, "that these are ***not*** children. They are grown-up minds in children's bodies. That is a very different thing."

"Oh, come on. They're very bright, but they're just kids." NaDii continued.

Greg interrupted. "Not so fast, NaDii. I saw the way Chii was looking at Bobby when he waltzed her around the dance floor. I may only be a human, but I know what a HaChii woman looks like when she's turned-on."

"Turned-on? Like sexually?" NaDii responded, "That's ridiculous, she's only eleven."

Greg looked over at FriiDa. "You saw it, didn't you? I heard you whispering something to Bobby when he came back to the table."

"Uh huh. Yeah, I knew what was going on and I tried to give Bobby a heads-up without making it too obvious to you guys."

"Wait a minute. Are you saying that Chii——that Chii has the hots for my son?" NaDii was aghast.

"I think she had a 'crush' before she met him. Then, when he was so much bigger and more robust than she expected from seeing him on the small screen, something changed. And that waltz around the dance floor——which by the way, I thought was very cute, myself, until I ***really looked*** at Chii during the dance—— Well, I think that was what sent things over the top."

"You're kidding! What does 'over the top' mean, and what in the world could that possibly have to do with Bobby?" NaDii was now moving over from aghast to downright bellicose.

FriiDa looked at Greg, who shook his head. Whether that meant ***no. you can't be serious*** or ***no. FriiDaa is not kidding*** she wasn't sure, but she assumed the latter and went ahead anyway.

"Sometime yesterday, she acted on it——"

"The ***polyadok*** lesson——" Greg said aloud, to himself.

"What?" NaDii asked.

"You were asleep. He told me Chii asked him to come over and help her learn how to beat her sister at ***polyadok***. He took the board and set with him and went over to her room for half an hour or so——"

"And he talked to ***you*** about it?" NaDii asked FriiDa.

"Yeah. I guess it's because I was the one who warned him at the awards banquet. And--he's a bright kid——since Dr. RuFii isn't around, I guess he decided he'd confide in me. He needed someone to talk to and this would be too embarrassing to talk to ***you*** about——"

"Embarrassing! He's an eight-year-old and this girl ***comes on*** to him. He must have been mortified!" NaDii said.

"Not exactly." FriiDa replied. "Remember, he was already very fond of her, even if he wasn't thinking about her in the terms we're talking about——"

"Your point?" a still-slightly-bellicose NaDii demanded.

"He went along with it." FriiDa explained.

"How far?" a somewhat subdued NaDii said softly.

"——All the way." FriiDa answered truthfully.

"Is he even capable of that?" Greg asked.

"Apparently." FriDa said.

"Wow! I'm impressed——" Greg said.

NaDii looked daggers at him and said, "Excuse us, FriiDa. I need to have a little private talk with Greg."

CHAPTER 22 - The Talk

At the back of the dining room, NaDii was speaking to Greg.

"Look, Mr. Testosterone. You may be impressed that Bobby is some sort of phenomenon of maleness, but I'm appalled. If these were ordinary kids, I'd say they were just playing around and laugh it off. If Chii were a twenty-five-year-old woman, I'd have her hauled into court for statutory rape. But actually, even though this was her idea, I think she's the victim here."

Greg looked at her with disbelief. "You're saying Bobby somehow took advantage of her and she was hurt? How do you figure that?"

NaDii gathered her thoughts for a few moments. "Chii obviously developed a bit of a 'crush' on our son, over the years of long-distance correspondence. Bobby may not have known how he was feeding-in to that with his surprise ballroom dance thing. It was really a very interesting way to show how much he appreciated her, but to her, that was a very ***romantic*** overture, because--FriiDa is right--Chii is ***not*** a little girl mentally. Both of these kids really have grown-up minds inside those bodies. It's just that they haven't had the time to adjust to it the way you and I have."

"Older and wiser, you're saying?" Greg elaborated.

"Something like that. When Chii took the next step, if Bobby had proven to be just a typical eight-year-old boy, he might have run screaming, or even with the best of intentions, he would have been a big flop, and that would have burst Chii's balloon. Instead, he -- and OK, here I'm going to give him credit for being a chip off the old block -- he probably outperformed her wildest expectations."

Greg absorbed that for a second. Momentarily he looked pleased, then processed things a bit further, and his expression turned to crestfallen.

"After that, she's probably head over heels," Greg concluded.

"That's an odd expression." NaDii said. "Don't humans ***usually*** have their heads located over their heels?"

"OK——figure of speech. I suppose it means a full 360 degree tumble, but it still means she has flipped for him."

"Makes sense," NaDii said, "he ***looks*** a couple of years older than her, and he might be that far ahead mentally, too. And also, he's ***exotic.*** Like you. You never know——some girls go for that sort of thing."

And she winked at him. Greg got the point.

"One of us has to talk to Bobby." NaDii said.

"I should do it." said Greg.

"OK. I won't argue with that." NaDii decided.

In the cabin, Bobby had just completed a tricky stratagem in his ***polyadok*** game with Vrii, wherein she had captured one of his Serfs, and ended up losing her Judge and the Princess in the exchange that followed. She had the kind of expression on her face that you see in an earthquake victim wandering around in the rubble after the village is flattened. She gamely tried to defend her Reeve, which was her last major player, by moving another Serf out to block, opening her Lord to attack from an unseen Lancer.

"Exile." Bobby softly said to Vrii.

She goggled for a moment. "Yes. My Lord is in Exile. I lose."

"Good game." Bobby said.

"Well, maybe a good learning experience." Vrii said reluctantly. "I want to go sit down with my board right now. I just can't see where I could have saved the game, once I took that Serf. I'd like to try out a bunch of variations. Oh! Chii wants to talk to you. I'll take my board and see you later."

She went away out of sight of the q-link, and Chii moved in. She stared at Bobby intensely for a moment, and said, "I thought the Abel Prize ceremony on Tuesday was going to be the high point of my life. But Wednesday is the date I've got circled on my calendar."

She looked at something off-screen for a moment. "Vrii's lost in the board somewhere. I don't think she'll come up for air for a while."

Then her attention returned to Bobby. "Wednesday." she said, simply, as though it were a whole paragraph, "Wednesday was everything I ever dreamed, and so much more. So ***unbelievably*** much more." And the intense look melted into something softer.

"Chii." Bobby said, and paused as though that, too, had been a whole paragraph. "Wednesday was something that should have happened after we were married. At least that's what I was brought up to believe. But it will be about ten years before we can get married and I have no idea what we can do about that." he explained. "I don't know if you thought about it, but I think it is just the sheerest dumb luck you don't have a clutch of eggs right now. If I'm not old enough to marry you, I'm certainly not old enough to be a father for your babies, either, and I've found at least a dozen cases on the q-net where girls your age became gravid."

"Bobby. That's a dozen out of millions. Besides, I was protected. Oh! can't talk now; Mom is coming——"

Bobby had just closed the q-net window when he saw Greg standing in the open door. Greg knocked ostentatiously on the door. "Bobby? Can I come in?"

"Hi, Dad." Then he thought, ***uh, oh.*** "Dad——How much of that did you see?"

"Enough to know that your girlfriend is smarter than I thought," he answered truthfully.

"She just got the Abel Prize, Dad, She's got to be pretty smart." Bobby said.

"We're not talking about mathematics here, are we?" Greg answered. "I just had a ***very*** interesting conversation with FriiDa about you and Chii."

"Hmmm——She told you about Wednesday, right?"

"Right. I suppose I should tell you that what happened to you Wednesday is a lot like something that happened to me. It's fortunate that, in your case, no eggs were involved."

"Was that about you and Mom?" Bobby asked.

"You must have wondered," Greg said, "why there aren't a whole lot of couples like us on Placet."

"There aren't ***any*** other couples like you ***anywhere***, as far as I know." Bobby responded.

"Don't take this wrong, son, but the only reason you exist at all is because we did something -- exactly the ***same*** something -- that you and Chii did on Wednesday, but we did it without any protection."

"I know that, Dad, and I also know that you guys had no reason to think that humans and HaChii would be cross-fertile, at that time. I can surf the q-net, just as well as you, you know. I looked up the story."

"Well," Greg sighed, "that saves me having a talk with you that I was planning to have when you were about twelve years old."

"***That*** talk? I knew about that stuff when I was ***three*** years old."

"In ***theory*** son. ***Reality*** is a whole lot different. Isn't it?"

"Isn't it just?" Bobby said.

"Was it when you told me you were going to give Chii some ***polyadok*** lessons? Was that when——"

"Yeah."

"And when you went out for ice——?"

"I asked Father Jack to hear my confession."

"Oh. And he——"

"Forgave my sins. But I——"

"Don't feel like that really solved anything——"

"No. Chii wants me——"

"Bad?"

"Yeah."

"Do you want her too, son?"

"Hell yes, Dad! I miss her every minute we're apart. I want her for the rest of my life. But what am I going to do?" Bobby cried.

"I think it may possibly be even worse for her." Greg concluded.

"Yeah. I think you're right." Bobby looked miserable.

Greg looked at his son. After this many years, he could read expressions on HaChii faces, and this one made him hurt inside just to look at.

"I've never thought children marrying children made sense," he said, "And what I mean by that is ages between sixteen and nineteen. Most people that age just don't have the maturity to be good spouses or good parents. Almost none of them have the financial wherewithal to support a family properly. Your Mom and I didn't even meet each other until she was 25 and I was 26——"

He thought for a moment and went on.

"That said——In the case of you and Chii, none of those things apply. After winning that prize, you're both independently wealthy. Not filthy rich, but you could support a family a lot bigger than mine, and do it in comfort. You're half the age of the 'children' I was referring to a moment ago, but there are other kinds of maturity, and although you haven't had much time for life experience, you're bright enough to figure out how to do anything well."

Bobby looked at him quizzically. "You're saying you'd support marriage?"

"No." Greg said, "You would both be totally illegal to marry in every jurisdiction on 25 planets. There isn't even any way to ***think*** about it. Frankly, even now, there ***still*** isn't any ***legal*** way for ***me*** to be married to your Mother."

"But the Pope——"

"In ***his*** eyes, we're married, so in the eyes of the Church, we're married, but there just isn't any legal jurisdiction for a HaChii marrying a human, so we're just living together in the eyes of the law. Room-mates only——"

"I didn't realize that." Bobby said. "So that makes me a bastard?"

"Literally, yes. And those other things you've seen people call you——mongrel, monster, et. cetera, they don't mean any more than that. You are the person you become. Names don't make you who you are. Ignore them."

Greg paused, waited to see if Bobby wanted to ask anything about that.

"Okay. So here's what I'm willing to do," Greg said, "If it is at all possible, I will try to arrange some way for you and Chii to have some time to yourselves. And please--your Mom will have my guts for garters if she finds out about this--so be careful. If it gets out that I helped, you guys are too young for anything really serious to happen to ***you*** legally, but they'll put ***me*** in jail for letting it happen. Do you understand that?"

"God yes, Dad." Bobby said.

"There's something else I wanted to say. This is me speaking, not the Church. I believe in God and for the most part I believe in the values the Church talks about, but--as long as it is done responsibly, I do not personally believe what you and Chii did is a sin."

"That's interesting, Dad," Bobby replied, "That sounds a lot like something Father Jack--the Holy Father--said to me Wednesday. He said 'Sometimes I'm not sure why a beautiful, loving act like that is a sin,' and I thought about it. I was mostly feeling guilty about what other people would think. The only thing I ***should*** feel guilty about is how it affected Chii——"

"Yeah. The emotional effect," Greg said, "She would have missed you when you were separated, anyway, because she wanted to meet you in person for so long and finally got to. But now, she is ***miserable*** when you are separated, because she has fallen in love with you and it is really a big-time, heavy-duty, industrial-strength love, not just a pre-teen crush."

"I got that, Dad. Boy, have I got that." Bobby said.

"Recrimination won't help anything, son." Greg said. "And if you want to have sex, the only thing I think is irresponsible would be if one of you got a disease and gave it to the other, or if you made a baby neither of you wanted to have. And that would be as bad as hurting Chii physically or emotionally, which I know you don't want to do."

"So that leaves the option of living together," Bobby said, "and Chii's parents would never allow that——"

"I don't think they would," Greg answered, "but you never know. I might find a way to talk them into it eventually. But don't hold your breath. I'd have to be persuasive beyond my wildest dreams of eloquence, to pull that off."

"You know, Dad," Bobby said, "Chii's father almost caught us——"

And he told Greg the story.

"Wow. That could have been ***really bad***. Half of me says God gave you the gift of camouflage for some other purpose than that, but the other half is glad you didn't end up banned from ever seeing each other again and especially that you didn't get hurt. If it had been my daughter and some guy——older or younger, I don't care——and my daughter was still only a child——it's easy to imagine things getting out of control."

"Bobby, I've been talking to you about ***not*** becoming a parent too soon, but I'm a parent myself, so I hope that doesn't sound hypocritical. So let me tell why you ***should*** be a parent some day. Here's what I think:

The gene pool is like any other home-made craft project. It could benefit from the use of a level and a t-square, sometimes.

Every time bright, responsible people decide ***not*** to have kids out of some misguided idea they are helping the planet, they leave the gene pool to get filled up at the shallow end. If the irresponsible and parasitic elements of society are the only ones who have kids, that can't go on for very long—— The gravy train runs out of gravy if the kids behave like the parents.

Darwin would say that's a violation of survival of the fittest. Because society wants to protect everybody, sometimes it ends up favoring its members who are--like a lot of home-made stuff--not on the level——

What I'm talking about is sometimes called ***eugenics.*** It got really bad press some time ago because of a guy named ***Hitler***. But his problem was, he defined fitness as whatever he and his cronies liked. It didn't really have anything to do with fitness, or goodness, or anything you and I can understand.

The general idea is sound, regardless of people who abuse it for their own purposes. My point is just that, if you know somebody who embodies the best in the HaChii race or the human race, or in your case, ***both***, encourage them to have kids. When they can do it responsibly."

"I don't think we're ready for that, either, Dad." Bobby admitted. "For one thing, I think we would have to know how we could get along in person, for extended periods of time, not just corresponding over the q-net."

I can't believe I'm thinking about getting an eight-year-old and an eleven-year-old together to live with each

other for a trial period. And I still don't have any very good ideas how to do it if I decide to, Greg thought.

CHAPTER 23 - Summer Vacation

One day a month later, Chii's Mom called Greg and NaDii. NaDii was in, Greg was out with Bobby and TiiNa doing some gardening, so she opened the message screen on the q-net.

"Hello, Mrs. Firestone." DriiLa said. She had learned the Earth mode of address, suitable as it may or may not have been in this case.

"Hello, DriiLa," NaDii replied, "How are BoTii and the girls?"

"Fine. Vrii is on Earth as the guest of the American Chess Federation, learning ***chess***. One of their young players has been staying with us as an exchange student, learning ***polyadok*** from some of our grand masters. The exchange has been a great learning experience for both of them."

"How delightful for Vrii! NaDii said. "And how is Chii?"

DriiLa's expression changed. "Frankly, I don't know what to make of Chii," she said, "She seems to be so melancholy and doesn't seem to take any joy in the things she usually likes to do."

"That's too bad. Has she told you anything about what's bothering her?"

"No. She won't talk about it. When she's home from school, she just spends most of her time in her room and only comes out for meals."

"That's not good. Are you sure she's not ill?" NaDii said, quite concerned.

"She doesn't seem to be. She studies hard and has top marks in all her classes, of course, but she seems to be distracted." DriiLa added.

Greg walked in with TiiNa just then. "Hi. Bobby's planting ***rugo*** roots, TiiNa got thirsty, so we came in for a drink of water." He then saw DriiLa on the monitor. "Hello, DriiLa. How are you?"

"I'm not sure. I was just talking to NaDii now, about Chii——"

Greg looked at NaDii.

"She's not doing so well. In fact, 'Down in the dumps' is the Earth expression that seems to fit best, here." NaDii said.

On the screen, BoTii appeared alongside DriiLa. "Have you asked them about the vacation yet?"

"Not yet." DriiLa answered him, "But I guess I'd better. Mr. and Mrs. Firestone?"

"Greg and NaDii, please," Greg said, "You don't have to be so formal."

"Greg and NaDii, then," DriiLa said, "BoTii thinks we should take that Summer vacation I've been putting off for the last three years, and take Chii to visit you on Placet. I know it's a big imposition, but he thinks it would cheer up Chii to see Bobby again."

Greg and NaDii looked at each other for a moment.

"That would be no imposition. We would love to have you come and visit." Greg said. "I remember you mentioned a Summer vacation when we said goodbye at the spaceport in Oslo."

NaDii added, "Greg and I have talked over some things we could do together if you were going to come to Placet. There isn't much to do here at home, but Placet has all kinds of recreation. Greg even mentioned a fishing trip, I think."

"Fishing trip?" BoTii said. "That sounds like fun. I'll ask Chii if she'd like to go."

DriiLa watched her husband depart. "I can bring my sewing machine and some patterns, and when we're not fishing, I can show TiiNa how to sew."

"I can help," Greg said, "I used to design and sew costumes when I was in the theatre group in college."

"You didn't tell me you could sew!" NaDii told him.

"It didn't come up much, in asteroid mining," he said.

BoTii returned. "She only screamed and jumped up and down a little," he said, "I think she wants to go."

Greg reflected that she was probably holding back, so as not to look too eager in front of her father.

"So, when do you get off work, and when can you get here?" Greg asked.

"Fourteen days," BoTii said, "two weeks, Earth reckoning, I guess."

"How long can you stay?" Greg asked.

"DriiLa has 30 days of un-used vacation time. That's too much, I'm sure——"

"No. It's not. We'll see you in two weeks, and I'll book the fishing campsite for three weeks. We can get in a week's sightseeing in Placedon afterwards, if you'd like, but please, take the whole time. Really. We wouldn't mind at all."

"Okay, if you're sure." BoTii said.

And they logged-out.

"I'll go out and tell Bobby." Greg said to NaDii.

The Firestones met the DriiBo family at Placedon spaceport. Chii had just turned twelve and Bobby gave her a birthday present there, in the concourse. When she unwrapped it, the box held a message-pad. She looked at him in puzzlement. "Open the message called 'For Chii' and start it running."

The music starts. Kettle-drums set up a contrapuntal back-and-forth beat. The violins come up. Instruments Chii cannot even identify become part of the polyphonic tapestry. Layers upon layers build a higher and higher level of magnificence. Then the voices come in, used at first as though they are instruments, beginning with a few and then swelling into a huge chorus. Then it ends.

Chii looked at Bobby questioningly. "Did you do this on your keyboard?"

"The Chicago Symphony Orchestra and the United States Army Chorus did it for me." he said simply.

DriiLa and BoTii had been standing on either side of Chii and listening in amazement.

"They all did this for her?" DriiLa asked.

"They are posting it on the q-net today. They did it because I asked them. They did it because they liked it. ***I*** did it for her, and so did they." Bobby said. "Happy Birthday."

"Thank you," Chii said, "for writing this piece of music for me."

BoTii whispered to DriiLa, "He's just going to keep doing things like this until our daughter marries him, isn't he?'

DriiLa whispered back, "And maybe even after that——"

They headed towards the baggage claim area.

"Come over here," Greg said as they rolled the bags out to the parking area. He walked to the back of a parking area, and there, in five or six spaces, stood a 20-meter version of FriiDa's space yacht.

"This is our new runabout. Hop in. We're heading for the FlaaMo fishing camp in Hwiss, the province just north of here."

The DriiBo's goggled at the staircase that dropped down on a signal from Greg's message pad. Alongside the staircase a hatch opened for luggage. Bobby stowed Chii's bags and Greg packed DriiLa and BoTii's.

Chii, BoTii and DriiLa seated themselves in a group of swivel chairs arrayed around a round table behind the pilot and co-pilot's seats. "Did you spend the Abel money on this?" Bo asked.

"This? Greg asked. "This was the income we got last year from NaDii's patent royalties on a kitchen appliance called a 'frim roaster.'"

"***I've*** got a frim roaster!" DriiLa said.

"Thanks!" NaDii said, and turning to Greg, winked and said "Cha-Ching!" Then she took the controls and lifted the vehicle off the parking lot.

"So, you're an inventor? What else have you invented?" DriiLa asked. Chii leaned over and whispered to her mother.

DriiLa turned pale. "***Really?***" she asked.

NaDii had spoken to Bobby, so she had a pretty good idea what patent Chii was describing to her mother. She waited until DriiLa's color had returned to normal, then turned around from the pilot's seat and asked, in an innocent-sounding voice, "You got one of those?"

DriiLa turned very bright pink. ***HaChii skin, just like a polygraph!*** she thought, grinning with her eyes at Chii.

Chii grinned back. ***She knows that I know!*** she thought. ***I wonder if Bobby told her?*** Then another thought, ***I wonder what else Bobby has told her?***

NaDii set the runabout down in a clearing next to a gravel beach. "Here's our camp-site." she declared.

Lowering the staircase to the ground, Greg and NaDii carried camp chairs and a folding picnic table out to the shoreward side of the craft, then unfurled the awning and sent Bobby and TiiNa out to gather fallen branches for kindling from the surrounding woods. Greg chopped up some of the larger fallen branches with a laser-axe. Then when the kids brought back armloads of kindling, he assembled the fire and lit the wood with the wide-beam setting on the laser. HaChii wood burned wet. Campfires were no work at all. It was one of Greg's favorite things about camping on Placet.

"What's for dinner?" Bobby asked. Greg brought out long forks and a kind of waffle-shaped folding wire gizmo. He put the buns in the wire frame and stuck a hot dog apiece on each fork.

"What do you do with these?" BoTii asked.

"You hold them over the fire, far enough away so they don't burn, and turn them. Dad will toast the buns; that's his thing. When they're done you put the hot dogs in the buns and eat them as a sandwich."

"Ahhh——" BoTii said, "Sandwich! I've had those in Oslo. So this is a sausage sandwich, right?"

"Right!' Bobby said brightly, "And there are all kinds of condiments you can add to the sandwich once you put the sausage in the bun."

"I like mustard and pickle relish," BoTii said, "DriiLa does too."

"Is there an Oslo style hot dog?" Chii asked Bobby, as Greg passed him a toasted bun.

"No. But I learned how to make a Chicago style one. Here——" he started to build her a sandwich with the hot dog he had just finished cooking, and used all the condiments, except ketchup.

"Mmmm." she said, mustard dripping off her chin.

They sat around the campfire afterwards, letting it burn down as nightfall approached. "This is nice, but do we have sleeping bags?" DriiLa asked.

Greg said, "I've got to show you the sleeping accommodations on this baby."

They walked down a corridor going back from the pilots' area in the runabout. There were three round doors set in the right side wall every four meters, and two on the left about six meters apart. Greg opened one on the right. Inside was a well-lit space about three meters by five. The space was a formed plastic capsule with a docking station for a message pad and a large screen to display its output. There was a raised section on one side with a mattress covered with sheets and a blanket. An air vent was visible, a control panel for the docking station, and a closet at one end of the room.

"Each one is self-contained and soundproofed; you can sleep through anything in there. There is a bathroom down there at the end of the corridor."

He opened a door on the left side of the corridor.

"The two on this side of the corridor are double rooms for couples. Pick whichever one you want. I'm going to ask if little TiiNa can have the single closest to the bathroom, if you don't mind."

Everybody got their luggage out of the compartments under the corridor floor, and took things to their rooms. They said their good-nights and closed the hatches.

Chii was unpacking night-clothes, and looking for the message pad Bobby had given her when a round section of the apparently solid wall at the head of her bed swung backwards and opened into Bobby's adjacent room. Bobby stood there holding the hatch and looking through the open circle.

"Guess what we rigged-up on this side of the ship?"

"I would have never known it was there," she said.

"I told my Dad everything. He said this was OK. Don't tell my Mom, or me and Dad are probably both cooked." Bobby said.

"Wow. He's OK with this? Does the other end open up into TiiNa's room?" she had too many questions at once.

"No. There's no connection to TiiNa's room. Look. If you don't want this, I can close up this hatch and nobody will ever know it was here." Bobby said.

"Don't want—— I was trying to figure out how I could sneak over after they were asleep, without getting caught," she said.

"Before we start anything——" Bobby said, "tell me about this protection you mentioned earlier."

She rummaged through her suitcase, and exclaimed when she found the message pad she had been looking for before. She set it into the docking station, rummaged some more and then held up a package that had been wrapped in some t-shirts. "Spermicidal sponge thingies. That's what I used in Oslo." she said.

"That's not one of the methods I found on the q-net. Where did you find out about them?"

"It was another one of your Mom's patents." Chii answered.

"Should have known." Bobby said.

——..

"Do we have to be quiet?" Chii asked at one point.

"Soundproofing!" Bobby reminded her.

Next morning, they came out of their rooms, looking extremely relaxed. Greg had already set up a griddle gizmo over the rebuilt campfire, where he was making pancakes with native berries TiiNa had found in the thicket when she went gathering kindling for the fire. TiiNa already had her plate of pancakes and was walking away as Bobby approached.

"Everything go OK?" Greg asked.

"***Extremely*** OK, Dad," Bobby answered.

His father gave him a quick grin and a pat on the back. "Try to pretend things are normal. Don't cling to her too much when everybody's looking. It'll cut down the chances of them getting suspicious."

"I'll try, Dad. But I've got to convince her to act that way, too."

"Tell you what. Let me talk to her." Greg said. Bobby walked to a chair.

Chii approached Greg, and as she was filling up her plate with pancakes, he whispered. "Hi. Everything go OK last night?"

"Magnificent." she whispered back. "Thanks."

"I'm glad," Greg said, "but while you're out and about today, try not to cling too much to Bobby so your parents don't get suspicious. Can you do that? If we can keep it looking platonic in the daytime, you'll have all the time you want together in the night-time? OK?"

"You've got it, Mr. F.," Chii whispered back.

"Just Greg, please." Greg implored. "And you've got six pancakes there; put a couple back. Come back for seconds if you're really hungry."

"Wow! I didn't even notice I was taking that many. I'm ravenous!"

She put back two pancakes.

NaDii, DriiLa and BoTii came over. Greg loaded up their plates. There were just enough to go around with two for everybody. "I'm going to start up another batch." Greg said.

"Don't bother on my behalf," DriiLa said. "This is plenty."

"I'd like some more," TiiNa said, after having returned with her plate.

"Well, you'll have to pick some more of those berries. Where's the basket you used before?"

"I'll get it, Dad," she said. Setting her plate down on the picnic table, she grabbed the basket off the back of a chair where it was hanging, and headed back to the thicket.

Greg had just finished mixing up a new batch of pancake batter when TiiNa came back with ***most*** of a basket of berries. He picked out a few stems, and dumped the basket's contents into the batter, stirring it in.

"Chii and Bobby love each other, don't they?" TiiNa said.

Greg blinked. ***It's that obvious, is it?*** he asked himself. To TiiNa, he said, honestly, "Yes. They do. Very much."

"Good. 'Cause when I went back there to get more berries, they were making out like bandits in the bushes."

Greg rolled his eyes. ***so much for fatherly advice.*** "Tell you what, TiiNa. If you see them doing that, slip away and don't let them know you saw them. They would be very embarrassed that they were caught."

"Oh, Jeez, Dad, I ***know*** that. I was quiet as a mouse; they never knew I was there." TiiNa shook her head ***what——does Dad think I'm some kind of infant?***

Got to remember, Greg said to himself, ***she only looks like she is three years old—— Well, she is three, but that doesn't count——***

Chii came back a while later. "Got any more pancakes, Mr. F.?"

Bobby came back a few minutes later with the same request. Greg gave him three more pancakes, as he had with Chii.

"Son?" he said.

"Yeah, Dad?" Bobby replied, talking around a mouthful of pancakes.

"Three words:" He pointed at the side of the runabout, and said "Soundproofing," then he pointed at the thicket where TiiNa had gathered the berries, "No soundproofing."

Bobby goggled.

Greg pointed at TiiNa, finishing her pancakes at the picnic table.

"Little ears have big eyes. Enough said?"

"Uhhh——Enough said, Dad."

Greg was using the last of the water he had boiled for coffee to scrub down the griddle. DriiLa and BoTii came over to Greg and asked, "So, when do we go fishing?"

He grinned. "NaDii will show you——"

Around back of the runabout, Using her message pad, NaDii opened a storage slot opposite to the side where they had put the luggage. This slot ran half the length of the runabout. They peeked inside to see what was in there.

There was a 6-meter fishing boat with rods, reels, tackle boxes, the whole works. NaDii pushed a button and a glow appeared behind the boat. Slowly, the boat floated out of the hatchway, suspended on the same kind of beam FriiDa had used to load them into her yacht. NaDii pushed a few more buttons, and the beam levitated the boat out, swung it out over the lake, and lowered it into the water just at the edge of the shore. Bobby grabbed the bow rope that was trailing on the shore, and tied it to a tree.

BoTii and DriiLa gaped.

"New toy." NaDii commented. ***Ever since FriiDa showed me one of these, I've wanted to use that line——***

"But——" BoTii said, "There's no dock——"

NaDii pushed a few more keys on the message pad. "No problem——"

And the beam lifted each of them up, levitated them out to the boat, and set them down neatly.

NaDii handed out life vests. Bobby, TiiNa and Greg helped tie the straps.

NaDii untied the bow rope, cast off and pressed a few more keys on her message pad. The boat began to move out from the shore. "Where's the motor?" DriiLa asked NaDii.

"The same beam that lifted the ship out of the runabout is propelling us across the water." NaDii said. "I've programmed it to take us to a deep spot that's supposed to have the best ***hargo*** fishing in the area."

"What's a ***hargo*** like, daddy?" TiiNa asked.

"About so long," he spread his hands out half a meter, "Lots of teeth. Sort of like an Earth fish called a Northern Pike. Great eating."

The ship stopped and they dropped anchor. "Let's find those ***hargo***," DriiLa said. She picked out a fishing rod and baited the hook, cast it out into the waters off the stern of the ship, and began reeling it in.

"You fished ***hargo*** before?" Greg asked. He was baiting his hook from the bait bucket as he spoke.

"Oh, yeah," DriiLa said, "They won't go for spinners and spoons, if that was what you were thinking. They only hit on live bait.".

Bobby, TiiNa and Chii were a little squeamish about baiting the hooks, but none of them wanted to let on that it bothered them, in front of the others. They soldiered on, but dropped their hooks into the water rather than casting out and reeling them in.

So, with NaDii Greg and DriiLa casting astern, and BoTii casting off the bow, it was Chii who got the first bite. "Wow!" she screamed, "I got one!"

The fish threatened to pull the fishing rod out of her hands, but Bobby got a hand on it, then both hands, controlled the rod, and gradually, inch by inch, they pulled the fighting fish in to the side of the boat, where Greg netted the ***hargo***, and lifted it up.

"Whoa! That's a big ***hargo***." BoTii said.

"We're going to eat tonight!" Greg said, as he put the fish in the live well.

They caught three more ***hargo***, and decided it was time to head back to shore. NaDii pushed a few buttons on her message pad, and——nothing happened.

"Ffurff!" she exclaimed. She fussed with the keypad for a while, realizing gradually that the batteries were low and the signal couldn't reach the shore. Greg hauled up the anchor and silently signaled to DriiLa. They each grabbed a paddle and began to row back towards shore. They were halfway back to the campsite before NaDii looked up and noticed the boat was moving.

Greg had finished building a fire, while DriiLa and NaDii cleaned the fish.

TiiNa was watching Bobby and Chii playing a game of ***polyadok*** on the picnic table. Chii was reaching for a piece when TiiNa interrupted her.

"Before you move that Serf, check out the position of your Judge, there."

"Oooh! I didn't see that." Chii said, "If I don't move the Judge, I will lose it in two moves. Thanks."

Greg stepped over to the table. "Bobby--so you finally decided to coach Chii at ***polyadok?***"

"Yeah. But TiiNa is doing better than me. She sees at least three moves deeper than I do."

"That's a bit scary," Greg said. "You can beat Vrii a fair amount of the time and she's a planetary champion in her age group. If TiiNa is better than you——"

"Yeah, Dad. If she wanted to, she'd ***murder*** Vrii and probably about half the adult grand-masters on Placet. I don't know how she does it, but she's ***dynamite***."

Greg looked at TiiNa. "You ever think about competing in a ***polyadok*** match?"

TiiNa looked up at him. "You think there's an age group for three-year olds? ***I*** don't——"

Greg looked at her. Like Bobby, she was large for her age. "You think we could enter you in the five-to-eight age group, as a five-year-old?"

"That might work." TiiNa said brightly. She took on a calculating expression. "I'd like to try that. But first, I'd like to learn sewing from DriiLa."

After dinner, DriiLa brought out a small rectangular box and three meters of fabric she had bought in Oslo. She clicked a small memory unit into a slot on the side of the box, switched on the box's power, and a three-dimensional projection of Chii's Abel prize gown appeared in the air above the box. She blinked, and it blew apart into individual panels of fabric, and then rolled back into the completed gown.

"Okay, TiiNa." DriiLa said, "This is the basic pattern for Chii's dress."

TiiNa pointed at the image. "It has to be smaller for me. I'm a meter one and Chii is a meter fifty."

"That's right!" DriiLa said, "Chii is a meter fifty tall. How did you know?"

"Lucky guess." TiiNa dismissed the question as though it were trivial. "So what -- we scale it down to 73 percent?"

DriiLa blinked, steered a cursor to 73 percent, and the diagram scaled down.

"Fine." TiiNa said, "But I'm stockier than Chii, so it will need to be wider ***here*** and ***here***," she indicated, pointing at the 3-D image in the air.

DriiLa blinked again, and the waist adjusted. Another blink, and the shoulders widened a bit.

"How are you doing that?" TiiNa asked.

"I control it with my eyes." DriiLa said.

"That's a good idea. Mom could use that instead of her message pad. That didn't do us much good when her batteries ran out——"

"Good thing there were paddles in the boat." DriiLa remarked.

"Well, Mom's kind of retro. She likes to have a backup plan if batteries wear out. There's a whole story that goes along with that (she looked around and noticed her parents were nearby) but I think I'll tell you that story some other time——"

"OK, I'll be waiting," said DriiLa, "Meanwhile, lay out that piece of fabric on the ground."

TiiNa laid out the rectangle of fabric until it was flat and free of wrinkles. "Is that OK?"

"Great. Now stand back." DriiLa blinked again. The beam sketching out the 3-D pattern unwrapped it into its individual fabric pieces again, flipped the pattern-piece projection down onto the cloth on the ground. She blinked a few times and re-arranged the pieces until they fit neatly on the fabric, then one more blink and all the outlines flashed ***very bright*** for a second.

TiiNa blinked at the afterimage, then she walked over to the fabric, where the beam was no longer shining. Each piece in the pattern had been neatly cut-out.

"Now we find out which edges are sewn together and then we see how it fits you," DriiLa said. She flipped up one end of the box and there were several spools of thread. Selecting one that matched the fabric, she placed it into a slot behind the spool caddy. Then she closed that end and flipped up the other. There was the sewing mechanism. She blinked. Two of the pattern pieces appeared in the air, and the projector showed how the two pieces should be stitched together. "Find me those two pieces." DriiLa said.

It was getting dark, and TiiNa could just make out the last two pieces. She brought them to DriiLa and rolled-up the leftover fabric with the cutouts.

DriiLa sewed the last two pieces into place, and held up the gown. "Want to try it on?" she said.

"Do I!" she took the dress into the runabout and changed in her sleep cubicle.

TiiNa came out in the dress, went forward and walked down the staircase. Bobby whistled. Greg turned, and he whistled, too. BoTii couldn't whistle, but he waved his grippers in the air. TiiNa blushed.

Chii looked her up and down and said, "That looks good on you. Maybe better than mine. You got anybody ***special*** in mind, that you're wearing it for?"

TiiNa blanched, "Just me right now. Give me a little time."

They sat around the campfire and talked as it burned down.

"I love your sewing machine." TiiNa said. "The problem with the eye control is I don't know what you're looking at. Is there a link on the q-net that would explain how that model works?"

"Sure. it's a Singer 2585-D; check out Singer Company's link on the q-net."

"Wow. The year I was born. Will do, Mrs. DriiBo." TiiNa said brightly.

"Ummm--TiiNa--HaChii names don't work that way. Chii's name is Chii Ix DriiBo because my first name is ***Drii***La and my husband's is ***Bo***Tii, but each of our last names come from our parents. My Mom and Dad, for instance, are named Fraa and Troo so I'm DriiLa Ix FraaTroo. My name didn't change when I got married."

"What were BoTii's parents named?"

"BoTii's Mom and Dad are AaNii and BiiRaa."

"So he would be BoTii Ix AaBii?"

"BoTii ***Iz*** AaBii. 'Ix' means 'daughter of' and 'Iz' means 'son of.'"

"Wow. That's complicated. In our family, everybody takes Dad's last name, so that's our last name, and that's it."

"But you lose everything about your mother. Nobody can tell you are descended from NaDii."

"Wow. You're right. That leaves Mom out completely. I never thought about that before, but it isn't fair to her, at all."

"So--what do I call you?" TiiNa finally got around to asking that question.

"Just DriiLa——or 'Reels' if you want to. That's BoTii's pet name for me."

"I think I'll just keep it at DriiLa, if you don't mind." TiiNa said.

CHAPTER 24 - Best Present

Two days later was Bobby's birthday. Chii and TiiNa had been planning something, he knew, but he hadn't quite been able to figure out what it was.

The morning had dawned sunny, BoTii and Greg had taken the fishing boat out at sunrise to get a head-start on the ***hargo***, while NaDii and DriiLa unfurled the awning so there would be some sun-shade over the picnic table at breakfast.

Bobby and TiiNa had gathered a fair amount of kindling, and Chii came back from her hunt with a fallen log that had rotted a bit, but still looked fairly sound. Bobby started to slice it into manageable firewood with the laser-axe when a buzz flew out of a cut end, followed by a swarm of them. Bobby backed off. ***Must have cut open a buzz hive,*** he thought. He herded TiiNa and Chii back to the runabout, and closed the hatch.

"Those can sting," he said, "And we've riled them up by opening up their hive. Let's let them settle for a while before we go back out."

Chii signaled NaDii's message pad. "Mrs. Firestone," she asked, "We cut open a buzz hive in the log, by mistake. Can you get my Mom and yourself in here ***quick,*** before they spot you?"

A shriek from outside indicated that they were too late. The swarm had found NaDii and DriiLa. Opening a closet, Bobby threw on one of Greg's jackets with long sleeves, put gloves on his hands, threw a blanket over his shoulder and tied a scarf over the lower part of his face.

Then he told the girls to back up. tossing the laser-axe to Chii.

"Cover me, and try to get any of the buzzers that make it in the door."

He popped the hatch and went out. Three of the buzzers that got in the door were crisped in a second and dropped to the floor. TiiNa gaped while they continued trying to sting the carpet as they died.

Bobby came back in the door dragging NaDii with one hand, and half-carrying DriiLa, who was wrapped in the blanket. He kicked the door shut with one foot, got DriiLa into one of the chairs in the cockpit, and placed NaDii gently on the floor while Chii zapped the dozen-or-so buzzers that made it in, while the door was being slammed.

TiiNa went over to DriiLa and pulled back the blanket. A couple more buzzers flew out and met with fiery death at the hands of Chii. DriiLa was shivering, and TiiNa was scraping out the buzz stings with her fingernails, rather than trying to pull them, which would squeeze in more venom. They would keep pumping for several minutes; the quicker they were removed, the less venom they would inject.

Bobby was doing the same for his mother. NaDii had more stings and was mumbling incoherently. Her color was pale blue and she could not stand. Chii killed the few buzzers that got free of NaDii as Bobby rolled her over and looked for more stings. He scraped out all he could, and then rolled NaDii over onto her back again, pushing aside the table in the middle of the cockpit so she could lay flat.

"Mom?" he cried, "Are you all right? Talk to me!"

But NaDii only moaned.

"Call Dad!" Bobby shouted to TiiNa "Get him back here ***fast!***"

TiiNa called while Bobby tried first aid. If NaDii was in shock, elevating her lower body so blood would reach the brain more easily was a priority. He pulled bedding out of the sleep cubicle where Chii had been last night and pushed the bedding under his mother's lower limbs and torso. He covered her with a blanket, and although he knew she was cold-blooded so this wouldn't really help much, it was first-aid for a human, so he tried it anyway.

Fluid was dribbling out her thoracic spiracles. Breathing seemed to be very difficult for her.

Greg and BoTii tumbled into the doorway and slammed the hatch. Chii zapped the half-dozen buzzers that got in from the swarm outside.

"Epi pen!" Greg shouted at Bobby, "First Aid Kit!"

Hurrying towards the front of the cockpit, Bobby pulled the first aid kit out from a drawer under the dashboard, handing it to Greg. His father, pulling out the epinephrine pen unit, removed its cover and injected it into NaDii's left walking tentacle. She was now a deep blue and her breathing had stopped.

Greg tried mouth-to-mouth resuscitation. One advantage of being a bellows-breather was the ability to force compressed air into somebody else's airway. He could see air coming out of NaDii's spiracles and forced more in. Additional fluid dribbled out as Greg continued rescue breathing. BoTii watched, distraught, knowing there was nothing he could do to help. He went to DriiLa and tried to comfort her.

Chii sent a distress call on her message pad. The nearest hospital was 20 miles south, in DiiXon, but they had a trac-drive ambulance, which appeared, hovering over the camp site, in less than a minute.

Two EMT's came in through the hatch. One looked at DriiLa, and began treating her, while the other pulled Greg aside to begin working on NaDii.

"Epinephrine does very little for HaChii," said the senior EMT to Greg. "I'm giving her our equivalent, and we're giving her forced oxygen, but she's not responding, so we have to take her to the hospital for further treatment." They asked BoTii to accompany NaDii, but he explained that he was DriiLa's husband, and the human male was NaDii's husband. The EMT's startled for a moment, then one brightened and said, "Oh. ***That's*** who you are!" He then escorted Greg and BoTii to the ambulance, with NaDii transported on a rolling stretcher and DriiLa being helped by the second EMT. Chii, Bobby and TiiNa trailed behind.

One EMT asked Bobby, assuming he was the oldest, "Can you stay behind here and watch the kids? We don't have room enough for everybody. We'll send somebody to pick you up in a little while, OK?"

"Sure. You take good care of our Moms."

The EMT's boarded their ambulance, and the three watched them take off.

Bobby shrugged out of the jacket, gloves and scarf. He scraped a few stings out of his cheek and around his eyes.

"That was very brave, Bobby." Chii said to him.

TiiNa asked him, with wide eyes, "Is Mommy going to live?"

He put his hand on her shoulder. "I don't know. I got her out of the swarm as quick as I could, and I gave her the best first aid I could. I hope Dad's rescue breathing was enough. He's the only one of us who could do that."

TiiNa looked down at her shoes. "Chii and I were going to give you your birthday presents after breakfast——" She hugged her brother.

Chii hugged him from the other side, "I'm sorry. This is the worst birthday ***ever***."

Bobby looked at her. "Would you mind if TiiNa and I pray for your Mom and our Mother? I know it doesn't make much sense to you——"

Chii nodded her head. "If you can teach me how to pray, I will try. If there ***is*** a God, and he's ***your*** God, then he's ***my*** God, too. What do I do?"

There was a table in the middle of the cockpit area. Bobby had shoved it aside when he lay NaDii down on the floor. Now he pulled it back into the middle of the room. Kneeling down and folding his hands, he rested them against the table edge. TiiNa did, too. Chii tried to do the same, with her grippers pressed together.

"OK, Chii, repeat after me——Heavenly Father——"

Chii and TiiNa repeated the words.

"Bless our Mothers and keep our families together——"

"Ease their suffering——"

"Return them to us——"

"And if you must take them, take them straight to Heaven——"

This was too much for TiiNa. She collapsed in a little pile on the floor. Chii finished the words Bobby had said.

"Amen——"

Chii repeated the unfamiliar word, and asked what it meant.

"'So be it,' or maybe, 'Let it be as God wills.'" Robbie answered.

"Let it be as God wills." Chii stated, then she bent down to comfort TiiNa.

A loud 'beep' from outside announced the arrival of a police cruiser containing two officers. It landed as the children walked down the staircase. They looked left and right for buzzers, but the buzz swarm seemed to have left. A policeman in tan stepped out of the small craft and greeted Bobby.

"You've grown." said Jii.

"Detective Jii? Bobby responded.

"It's Chief Jii, now. I took the job in DiiXon, the small town where the KissBii hospital is. It's a lot different from big-city life in Placedon, but things still happen that need police work. I'm sorry to hear it was your mother who was injured so badly. Is this your sister?" He looked at TiiNa.

"Yes. TiiNa, this is Chief Jii. We know each other from something that happened before you were born."

TiiNa took Jii's gripper and released it without shaking it up and down, which was proper HaChii protocol.

"And who is this?" Jii asked, looking at Chii.

"This is my——girlfriend, Chii." Bobby told Jii, "Her mother was injured and is also at the hospital."

"Well, I'm here to give you a ride." the Chief said, "and I'm sorry to hear that Chii's mother was injured also. Come along; there's room enough for everybody."

The trip took a few minutes. At the end, Jii swung the craft down out of a cloud bank and landed on a pad on the roof of the hospital. Closing up the craft, he sent the other officer back to the station, and walked the children in to the emergency room.

BoTii came out of a cubicle and said to her, "DriiLa is doing well. They may be able to clear her to go in a few hours."

"Can I talk to her?" Chii asked her father.

"Sure. Come in here." He led her into the cubicle.

DriiLa was sitting up in the bed, looking alert if a little puffy around the eyes. She had sting marks on her face and shoulders.

"Chii!" she said, and hugged her daughter. She looked at her for a minute.

"If Bobby hadn't scared off the buzzers and wrapped me up in that blanket——is he here?"

Chii said he was, and asked him to come in.

"Hello DriiLa. How are you doing?" he asked.

"Not bad, thanks to you and your sister," she said, "They said the way she scraped those stings out of my skin saved me from a much worse reaction."

"I'm glad." Bobby said. Then, "Is my Mom here?" he looked around.

BoTii looked at Bobby and TiiNa. "I'm afraid she's not. They took her upstairs to intensive care." Looking at Chief Jii, he asked, "Could you show them where Intensive Care is?" I'm going to stay with my wife."

"Sure. Bobby and TiiNa, come with me——."

"Dad?" Chii asked her father, "Can I go with them?"

"Mom will be OK." he told her, "Go with Bobby and TiiNa. I'll see you in a little while."

Jii led them upstairs. He walked over to the nurses' station and asked where Mrs. Firestone was located and was told to go to Room 335.

The Chief led the children in to the room. Greg looked up at them red-eyed.

"How is Mrs. Firestone doing?" chief Jii asked Greg.

"She's on life-support." Greg answered. Jii gripped Greg's hand, and left.

Greg gestured the children toward the bed. They could see she was connected to machines and tubes all over and was very still. Air was being forced into her mouth and seemed to be passing out of her spiracles freely. Her face was swelled so that her eyes were squeezed shut. Her arms and grippers were also much bigger than their normal size. Her color was cyan with red spots, rather than the blue they had seen when she was taken out on the stretcher.

Bobby knelt beside the bed and began to pray silently, and so did TiiNa.

Chii approached Greg Firestone, took his hand in her gripper, and squeezed. "I'm so sorry. I brought in the stupid log for the fire, that had the buzz hive in it."

Greg looked up at her. "You couldn't have known it was there."

"No. but I feel ***terribly*** responsible," she said in a very small voice.

Greg stood up and held her while she shook and whimpered.

Bobby and TiiNa had finished praying. They stood up and looked at their mother for a while. Chii looked at their faces and realized she had gotten so used to their unusual human-style eyes that she really didn't see them. At this moment, however, they had tears running down their faces, something that HaChii eyes did not do.

She looked back at Greg, and tears were running down from his eyes too.

There was a big lump of pain in her chest, because there was nothing she could do to help. Then she thought of something.

"Bobby? Can I borrow your message pad?" she asked.

He handed it to her wordlessly, and didn't even ask why she wanted it.

She stepped out into the hallway, and checked Bobby's list of contacts. There was a link marked 'Father Boyle.' She clicked it.

A human male answered. "Hello?" he said.

"Hello, Father Boyle?" she said. "I'm Bobby Firestone's girlfriend, Chii."

"Yes?" he asked, puzzled.

"NaDii has been very badly injured." she said.

"O my. Does she need the Last Rites?" Father Boyle said.

"I don't know." Chii said, "It might be that bad. I'm not a Christian, so I am not sure what you're talking about. But there's no chaplain in this hospital, and I think Greg may need some support. So do Bobby and TiiNa."

"Where are you, child?" the priest asked her.

"It's a hospital in DiiXon. I heard them call it KissBii hospital."

"I know the place. Sit tight. I know a pilot who can get me there in twenty minutes."

Fifteen minutes later, Father Boyle came striding down the hallway towards room 335. Chii hailed him and they walked back into the room. Father Boyle conferred with Greg for a few minutes.

The priest spoke to NaDii, and receiving no response, began the rites of conditional absolution and unction. At one point, he asked that Chii join them in prayer. She asked for his guidance, and carried out Father Boyle's instructions to the best of her ability.

Afterward, Greg asked Father Boyle, "Why did you insist on including Chii with us since she is not a member of our family or our Church?"

The priest replied, "She was the one that asked me to be here. If NaDii is going to die, Chii asking me to be here to prepare her for judgment was the ***single greatest act of love she could offer.***

Bobby has told me how he would like her to be a member of your family, and today, I understood why. I hope I can marry them some day. I ***wish*** I could marry them today. She may not be ***Christian in upbringing***, but she is ***Christian in character***, if that makes any sense."

"It makes perfect sense to me, Father; I'm glad my son found her." Greg said.

"I would like to speak to Bobby and TiiNa." Father Boyle replied.

Greg went and got the children. Both were bearing up stoically, but the tears were still running down their cheeks.

"Bobby and TiiNa," the priest began,

"I want you to know that the Sacrament you just saw is not just an admission that your mother is dying. It is also a Sacrament for healing. If the Lord wishes, he may either take her or heal her. For now, I would like you to remember that I profoundly hope ***and pray*** that the Lord will heal her. Is that understood?"

"Yes, Father." They both said.

"Now," he said as he turned to Greg, "I'm going downstairs to see if there is something worth eating in this hospital's cafeteria. Call me if anything changes. Chii has my message-pad link. Goodbye." And he left the room.

Chii walked over to Bobby. "You and TiiNa are so upset," she said, "I don't know if I did the right thing."

Bobby gaped in disbelief. "You're an angel. Don't even ***think*** that way."

And TiiNa joined him. "Now I know why Bobby loves you. I agree with him. You ***are*** an angel, even if you don't know what that is, yet. If he doesn't marry you, I will never forgive him——"

Next, Greg joined them, and grasped her grippers in his hands. "Chii, you are a good friend, and you are going to be a ***great*** member of this family."

And finally, Bobby held her and said what he should have said a long time ago, legalities or no legalities, "Chii Ix DriiBo, will you marry me?"

And she said, simply, "Yes."

Bobby turned to his Father, "Now ***that*** is one really ***great*** Birthday present."

"And it's ***about time!***" NaDii said, from inside her oxygen mask.

Everyone swiveled around and looked at her, and their faces lit up.

Chief Jii gave TiiNa, Chii, Bobby, DriiLa and BoTii a ride back to the camp site early in the afternoon. Greg stayed with NaDii, who was out of danger but would be in the hospital at least a few more days. On the way back, Jii and Bobby took turns telling Chii and TiiNa the story of how they met and what had happened with the Denny Harris case.

"For a guy who doesn't get out much, you know some of the most ***interesting*** people." DriiLa said to Bobby.

The fishing boat had been pulled up on shore and loosely tied to a tree stump when Greg and BoTii had come in on the run; BoTii asked Bobby to tie it up a little more securely, so he went over and threw a couple more half-hitches over the stump, tightening the rope and making sure it was secure.

TiiNa and Chii were helping BoTii furl up the awning, while DriiLa rested in a lawn chair.

"You know, Bobby asked Chii to marry him today?" TiiNa asked BoTii.

"No. I hadn't heard." BoTii said, as though marriage proposals from nine-year-old suitors were the most normal thing in the world. "What did she say?"

"She said 'Yes' of course." Chii answered, as she finished rolling up the awning.

"That's what I expected," BoTii responded, "You can't get married yet, but at least you're engaged."

"Is that OK with you?" TiiNa asked.

"The idea takes a little getting used to." BoTii answered honestly. "How do you feel about it, Reels?" he asked his wife.

"Let's see," she said, "He's brilliant, brave, heroic, plays a great piano, dances like a dream——did I say heroic?——"

"Sounds like she's still making up her mind." BoTii said to TiiNa, and winked.

Bobby came back. "You know, if you're starving, like I am——there's a charcoal barbecue grill in the same cargo bay where the fishing boat was. Also, there's charcoal. Did you guys get any ***hargo*** while you were out there?"

"Got a couple in the live well," BoTii said.

"I'll go get the grill." Bobby said, "Somehow, I don't feel much inclination to start a wood fire right now."

BoTii and DriiLa looked at the cut sections of log with the same regard a canary looks at a cat. "Could you make that stuff go away?" DriiLa said, to no one in particular.

Bobby, in the cargo bay wrestling with the charcoal grill, stopped to activate something in the back of the bay. A beam shot out of the cargo hold and the logs silently lifted from their locations, arced over the water, and splashed into the lake a hundred meters out, one by one.

As Bobby carried the grill out to the front of the runabout, he remarked, "Like Mom said earlier--new toy."

Once the charcoal was down to red coals and white ash, Bobby and TiiNa fetched and cleaned the fish--not without some complaining from TiiNa--and placed them on the grill. Bobby added some salt, pepper and herbs, a touch of butter, and covered the grill with its lid.

"Mmmm. That was good." Chii said after they finished the meal. She then addressed her Mom, "Did you include 'great cook' on your list?"

"Greg seems to know fishing and camping, and he's taught you pretty well." BoTii said to Bobby.

"That's right," Bobby said, "Dad used to fish for Northern Pike out at the Loch Raven reservoir with his father when he was a kid."

"That's on Earth?" BoTii asked.

"Yeah," Bobby said, "Near Baltimore. I guess most of this stuff (he pointed at the boat and fishing gear) was like stuff his Dad had."

"Where's his Dad now?" BoTii asked.

"He died in a mining accident when my father wasn't much older than I am."

"And Greg went into mining anyway?" BoTii asked.

"Family business. 'It's in the blood,' he told me. His Firestones have been miners for hundreds of years.

"And have NaDii's family been inventors before?" he asked.

"I'm not sure. NaDii's Dad, Bii, is an engineer. Maybe he has patents. You know, I've never even looked——"

Thus it was, that later that evening, after everybody had turned in for the night, that Bobby was surfing the HaChii Patent Office with his message pad, when the hatch opened and Chii looked in. She climbed into the bed with Bobby while he hunted for 'Bii Iz SiiFii' among the patent holders.

"Look here," he remarked. "My grandfather has two patents for improvements in the trac drive. He's a propulsion engineer. I never knew that."

"Wow," said Chii, "That's interesting. But look here, where he uses the Bii-Yanang equations. Wait! is he the 'Dr. Bii' of the equations? Oh! of course, he is—— But here," she went on, "if you changed the parameter to——"

"Yeah, but here——" Bobby pointed out a possible improvement.

And by the end of twenty minutes, they had a method for doubling the contraction factor while only increasing the power consumption by 10 percent.

"This looks like you should apply for a patent." Bobby said.

"WE should apply for a patent." Chii replied, and they submitted the design modifications jointly.

"Now," said Chii, "What were you thinking about doing for the ***rest*** of the night?"

In the middle of the night, TiiNa was coming back from the bathroom when she saw the door opening at the sleep cubicle Bobby had gone into. Chii stepped out. ***Interesting!*** TiiNa thought. She pressed up against the wall and merged in with the background. ***Bobby isn't the only one who knows how to do this——***

Chii walked right by her without seeing anything. The door she exited had been left open a bit. As Chii went in and closed the bathroom door, TiiNa crossed the hall and peeked into the doorway of the middle bedroom cubicle.

Bobby appeared to be asleep on the bed. TiiNa slipped in, entered the closet and blended in with the blankets and sheets stacked here and there. She slid the closet door shut part-way, leaving enough of an opening to peek through.

Chii returned a few minutes later. She snuggled up to Bobby and appeared to be going to sleep. ***Not very much interesting here,*** TiiNa thought. ***Maybe I'll slip out after they're asleep.***

Then Bobby woke up. Chii was not going back to sleep at all. Whatever she had done had awakened Bobby completely, and TiiNa watched, still and quiet, as they started, and finished, what she had been expecting them to do.

At one point, Chii had arched up from the bed and had her head thrown back with an expression on her face resembling extreme pain. That was slightly surprising to

TiiNa. She had heard and read about sex, of course--her parents had not closed off any area of the q-net to her, and probably couldn't have made it stick even if they had tried, but none of what she had read about making love suggested ***pain***. She almost jumped out of the closet to help when Chii cried out, but thought better of it. Afterward, Chii and Bobby looked so immensely relaxed and comfortable as they drifted off in each other's arms that she doubted her first impression.

TiiNa suspected the expression she had seen on Chii's face related to pain about the way a cup of hot chocolate related to a cup of hot coffee.

After both Chii and Bobby were quiet and still, TiiNa slid out of the closet, silently opened the door, and slipped out of the room.

CHAPTER 25 - Board Games

Greg and NaDii returned to the runabout in time for the last week of the fishing vacation. At first, NaDii tired too easily to do much, but after a few days, she went out in the fishing boat with the others. They had caught enough ***hargo*** that they had a cooler full of them, chilled down in the cargo area where the boat and the barbecue had been. In addition to ***hargo,*** there had been several other kinds of small pan fish, and a second cooler partially filled with those ensured they would be bringing home good eating for both families, for months to come.

Two days before they were scheduled to pack up and leave for Placedon, a message request came in on NaDii's message pad. She opened the screen, and there was her father, Bii.

"Hello, Daughter," he said, "Can you get your son over here?"

It seemed a strange way to ask to talk to Bobby, but she called him over. Both of them looked at the screen, and Bobby spoke to his grandfather:

"Hi Grand-Dad, what's up?" he said.

"***You*** are!" he said, "***Way***, way up, in my estimation. Where did you learn trac drive engineering?"

"Oh, ***that***," Bobby said, almost embarrassed. His mother looked puzzled.

"***Oh That*** is going to double the speed of most trac-drive vehicles," Bii said, "and it came to my attention because somebody at the patent office is a fan of your mother's——" NaDii looked slightly embarrassed.

"That would probably be the Director. I've seen her talking to Mom on the q-link" Bobby responded.

"She put two and two together when she saw the name of the patent applicant, and called me to see what I thought about the patent application. Which, by the way, is brilliant."

"Thanks, Grand-Dad."

"And I recommended that they fast-track it for approval. Your patent is going to be approved two or three days from now. Thought you'd like to know."

"That's very quick," Bobby said.

"Not as quick as one of your Mom's patents——but that's a story for when you're older," his grandfather said, turning slightly pink.

"You mean the BrropCo Model 37?" Bobby said, watching for his grandfather's reaction.

Bii turned even pinker, "You know about that?"

"They never did put child-lock restrictions on the Patent Office's q-net files, Grand-Dad," he explained.

"I doubt they ever thought it would be needed." Bii chuckled ruefully, "At any rate, grandson, you have made me proud. But I want to know something. Who is this 'Chii Ix DriiBo' listed on the patent with you?"

Oh, might as well introduce her, he thought. "Hang on a moment——" he said, then he shouted "Chii! Could you come over here for a moment?"

Chii walked over. Bobby pulled her to him and put an arm around her. She looked somewhat embarrassed, but put an arm around Bobby too, and looked at the message pad.

"This is Chii Ix DriiBo," Bobby explained to his grandfather, "mathematician ***extraordinaire*** and the love of my life," he said.

"Chii, this is my grandfather, Bii Iz SiiFii," Bobby explained to her.

Bii seemed taken aback. "Well, she's certainly lovely, but -- wait a minute! She's the girl you won that prize with on Earth, earlier this year——"

"That's right, Grand-Dad. I didn't think Mom would have let that go by without bragging to you about it——"

"Sorry. I guess I don't take things that happen on Earth as seriously as I should. But this——"

"Sounds like you like our design, Grand-Dad."

"Not as much as General Spaceframes and ZyssCraft are going to like it. I'd love to see how they are going to fight it out to get the rights from you two to build the new engines."

"Dr. SiiFii?" Chii asked Bobby's grandfather, "Do you know a good lawyer who can help negotiate this kind of deal? I don't think Bobby or I have enough expertise to do that without getting--'taken'--is the term, I'm thinking."

"You've got a sharp girl, there," Bii said, looking at Bobby, "Here's a link to a corporate lawyer at my engineering firm who will help out. It will cost some money, but I understand you have got some of that from the award."

"Yeah." Bobby said, "we've still got some of that left," and he winked at his Grandfather. "I hope this won't cost more than it's worth."

"Bobby," Bii responded, "and Chii. After the Big Two get done fighting this out, there should be ***plenty*** to pay your lawyer. Trust me——"

Bii looked critically at the two of them, tilted his head to one side, and said, "One more thing--and correct me if I'm out of line--because you two are way too young to be romantically involved, and yet——I see something in your eyes, Bobby, that says '***This is the one***.' Is that true?"

"I ***said*** 'love of my life' already, didn't I?" he said, and hugged her closer.

That afternoon, Greg and Bobby went out to fetch some firewood. Greg said they should cut up firewood away from the camp, and then bring the pieces back, so that if there were any more buzz nests, the swarm wouldn't attack the camp site.

They were fortunate in that the first fallen limb they found and chopped up with the laser-axe proved to be uninfested. Greg and Bobby brought the logs back to the camp site while TiiNa and DriiLa rounded up some kindling. When all the wood and twigs were assembled, Greg adjusted the laser axe beam to wide-focus, and used it to start the kindling. By the time it became dark, the fire was blazing merrily. Everybody sat around the campfire roasting hot dogs, toasting buns, and trying to keep marshmallows on the forks until they turned golden, without starting them on fire or having them fall off into the flames.

"Is this what you do on Earth when you go camping?" BoTii asked Greg.

"Pretty much," Greg responded. He turned to DriiLa. "You grew up going on fishing trips, right? What are HaChii camping trips like?"

"Well, we go out in boats and catch fish, of course," she said, "and the tackle and rods might be a little different, but not that much. We also cook things over campfires, not just the fish but ***ba-hong*** roots, which we wrap in foil and put in the fire, and we roast ***xii*** fruit over the fire, like you do with marshmallows. They are a favorite with the kids. We sit around the fire and tell stories. And we play ***polyadok*** or cards. There is an Earth card game called cribbage that became very popular a few years ago."

That made Chii think. She had been playing ***polyadok*** with TiiNa earlier in the day. TiiNa never lost, but Chii was learning a lot about strategy from the little girl. "Mrs. Firestone?" she asked NaDii.

"What is it, Chii?"

"I'd love to get TiiNa into a ***polyadok*** match with Vrii."

"Face-to-face? I'm not sure how that could be arranged." NaDii replied. "She could always play your sister by q-link," she said.

"But Vrii would assume if TiiNa played well, Bobby was feeding her moves from off-screen. If she played her directly——" Chii said.

"I see. But Vrii plays all her games on Gracet, doesn't she?"

"Not all. In eight weeks, she's playing a round-robin with twenty players in the 8-to-12 age group, in Cluret, right here on Placet."

"That's MeBlii and ChuuRi's home town. If we visit them, TiiNa could visit with their daughter RiiMaa, who is the same age."

"And play ***polyadok*** with my sister, Vrii, who is the same age socially——" Chii concluded in a somewhat snarky tone.

TiiNa came over. "That sounds like fun. Could we visit MeBlii, ChuuRii and RiiMa? RiiMa is so much fun, like a little sister," she asked her mother.

"RiiMa is two weeks older than you," NaDii told her, "but you're right, she ***is*** like your little sister. I think we ***will*** make that trip."

"Oh, Goody! And I'll get to play Chii's snobby sister too!"

Two days later, when they flew back to Placedon Spaceport, and said their good-byes, Chii hugged Greg and whispered to him, "Thanks for everything. I think I have my parents convinced Bobby is for me. The next challenge will be the civil authorities——"

That's going to be an interesting battle, Greg thought, as he waved good bye.

Since Bobby had gotten ahead of anything his parents could teach him through home-schooling, his parents had left his education mostly to his own choice of what to study on the q-net. The civil authorities of Placedon, however, felt obligated to periodically send 'visitation' evaluators, to check on his progress. Since they could never find any deficiencies in his knowledge, they had never been able to challenge his home-schooling. Although Bobby didn't think about it too much, he occasionally worried that there was an element of suspiciousness in the bureaucracy that could cause trouble later.

His summer vacation trip had altered his view of the world, however.

Trouble with the civil authorities was the last thing he needed now. He had spoken with Chii about one of the ways they could be together. In his q-net peregrinations, he had discovered something called 'emancipated minor' status. It would involve being financially independent, getting the parents' OK, and getting the approval of the civil authorities. In the HaChii Confederation, that meant a court would have to approve.

One way to convince the court his home-schooling situation was not a problem would be to get a college degree, or preferably several. Without explaining why, he asked his parents if they would release some of his Abel money for him to pay tuition for on-line courses. Since they had already been paying for on-line home-schooling resources, they thought there was nothing unusual about his request, except that college courses were involved. And if that surprised them, they didn't say so.

He was surprised to find that he needed to pass a general educational development test before he could enroll in college classes. In Placedon, that required him to appear at a nearby community college for testing. He told his parents he was going to North Placedon Community College, and said he would be back in the afternoon.

Because he could superficially pass for a teen-aged HaChii male if he wore gripper mittens and was not examined too closely, he was able to blend in and take the exam at the testing center without attracting attention. In each section of the exam, he finished in less than half the time allotted, and waited with the exam form face down on the table and his hands in his pockets, until some of the other examinees began bringing up their forms, then he brought up his. At the end of the day, he returned home, told his parents he had completed his exams and went back to working on a musical composition he had been involved with before he left for the fishing trip.

The next day, his test results were reported to him. To his satisfaction, he had not missed any of the questions, so he went to North Placedon Community College to pick up his certificate. Somewhat to his surprise, he received the certificate and an offer of a scholarship to the college. Offering his regrets, he went back home and enrolled in the original four-year online university program he had planned on--a double major in mathematics and physics. Each day's coursework took only a few minutes of his time, so it didn't interfere with his routine very much. He figured he could finish the degrees in a couple of years, and at that age, might have a better chance to apply for the emancipated minor status.

TiiNa found that the local public school, North Placedon Middle School, had a ***polyadok*** club. She inquired if she would have to enroll in classes at the school, rather than continue on-line home-schooling, but found that it was an after-school program not funded by the public school; she could enroll with no questions asked. Which was just as well--she enrolled in the 8-to-12 age group--never mind that she had actually just turned four, and was large for her age. She let them think she was a smaller-than-average eight-year-old.

Like Bobby, she could pass for HaChii in most circumstances. Special contact lenses made her eyes appear HaChii-normal. Her hands were the problem. A long dress could cover the fact that she had feet at the end of her walking-legs, but the only way to camouflage her hands was to wear HaChii gripper-mittens. She explained that she had been injured and had deformed grippers for which the mittens provided some protection to the injured parts.

The excuse was accepted, and she was allowed to play.

By the end of the week, she was ranked first in her age group, and there was guarded optimism among the players at North Placedon, regarding the week-end match with the Cluret Middle school group, to whom they usually lost.

That weekend, they didn't. And over the next four weeks' competitions, leading to the City championship, TiiNa moved up the ranks undefeated, not only winning each match, but coaching other members of her team to defeat opponents who had previously said disrespectful things about Placedon Middle School players.

A week before the visit and round-robin challenge match with the Gracet planetary champion (8-12 age group) the City championships were held. In previous years, this had been a time-consuming process, involving a lot of games ending in draws. TiiNa won her quarter-final game in 20 moves, a record. She won her semi-final game with a little more effort, taking 30 moves to defeat the previously-undefeated City champion. And finally, the day of the final game, she faced an opponent who looked all of fifteen, but was competing as a twelve-year-old. With Greg and NaDii watching her on the q-net, she made her first move. Twenty-five moves later, her opponent conceded the game, seeing inevitable Exile in three moves.

TiiNa was now in position to be one of the twenty players who would face Vrii in the round-robin match the following week-end.

Bobby continued his studies, and spoke with Chii on the q-link every day. She, too, had begun college classes with a view toward a double major in propulsion engineering and mathematics. They had enrolled in the same on-line university and had many of the same courses. When they could, they worked on homework together. They also plotted their strategy for the day when they could apply for 'emancipated minor' status.

Vrii Ix DriiBo rounded the group of tables, having made one move at each of the 20 ***polyadok*** boards. At each table, she examined the board position, made her next move, and moved on. At first, she hadn't noticed the strange little girl with the gloves, but on this, her fifth visit to the table, she was beginning to see the possibilities of a real competitor on the other side of the board. She made her move, and walked on, but was troubled at the limited number of board positions she could take advantage of.

Next time around, she stopped, looked at the move that had just been made, and began thinking about defense, instead of simple attack. She spent more time there, then moved on to the other challengers.

Five moves later, she was losing pieces on table 14, and was beginning to worry about the outcome of that game. At the rest of the tables, she was mopping up, as usual.

Three moves later, she conceded at table 14. She asked the little girl to stay, and finished the other games. Then she went and sat down at table 14 as the other players packed up their pieces.

"Could I play you a game, right here, without the rest of that sideshow?" she asked TiiNa.

"Sure," TiiNa answered, "I'm game if you are," she winked.

Having recently studied chess on Earth, Vrii noticed halfway through the game, that her opponent was using moves like those she had seen in chess games played by a 20th-century champion named Bobby Fisher. She could recognize the type of strategy, but couldn't compete with it, and had to concede again in ten more moves.

Stunned, she asked her diminutive opponent what the gloves were about. She had been told a story about injured grippers, but was skeptical, given the dexterity with which her opponent moved the pieces despite her supposed injuries.

"Oh, heck——Might as well show you." TiiNa said, and pulled off her gloves, and taking a contact-lens case out of her pocket, blinked out her contact lenses, putting them away. She then looked up at Vrii.

"TiiNa, Bobby's sister!" Vrii exclaimed.

"Don't tell them how old I ***really*** am——" TiiNa asked. "They think I'm a smallish eight-year-old."

"I know you're younger than Bobby——" Vrii said, "but I've forgotten--how much younger?"

"I turned four a few weeks ago, not that I look that age." she replied.

Vrii paled. "You're better than Bobby," she said.

"Yeah. He tells me that, too. "TiiNa said.

"And he's hell on wheels, for a nine-year-old." Vrii said, "although he never demolished me as thoroughly at ***polyadok*** as ***you*** just did."

"Believe me, he's hell on wheels for ***any*** age. I'm just a better ***polyadok*** player than he is, but he's so much better at everything else."

"My mother told me he saved her life. Is that true?"

"Yeah. I think the word she used for him was 'heroic.'"

"And my sister——"

"Well, I'm sure she's told you about him——"

"Like what?"

"Like how he asked her to marry him."

"Awww——That's cute! Puppy love——"

TiiNa looked askance at Vrii. "I guess she hasn't told you as much about him as I thought. A ***lot more*** than puppy love, is all I'm going to say."

"Aw, go on!" Vrii reacted. "They're just kids."

"You weren't there," TiiNa said, "There's a lot more to it than you think."

Vrii decided to change the subject. "Has Bobby been coaching you at ***polyadok***? He never even told me you played."

"No. I've been coaching him and Chii for the past few weeks, and I think they'll ***both*** be in shape to take you on, the next time you play them."

"Bobby, I'll grant you, is a challenge," Vrii said, "but my sister? Please! She'll be a sacrificial virgin put on the altar for slaughter."

"Interesting turn of phrase," TiiNa rebutted, "but you might be surprised by how hard she's going to be to slaughter, and she's ***sure no virgin***."

Vrii turned a light gray color. "***Surely***, you don't mean that——"

"I caught them one night this Summer." TiiNa said, "They never knew I was there. But it was interesting to watch——"

"I'll ***bet***——" Vrii was almost white. "My God——"

"I didn't think you guys believed in God——" TiiNa joked.

"For this, I might make an exception," Vrii replied, then, "Tell me about the 'never knew I was there' part..?"

TiiNa put her hand on the ***polyadok*** board. For a moment, it just rested there. Then, it was gone. Vrii reached out and touched the hand. She could feel that it was there. but the colors just merged in and matched the board so perfectly from her vantage point, that it looked as though the hand had vanished at the cuff of TiiNa's blouse.

"Bobby can do that too, I remember——" Vrii said, "I can see how that would be convenient——" she had a strange, speculative look on her face.

"It's gotten both of us out of tight spots more than once," TiiNa said.

"Like what?" Vrii asked, intensely curious.

"I'd rather not say." she answered, mysteriously.

"But one of them involved my sister and your brother?"

"Like I said——"

"By the way, Chii said 'Yes.'" TiiNa added.

"To what?" Vrii seemed to have lost the context.

"To his marriage proposal."

"Still sounds like puppy love to me. What do you think about it?"

"Me? I'm halfway in love with her myself. You're probably not going to understand this, but let me tell you what she did when we thought Mom was dying——."

——and she told Vrii the story——

"You're right. I don't know anything about your Gods, or religions. But from what you've told me, it sounds like Chii ***does***, and she knew ***exactly*** what to do at a terrible time like that."

"I know it's a strange idea to you, but let me tell you, that impressed all of us ***beyond words***. Even the priest thinks Chii would make a dandy wife for Bobby, and feels that it's a shame they're too young to marry legally."

"Wife——" Vrii mused out loud, "I just can't get my head around the idea of my sister being somebody's ***wife***——"

"Is it any easier to think of her as somebody's lover?"

"Ummm—— no——" Vrii said, "Actually that's not any easier, at all."

Then she looked at TiiNa. "And I can't believe I'm talking about this to a ***four-year-old.***"

"——And I'm a typical four-year-old, ***how****?"* TiiNaa asked.

Vrii looked at the ***polyadok*** board. "I guess you've got a point. If I play you again, I'm going to get ***creamed***, aren't I?" she said, as she set up the pieces.

The girl has a death wish, TiiNa reflected, and then made her first move.

CHAPTER 26 - Confidences

TiiNa was talking with MeBlii as she and RiiMaa played with dolls.

"This is great, Auntie May! I'm so glad Vrii came to Cluret. Being able to visit you and RiiMaa ***plus*** cleaning Vrii's clock was a two-fer that was just ***too good to be true***."

"Sounds like a grudge match. But what did Vrii do to you?" MeBlii asked.

"Nothing. But you should hear the way she disses Bobby and Chii sometimes," TiiNa said, "so full of herself. Like ***polyadok*** is everything and nothing else they ever did was worth anything. That really frosts me."

"Well, when you put it like ***that,*** I can see why you wanted to hand her head to her on a platter. So--***did*** you?"

"All that, plus several other parts of her anatomy as well—— " TiiNa said.

"Well, ***that*** must have been satisfying." MeBlii concluded.

"Not exactly. I kind of--lost it--when she was belittling Chii, and I told her more than she should know——"

"You really like Chii, don't you?" MeBlii asked TiiNa.

"Love her to pieces. If Bobby hadn't proposed, I would have done it for him——if Dad didn't get ahead of me——" she said, as she was helping dress one of RiiMaa's dolls as the Princess.

"Wow! That's a pretty big endorsement." MeBlii said, as she rigged up a miniature horse carriage for the Princess.

"The only thing stranger than the idea of a twelve-year-old bride who is ***qualified*** to be a bride," TiiNa said, as she arranged Prince Charming's costume for the grand ball, "is the idea that my nine-year-old brother is ***totally qualified*** to be a groom."

"Is that as strange," May asked TiiNa, "as a four-year-old who thinks she is ***qualified to judge***?"

"Trust me, Auntie May, I know ***way too much*** for a four-year-old," TiiNa said.

"***That,*** I can believe——"

So they got the Princess ready to go to the ball and meet Prince Charming——

Later, after they had put RiiMaa to bed, May sat down with TiiNa.

"OK, now you've got to tell me, what did you tell Vrii you shouldn't have?"

"Jeez, Auntie May," TiiNa said, "it's something I shouldn't even tell ***you***."

"TiiNa, you know me. What is so bad you couldn't tell me about it?"

"Well, it's what I did as much as what they did——" TiiNaa said.

"We're not getting anywhere here—— Do you need me to promise not to talk about it with anyone?" MeBlii asked.

"That would help. Talking about it may be as bad as what I did and what they did." TiiNa answered, which didn't clear anything up for MeBlii.

"I promise. In the name of God, I promise——My lips are sealed, OK?"

"That's--got to be good enough--I suppose. I talked to Father Boyle about it in confession, and I know ***his*** lips are sealed—— OK."

"Well?"

"I told Vrii that her sister isn't such an infant as she thinks, and that I caught her and Bobby making love in Bobby's bedroom."

"Yipe! That ***is*** more than a four-year-old should know about."

"Yeah, but it isn't exactly true——"

"About them?"

"No. About me. I snuck in and watched them. It isn't about them doing it where I would have a chance to see. It's about me sneaking in to watch."

"I guess that ***is*** a sin. I can see why you told Father Boyle in confession."

"Ffurff! It's more than a sin. It's actually a felony on the books. They call it 'voyeurism.'" TiiNa replied.

"Well, yeah, but I think you'd have to be an adult before anybody would prosecute you for it. You're a kid. Kids are curious."

"So are adults. Or doesn't that apply here?" And she winked at MeBlii.

"Oh Fleep! I guess it does——" She looked at TiiNa, tilted her head to one side, "You are, for damn sure, the most grown-up four-year-old, ***ever***."

"Shooting my mouth off, if that isn't a crime, it's probably a sin, anyway. Now I don't know how it's going to keep from getting back to Chii's parents. ***Really*** stupid of me——"

"Well, if you betrayed a confidence, I could call that a sin, but at best, this is——"

"Mischief. Worse, it could wreck things for Bobby and Chii, who really ***should*** be together. They're ***perfect***——"

MeBlii shook her head for a moment. ***Too much knowledge, too fast——***

"Are they a perfect match mentally, or physically, or what? I'm ashamed I'm even ***asking*** this question——"

"Hell, no, Aunt May. It's a ***good*** question. I've seen both--and as far as I can judge--and yes, OK, I'm only a four-year-old--they're perfect for each other mentally ***and*** physically. You know they've done work together that belongs in the Nobel Prize category of really intense stuff——"

"So I've been told. Not that I can follow one percent of it, they are so far ahead of anybody I know at that age--except maybe you."

"Give me time. I'm not that age, yet. But seriously, if I had to characterize what they are like together physically, I'd have to go to rock 'n'roll lyrics——"

Such as——?"

TiiNa thought for a minute. "Well, like 'she was giving what she got,' and Bobby 'hit her with his best shot,' and stuff like that."

"They're that good together?" MeBlii said, "But are they doing it ***safely***?"

"How do ***I*** know?" said TiiNa, "But they're two of the smartest people I know, maybe the smartest people on several planets. If ***I*** know about it, I'm ***sure*** they do."

"Oh, Ffurff, that is ***way*** more than I wanted to know. You don't use birth control ***yourself***, do you?"

"Oh, please! I'm ***four***. For me this is all ***theoretical.***"

"Thank ***God***——"

"I suppose there's one other question I should ask," MeBlii said.

"What's that?"

"How could they ***not*** know you were there watching them?"

Rather that explain, TiiNa simply shrugged out of her clothes, closed her eyes for a second, and disappeared.

"Holy Mother of God!" MeBlii exclaimed.

TiiNa reappeared, and opened her eyes. "Camouflage." she said.

"Camouflage? That wasn't camouflage! It was ***invisibility!***" MeBlii said.

"Only from the direction you were looking from; anybody looking from the side would still be able to see me. But for a lot of purposes, it's good enough."

"***More*** than good enough. Do you realize what the spy agencies would do if they knew about that?" May asked.

"Me and Bobby would disappear for real." TiiNa replied.

"Bobby, too?" MeBlii said in astonishment.

"He's better than me. At least he was——"

"I never knew about that. Then again, when would it ever come up in conversation?" MeBlii mused to herself.

Word got around that the odd little girl with the mittens had won her match in the round robin session. TiiNa was already the city champion of Placedon, so she wasn't surprised when she was invited to try out her ***polyadok*** game against the (8-12 age group) planetary champion of Placet.

"Hi. I'm Shaa," her opponent said, holding out a gripper. TiiNa took it in her mitten and gave it a squeeze in the HaChii fashion.

"You know, all those ***polyadok*** boards had a recording mechanism in them. They recorded every game played on them." Shaa said.

Taken aback, TiiNa said, "No. I wasn't aware of that."

Board 14 showed two ***additional*** games after you beat Vrii." Shaa said.

"I suppose it did. They were off the record, I thought——"

"They shouldn't have been. Game 3 in particular, is one of the most brilliant ***polyadok*** games I've ever seen played. If you play like that today, I'm doomed," Shaa explained.

"You want me to take it easy on you?" TiiNa said in a skeptical tone.

"Ffurff, no. Give me your best shot." said Shaa.

Your funeral. TiiNa thought, "OK. You've got the first move——"

She played an even better game than she had against Vrii. Shaa didn't have a chance.

Then they played nine more games. Result 10-0.

"You know. I expected that." Shaa said. She held out her gripper to TiiNa, "Congratulations! You are planetary champion of Placet——"

"Well, thank you!" TiiNa said, "You don't seem as disappointed as I would expect. Vrii didn't take it nearly this well."

"Kid," Shaa said (and it was obvious she was considerably older than TiiNa) "you don't know how honored I am just to have played those games with you."

"That was--" TiiNa teared up, and tried not to let her HaChii opponent see, "--the most selfless thing I've ever heard——" and she reached out and hugged Shaa, "You are a ***good sport*** and I thank you for ten wonderful games——"

"No. Thank ***you***." Shaa said, and held up the board. "These games are priceless. They are going into the history books." she said. Then she set the board down, reverently. She called over the judges. "We have a new planetary champion." she said simply.

Two days later, TiiNa received a message on her message pad. She saw that it was from a HaChii adult male. "Mom!" she called. "There's a message here from an adult guy. Do I open it?"

NaDii looked at the thumbnail attached to the window. "Let's see what he wants. I'll stay with you in case he's a weirdo——" she told her daughter.

"Hello, TiiNa," said the male, "I'm MorPhii Iz PaaWul, the ***polyadok*** Planetary Champion of Placet."

Hello, Mr. MorPhii," TiiNa said, respectfully, momentarily forgetting that 'mister' was an Earth term of address.

"I have a student named Shaa." MorPhii explained. "She said I should play you a few games of ***polyadok*** sometime."

TiiNa looked at her mother, "That OK?" she said.

"These are off the record?" NaDii asked.

"Of course. I wouldn't be allowed to compete professionally with an eight-year-old, for goodness' sake."

"Ummm--right!" said NaDii, cheerfully sidestepping the fact that TiiNa was a ***long way*** from being an eight-year-old, "I don't see any harm in that——"

"How about we play now?" TiiNa said.

They played five games. The first, TiiNa lost (a new experience for her). The next two were draws, which took a lot out of both players. But TiiNa won the last two games.

"You get better with practice." MorPhii said.

"Who doesn't?" she said.

"You don't get my point," MorPhii said. "You just got ***better than me***, and I've been playing ***polyadok*** for forty years, against the very best. Do you have any idea how ***good*** you are?"

"Ummm——Well, I ***feel*** like I did pretty well."

"My dear," MorPhii said, "***pretty well*** is for amateurs. You are the best professional I ever have played. Any age group, any era. After game four, you could be giving me lessons. Game five——" he put his head in his hands.

"Oh, dear," she said, "I hope I didn't hurt your feelings——"

He looked up, and said, "Feelings have absolutely nothing to do with it. I'm just going to ask you a favor."

"What?" TiiNa said apprehensively.

"I said these games would be 'off the record,'" he said.

"That's OK." TiiNa answered. "They never happened——"

"No! No! No! That's not what I mean! Game five—— I'd like to make an exception—— That game was too brilliant ***not to publish.*** Could I put it on the record——on the q-net?" he pleaded.

"Mom?" TiiNa asked, "Would that be OK?"

I may regret this later, NaDii thought, but she said "That's OK, dear."

"I'd like to speak to your mother privately. Is that OK too?" MorPhii said.

"Sure. 'Bye, Mom.'" and TiiNa walked away.

"I don't know your name," MorPhii said, "but your daughter addressed me as 'mister' which is a form an Earth person would use. And she keeps her grippers covered by mittens. Are you NaDii Ix ChiiBii?" he asked.

"Yes. Yes I am." she admitted.

"Then your daughter is TiiNa Firestone." he concluded.

"I'm sorry if we've deceived anyone——" NaDii said. "She plays under the name of TiiNa Ix DriiBii."

"No! That's OK! You were just protecting your daughter. I have read about the bigots and the death threats," MorPhii said, "Maintaining a HaChii identity is fine, and I will never give away your daughter's secret. But I wanted you to know that if ***I*** can figure it out, it is something ***other*** people can figure out, too. ***That*** may be dangerous."

"Yes——I'm afraid of that. Bobby's already been shot at——"

"I didn't know that! But it doesn't change anything. I wanted to tell you something. I can use the q-net. I also know TiiNa is not an eight-year-old—— Now that I have seen what your children can do——"

NaDii waited, silently.

"They are going to take over. From HaChii, from humans. They will replace us, because they are better. And our worlds will all be better for it. Only--there will be people who don't want it to happen. It terrifies them. People--both HaChii and human--will try to stop it by any means necessary. The less they know about TiiNa and Bobby, the better——"

"I've been practically keeping them prisoner, now." NaDii said.

"And you can't do that forever, I know," MorPhii said, "nonetheless, if there is some way to protect them--***anything***--do it."

"Thank you, Mr. MorPhii," NaDii replied, forgetting for a moment that it was an Earth form of address herself. It seemed right, in this context.

"And that game——" MorPhii said, "I'm going to publish the name of my opponent as "TiiNa Ix DriiBii" would that be OK?"

Not much of a disguise, but OK, she thought, "I would be honored." she said.

CHAPTER 27 - Gold

The Firestone household was awakened by a raucous alarm from the main message screen in the living room. Bobby was up first, and got the message.

Chii's face appeared on the screen. Bobby was so happy to see her that he just looked at her and didn't say anything for almost a minute. By that time, the rest of the family was up and standing in front of the screen in their pajamas. "Ask her what's up, Bobby." Greg directed him.

"Oh Hi, Chii!" Bobby said, "What did you wake us up for?"

"Take a look at your mail this morning," she said, "and open the one that says 'Karolinska Institute' first."

"OK. But what the heck is the Karolinska Institute?" Bobby said. He turned to his parents, who both shook their heads in incomprehension.

He found the mail message and then opened it:

Stockholm,

Monday, October 6, 2588

The Nobel Assembly at Karolinska Institutet has today decided to award

The Nobel Prize in Physiology or Medicine 2588

jointly to

Chii Ix DriiBo and Robert Firestone

for the discovery of

"how the fractal mathematics of DNA produces organized structure in multi-cellular organisms."

Bobby stood, paralyzed, in front of the screen. Greg grabbed him around the shoulders. NaDii screamed, and TiiNa, scrutinizing the message, said to him,

"That's the Big One, isn't it? Even bigger than the one for Mathematics."

"It sure is, Little Sister." Bobby said, breathlessly.

"It comes with a shiny gold medal." she said, somewhat facetiously, "Can I wear it sometimes?"

"It might be a little heavy for a necklace." Bobby said, distractedly, as he pursued a q-net search.

"As I recall, it also comes with 30 million credits." TiiNa added in a nonchalant tone.

"Thirty ***five*——**" Bobby corrected.

This time they didn't jump up and down. It was too big for that. They just all kneeled down and prayed.

They had forgotten Chii. She waited until they were finished with the Lord's Prayer. Out of the corner of his eye, he saw Chii mouthing the word, 'Amen.' with his family, as they finished.

"Hey! Over here!" Chii said. Then the screen split into two images, and the second one was FriiDa. "I hear you guys could use another ride to Scandinavia," she said.

"Well--We've got a pretty nice runabout, but yours is nicer——" Greg said.

"Yeah. And I just upgraded to one of those new Firestone-DriiBo motors——"

"Oooh! I hear those are ***fast***," Chii said, and winked broadly.

Vrii walked in and peered curiously at the screen. "Morning Chii. What did you get in the mail?"

"Nobel Prize." Chii said casually.

Vrii goggled. Looking into the screen and seeing Bobby, she said to him, "She's shitting me——?"

"Language, Vrii," Bobby answered, "And by the way, fuck no, she's not."

NaDii scowled at Bobby; Greg roared with laughter.

BoTii appeared on the screen. "Well done, Bobby! Never mind Vrii; she doesn't think there's anything but ***polyadok*** in the world."

"Then she needs to talk to TiiNa." Bobby said.

"Hi Vrii," TiiNa said cheerfully, "MorPhii Iz PaaWul told me to say hello to you after our last match."

Vrii goggled again. "You played Grand-Master MorPhii?"

"Our last game is posted on the q-net. Here's the link." TiiNa said, and she waited while Vrii looked it up and stepped through the game.

Vrii's eyes widened. She looked up. "You took it easy on me." She fast-stepped through the game again. "In fact, you threw me cream-puffs compared to this." She backed up and stepped through the game a third time.

"There are no words——" Vrii said, simply, "I'll simply ***never*** be this good."

"Here's my point, Vrii." TiiNa said, "This Nobel Prize thing. It's a ***hundred times*** as important as that. And that may be an understatement. But if it matters so much, play a game of ***polyadok*** with your sister. I told you I've been coaching her. See how she does now."

Vrii said nothing. She turned to her sister and looked at her quizzically.

"'Bye, TiiNa," Chii said, and closed the link as she approached her sister with a ***polyadok*** set in hand.

"I'd love to see that game." Bobby said.

Bobby sent a mail message to Professor O'Brien, his advisor for the on-line physics classes he was taking, explaining that he might be unable to complete coursework for a couple of weeks around December 10th.

The Advisor linked in on-line, and asked what the circumstances were, so Bobby referred him to a q-net link and waited while the advisor read. He had chosen a university on Earth, which made things simpler, as his Professor did not read or speak HaChii.

O'Brien turned very white and looked as though he were about to pass out. He then recovered himself and said, "This isn't your father, is it?"

Bobby said no, it was him.

"Of course, take as much time as you need. Although if you want to work ahead, I could give you the rest of the course-work for the semester."

"OK." Bobby said, "I'll have it back for you tomorrow."

O'Brien goggled, then he said, "Of course. I should have expected that."

Then he thought for a moment. "Why are you even taking these courses?"

"I should have a degree." Bobby answered, "But I'm only nine years old--I haven't had much time to tackle that."

"Only nine——" the Professor was silent again. Then, "and how old were you when you did the Nobel work?"

"Mostly when I was five and six." Bobby admitted, "I probably should have looked into getting a college degree earlier, but I got busy with music."

"Those Robert Firestone albums I've got; is that ***you***?"

"Sure. I do Symphonies, Concertos, Sonatas; I've even done some church music."

You're HaChii. They must mature faster than humans——"

He held up his hands, "Only partly HaChii. They don't mature any faster than humans, but I'm both——and neither——apparently, for me, all bets are off on how fast I mature. It seems to be true for my sister, too."

"Look. You shouldn't be wasting time chasing paper at the speed of mundane humans. There's another way. You can take a proficiency exam--sometimes called a CLEP exam--for practically every class on the curriculum."

"Could I still get a degree that way?" Bobby asked. He had never heard of this short-cut.

"You would still have to take some percentage of standard course-work. But frankly, I think I could arrange for that to be a couple of semesters' courses, at most." O'Brien said.

"Can I take a CLEP test for this course?" Bobby asked.

"Sure. Actually, that would be easier than me sending you the rest of the coursework. Can you go to the community college where you took the GED to take the CLEP tests?"

Bobby agreed that he could.

"How about I send the tests for the core courses in the curriculum, a couple every week? You've got a couple of months before the Nobel. If you take a couple of tests a week, we should have most of that done by the time you leave for Earth."

"Oh!" Professor O'Brien added, "The tests cost about 100 credits apiece; can you handle that?"

"The Abel Prize gave me 20 million credits." Bobby said, "I've spent a few thousand, but I don't think this will be a problem."

"You won the Abel Prize for Mathematics?" O'Brien goggled again.

"Yeah. About six months ago," Bobby answered. "It's on the q-net."

"Give me the name of the College; I'll send the tests for Classical Physics, Modern Physics and Calculus, this week. If you did the Abel and Nobel work when you were--five--(he shook his head)--this will be trivial for you now."

"Thanks. (Bobby typed in the name and location of the Community College) How do I pay for this? Remember--I'm nine, so I have to get my Dad to release the money."

"I'll give you a link for the Bursar's Office. Have your Dad send them the 300 credits for this week; I'll arrange things for the same every week. Is that OK?"

"Fine. One more question. Can I visit you when I'm on Earth?"

"I'd be honored. Here are the co-ordinates of my home. (he gave him latitude and longitude) I don't actually go to a University to do most of my work; it's almost all done on-line from my home. Is that OK?"

"Sure. See you in December."

Delighted with his discovery of CLEP testing, Bobby called Chii.

"Hi Bobby. I love you." she said simply.

"You too." Bobby answered, then said, "Have you ever heard of CLEP tests?"

"No. What's that?"

And Bobby filled her in on the details.

"So I can contact Professor O'Brien and set up the same thing?"

"I expect so. I doubt he knows you are twelve years old. So break that to him easy, and then let him know about the Nobel. I practically shocked him to death when I broke the reason why I needed to skip course-work for a couple of weeks around December 10th. Then he came up with this CLEP idea. It sounds like the answer to a lot of our problems."

"I'll say!" Chii exclaimed, "and I'll tell him I'm going to be with you when you visit him."

"Chii? One question. How did your ***polyadok*** game with Vrii go?"

"Tied. Then I won the next two. Say thanks to TiiNa."

"OK. We'll be seeing you in eight weeks——"

"Love you. 'Bye."

During the next six weeks, Bobby went to North Placedon Community College three days a week, to take CLEP tests. By that time, he had completed most of the required courses in his physics major, and about half of those for mathematics, but was informed that essay examinations were needed for most of the liberal arts courses. He decided he would save that experience for after he returned from Stockholm, with one exception. He had chosen a course in public speaking for one of his liberal arts credits. With the help of Professor O'Brien, he had received permission to submit his Nobel Lecture as the proof-of-proficiency in public speaking, and O'Brien's colleague, Professor Lafeber, agreed to accept submission of a recording of the Nobel Lecture in completion of the public speaking course. The same arrangement had been made for Chii, and, confident that a few small adjustments to their Abel lectures would suffice, they approached their upcoming trip to Stockholm with confidence.

King Oscar VI of Norway had called King Gustav Adolf XIV of Sweden with a little unsolicited advice.

"Make sure you give the Physiology and Medicine laureate, Robert Firestone, a chance to perform at the Concert after the Nobel Ceremony." Oscar said.

"Is he any good?" Gustav asked, innocently.

"Let him play the piano. If you do, you are in for a treat!" Oscar replied enigmatically.

After the conversation, Gustav did a quick q-net search for piano performances by Robert Firestone. He found dozens, and picked one at random. It was Firestone's Symphony No. 4, with Bobby and TiiNa performing the 'four-hands' piano sections. He played it, not expecting much, considering that the pianists were eight and three years old at the time.

"Gud i Himmelen!" Gustav exclaimed.

FriiDa checked with the Firestones about four weeks before the trip was planned.

"Here's the itinerary we've worked out with the people from Stockholm: December 4th, we fly you and your guests to Gracet to pick up Chii and her family. Next day we head for Earth, arriving Arlanda Spaceport the afternoon of the 5th. There is a high-speed train from the spaceport to the Stockholm City Center. We will be staying at the Radisson Blu Royal Viking Hotel over a relaxing weekend, then Monday, you and Chii will give your Nobel lectures at the Karolinska Institute. Tuesday there is a press conference and photo-opportunity. Wednesday afternoon's the award ceremony at

Stockholm Concert Hall and in the evening you go to the banquet at Stockholm City Hall."

"Then a little sightseeing?" NaDii said.

"We'll see," FriiDa said, guardedly, "I'm still worried about security."

NaDii took Greg aside and whispered to him.

"I think we're OK with that," Greg told FriiDa, "NaDii has made some security plans that might help——"

As time drew close, DriiLa worked on Chii's ball gown, and TiiNa, working over the q-net with advice from DriiLa, tackled the project of making a formal black tailcoat for Bobby. Bobby was startled when he tried it on for the first time. The fittings and adjustments he expected were not needed.

"It fits perfectly." he said to TiiNa. "But you never took measurements——?"

"Piece of cake." TiiNa said.

Skeptical, Bobby decided to test her. He pointed at a railing along one wall of the kitchen they were in. "How long is that rail?"

TiiNa glanced at it for a moment "eighty-four centimeters," she replied.

Bobby pulled out a meter stick and measured. It was eighty three centimeters, 8 millimeters. "How did you do that?" he asked.

"Not sure." TiiNa answered. "It just looked too small for eighty-five and kind of long for eighty-three——"

"Ohhh——Kay——" Bobby said, thinking, ***Damn**, she's good. No wonder the suit fits——*

The Firestone family went to Mass every Sunday. Early in November, they asked Father Boyle if he would like to join their party as their guest at the Nobel Banquet. He graciously accepted, on condition that he could have someone fill in for him at the Chapel, on what would be the Feast of the Immaculate Conception, Sunday, December 7th.

He was somewhat surprised to find a message in his inbox, stating that a priest would be arriving on the Earth-to-Placedon shuttle December 3rd. That surprise related to the fact that he hadn't yet requested a replacement. Then again, he knew that Bobby had the code for a private link to a certain individual in Rome——so in retrospect, he wasn't so surprised, after all.

All the living grandparents and NaDii's siblings had been invited, MeBlii, RiiMa and ChuuRii had agreed to come, and Greg's human friend Rob had agreed to meet them in Stockholm with a guest, whom he promised-somewhat mysteriously-he would introduce them to, after the Nobel ceremony.

DiiRa asked Bobby if he would accept an invitation to perform at a concert with the Stockholm Philharmonic on Sunday Night, and Bobby agreed. He would be joined by TiiNa, and they would perform the piano part of Firestone's 4th Symphony. However, Bobby placed one condition on his performance--that he be allowed to perform a short piano solo after the Symphony. The concertmaster was delighted to comply, even though Bobby was somewhat mysterious as to the purpose and theme of his solo.

Thursday, December 4th dawned warm and muggy. And why not? The Earth date of December 4th had no relevance to the seasons on Placet. At this moment it was late Summer on Placet, and Placedon had just come through a hot spell.

The back yard became crowded with Greg, NaDii, Bobby and TiiNa's visitors as the sun rose. RiiMa, MeBlii and ChuuRi had arrived Wednesday night and slept over. Grandma Chii, Grand-Dad Bii, and all seven of NaDii's siblings, plus two of their wives and three of their kids, had arrived, had stayed overnight at a nearby motel, and were now in the large back yard with everybody else, awaiting the appearance of FriiDa's space yacht. Father Boyle joined them shortly after sunrise, having turned the Chapel over to Father Wojciechowski, from Chicago, for the week. DiiRa, living closest, was the last to arrive.

All twenty-three of them peered upwards, and little RiiMa was the first to see when the cigar-shaped craft hove into view, cruising down the Placedon River towards their location from the distance. As the space yacht ***Good Vibrations*** hovered above them and the loading-bay doors opened, Father Boyle just had time to inquire, "How do we embark?" when the same lifting-beam system FriiDa had impressed Greg with earlier, picked them all up and drew them upward into the yacht.

They looked around the 100-meter yacht, with most of its crew of five giving their guests the grand tour, as FriiDa helmed the ship, lifting into space for five minutes before placing the ship on autopilot.

Bobby took most of the younger HaChii up to the observation deck, where he regaled them with stories about what they were seeing, as the view showed their home planet receding. Once the ship was comfortably out of Placet's gravity-well, he warned them to cover their eyes if there were made squeamish by looking at contracted-space, so of course none of them did. Little RiiMa squealed for a second as the Universe corrugated into contracted-space in the direction of their movement. Bobby pointed out that, to everybody living in that space, their own lives and perceptions of the Universe did not change; it was only from the perspective of passengers on this ship that space was different. Then the ship, traveling in the direction of the planet Gracet's stellar system through contracted-space crushed 600,000 to one, sped up to 90 percent of light speed.

Then Bobby took them down to the lower levels. "This ship sleeps 35, he said, pointing out the cabin doors. The galley downstairs can feed 50——"

And he went on in that vein until even the oldest and most mature cousin was bored. "Let's get Breakfast!" That individual wisely suggested, and they all headed for the dining room by the galley downstairs.

By early afternoon, the swirling white cloud patterns etched against Gracet's blue background loomed in the forward view screen.

"This is flight GV74494 out of Placedon Spaceport, requesting clearance for landing at Gracedon Spaceport, as per flight plan GV60646-A." FriiDa stated.

"Flight GV74494 cleared to land in 023 minutes, on landing pad seven," the tower replied.

FriiDa greased it in, right down the line, and set ***Good Vibrations*** down light as a feather.

"Couldn't you have just come in by Chii and Vrii's house?" one of Brii's daughters asked.

"Sure." FriiDa said, "But it would make the Customs Agents really mad——"

"They need to inspect the ship and passengers, before they let us leave the ship," Bobby explained to his cousin, "They don't want us bringing anything in to their planet that might harm the wildlife or the people."

"Oh. That makes sense," the little girl replied.

After the inspection, the yacht was allowed to lower its staircase. As expected, BoTii, DriiLa, Vrii and Chii were there waiting.

Chii pretended not to be ***too*** excited about seeing Bobby, but her pale-lavender skin color gave her away. Her father pretended not to see, and let her go up the staircase first. Bobby took her gripper in his hand, and they walked into the ship.

TiiNa appeared at the top of the staircase and waved to Vrii, who boarded next. As she reached the top, she addressed TiiNa:

"Do you have the other games you played MorPhii in your pad's memory?"

"Sure!" TiiNa replied. "Come over to my cabin and I'll show you! Do you know, I actually ***lost*** one game to him? I think I heard you refer to that kind of thing as a 'learning experience,' some time recently."

"And--***was it***?" Vrii asked, curiously, as they walked to the cabin.

"He never beat me again," came TiiNa's reply. Vrii rolled her eyes. ***This can not be happening,*** she thought. Then a moment later reflected on her own experience versus the precocious near-toddler. ***Well--Maybe it can***——

TiiNa opened the files on her message pad. Vrii flopped down onto the bed, and started stepping through game one—— "What happened to you here? What were you thinking?" she asked. And TiiNa started to explain——

And Vrii found out that this was, ***indeed,*** a learning experience.

BoTii and DriiLa checked out the couples' cabins and picked one out. Greg and NaDii picked out another. Two more had been assigned to NaDii's married brother, Baa, her sister Brii, and their spouses.

Chii and Bobby were relegated to widely-separated 'singles' cabins assigned by FriiDa, amidst all the other youngsters.

Well, she's the Captain, Chii reflected, and started unpacking her luggage.

The new guests from Gracet were introduced to FriiDa and her crew.

"This is your Mom's college room-mate?" Chii asked Bobby, after shaking hands with FriiDa.

"It's her ship. She owns BrropCo. But you probably knew that——"

"I'm going to ask you to look at the other crew members," Bobby told her, "especially RaaGii, the cabin steward."

"OK," Chii said, puzzled, "I've got his face fixed in my memory."

"Good." He said. "Put in a call to Room service after you go to bed. Order Oysters Rockefeller."

"Hmmm. All right. I trust you know what you're doing——"

"You bet."

Bobby and Chii ate dinner in silence, with an occasional quizzical glance from Chii towards Bobby as the only signal that he had intrigued her. She remained puzzled because she could not imagine what his plan might be.

NaDii's family introduced themselves to Vrii and her parents, and they traded stories about TiiNa, Chii, Vrii and Bobby. MeBlii and ChuuRii added such stories about Greg and NaDii as could be repeated in mixed--and youthful--company. And TiiNa and Vrii spent the moments between each course of the dinner, stepping through ***polyadok*** moves on TiiNa's message pad——

Several hours later, in her cabin, Chii changed into her pajamas. Then, she messaged to Room Service and ordered Oysters Rockefeller. Shortly, there came a knock at the door. There stood RaaGii in his uniform, holding a platter with a cover.

"Bring it in," Chii said, "You can set it here."

The steward placed the tray onto a chest of drawers. He then took the plate of oysters off the tray, and set the cover and tray outside the open door. Chii was rummaging through her luggage to find some coins for a tip, but saw RaaGii walk up ***outside***, taking away the tray and closing the door.

She looked back at RaaGii standing next to the door ***inside*** the room. Suddenly, the uniform disappeared and he wasn't RaaGii anymore; he was Bobby.

She shook her head and blinked her eyes.

"You knew I could do that, didn't you?" Bobby asked.

"It makes sense, ***now that I've seen it***." she answered honestly.

"As far as anybody outside knows, RaGii brought the oysters and then brought back the empty tray. I just asked him to come here at this time and pick up an empty tray from cabin 32. The guys at Room Service are sure they gave that tray to RaaGii, so they expected him to be bringing it back empty."

Chii still looked puzzled.

"Oh, yeah. I gave him a ***big*** tip——" Then she grinned with her eyes.

"And where do they think ***you*** are?" she inquired.

"In my room." My parents saw me go in, and saw the room steward come out, after making up my bed. "They gave him a tip for helping out——"

Bobby held up the coin.

"Oooo! You're devious!" Chii said, "Come on over here——
"

She took the contents of one oyster out with a fork, and placed it into his mouth. He took the fork from her and reversed the process with the second oyster. "Mmmm! These are ***scrumptious***! What's in them?"

"These are the ones made with absinthe," he answered, then he gave her the rest of the recipe. And they took turns with the rest of the oysters.

"Are you sure this is the right time?" he asked.

"It's ***exactly*** the right time——" she answered.

"And you're ***sure*** you want to do this?"

"***Absolutely.*** Don't you?"

"***Yes! For sure***!" he said.

They turned out the lights.

Later, Chii cried out three times, then ended with one more loud cry. Bobby responded with a cry of his own. Then all was quiet.

"Did that work?" he asked a few minutes later.

She fumbled around in the bedclothes for a few moments, then stopped.

"Yes!" she said, "Yes! It worked!"

He heard the chest of drawers open and close. Time would tell. They would check tomorrow.

He hoped the soundproofing in FriiDa's craft was as good as his father's.

The next morning, Chii dressed for breakfast and stepped out of her cabin, heading for the dining room by the galley.

A few moments later, the door she had left ajar closed itself. If somebody had been looking, they might have seen something like heat ripples in the hallway momentarily moving down to cabin 12. The door to cabin 12 opened, and a few moments later, Bobby peeked out of the door. He ducked back in and came out a few minutes later, dressed for breakfast. Chii's parents, having heard the door open, looked out of their cabin and saw Bobby step out.

"Good morning, Bobby." DriiLa said, "We'll meet you downstairs for breakfast in a few minutes."

"See you in a few." Bobby replied. And he walked downstairs.

Arlanda Spaceport, near Stockholm, Sweden: Friday, December 5, 2588. Two men met under a sign reading 'Arlanda Utrymme Flygplats.' The taller, sandy blond fellow in a khaki hunting jacket held out a hand.

"Ulf Schultz, ***Verbindung Der Echten Menschen,*** Northern Division Field Commander. Welcome to Stockholm." he introduced himself.

The shorter, balding fellow in denim overalls and a checkered flannel shirt took the hand and gave it a shake.

"Billy Bob Wilson, ***United Klans of America,*** Grand Kleagle of the Eastern Sector. Pleased to meet you. Wanna see the gear I've brought? It's pretty clever stuff——"

They walked away, towards the Arlanda Express station.

After breakfast, FriiDa's yacht, which had been orbiting Earth, got clearance for approach to Arlanda Spaceport. Customs inspection after landing would take about an hour and a half.

Father Boyle was on the observation deck, looking out the forward viewport, and taking in the view of his home planet, Earth. He would be seeing some members of his family for the first time in years, a circumstance which would not have been possible without Bobby, he reflected. When Bobby and Chii walked up to him, he was delighted to see them, and thanked them again for making this possible.

"Father?" Chii said, "We have been talking, and there is something we would like you to make possible for us, as well."

She and Bobby described their plan, and asked Father Boyle if he would be willing to help them out.

"Would Chii want to be baptized at the same time?" the priest inquired.

Bobby looked at her, curiously. "Yes," she said, "I've been studying. I think I'm prepared."

"Can you come to my cabin while this inspection is going on?" said Boyle.

"Sure. Now is a good time." Bobby agreed.

They left the observation deck.

Upon arrival at Arlanda, the Nobel party gathered their luggage and boarded the high-speed train for Stockholm city center. In less than twenty minutes, the Arlanda Express delivered them a short distance from the Radisson Blu Royal Viking Hotel. If they expected an uneventful arrival, as they had in Oslo, that expectation was quickly dashed, when hundreds of reporters and photographers mobbed them as they entered the lobby.

"Which one is Chii!?"

"Where is Bobby Firestone?"

"So, What do you think about your (daughter, son, grandson, cousin) being the youngest ever to receive a Nobel Prize?"

——and so forth——

An hour later, they were finally checked-in and in their rooms.

Bobby, TiiNa, his parents and FriiDa were in their suite, at last, thoroughly rattled by the media circus they had just escaped. Bobby was looking over the itinerary FriiDa had put together.

"Was this the relaxing weekend part?" Bobby asked FriiDa.

"I may have been a ***tad*** optimistic about that——" FriiDa replied.

Bobby's message pad beeped. He opened the link, and there was Chii.

"Did you make it through OK? Are you settled in?" he asked her.

"Barely. But I got in with——(she realized he was in the company of his family)——our ***item***—— and it's un-harmed."

"Thank God," Bobby said, and realizing the company he was in, also, added, "So--does it show a ***positive charge*** or a ***negative charge***?"

"A ***positive*** one. A very positive one!" she answered excitedly.

Then she closed the connection.

"What was that about, Bobby?" TiiNa asked, curiously.

"Oh. We built an ionization detector for the physics lab course we're taking," Bobby said, expecting that would settle the issue with TiiNa.

"Really? How does it work?" she asked.

Oh, what a tangled web we weave, when first we practice to deceive, Bobby said to himself. Then he started describing a circuit with field-effect transistors, red and green display lights, and an antenna. By the time he'd finished making it up, he had an electronic device that would probably ***actually work***——

A few minutes later, after TiiNa had left, he keyed in the link information for Professor O'Brien. The window opened and Professor O'Brien eyed him somewhat owlishly.

"It's **six in the morning**, Mr. Firestone," he said.

"Sorry. Did I call too early?"

"No. I was awake——barely. What's this call about?"

"Well--first I wanted to let you know I've arrived in Stockholm."

"Where it's five hours later than here——OK, you're forgiven. What else?"

"I wanted to know if this idea I had for an electroscope would work. Suppose I have a p-channel and an n-channel field effect transistor, attached to a short antenna at their gate contacts——" and he continued the description.

O'Brien made a few quick sketches, did a couple of calculations, and agreed that it would be sensitive enough to detect atmospheric ionization.

"Now build it for me," he said, "and I'll give you proficiency credit for Physics 347L--Basic Electronics Lab."

"Cool! I'll order the parts on the q-net and have it built by the time I visit you after the ceremonies are finished here."

After careful consideration, all 24 members of their party agreed that trying to go outside without traveling incognito would be fundamentally insane. They ordered lunch from Room Service.

That would work for a while, but they felt bottled-up in the hotel. The basic problem was--how to blend in and look 'incognito' among Swedish people if you are a HaChii——

Bobby and TiiNa whispered to each other. They walked into the bedroom and changed into some Earth-style clothing. Then they walked out and called their father Greg over to look. Bobby put a hat on and transformed himself into a very plausible-looking Swedish young man of about sixteen. Wearing a warm Fall coat and beret, TiiNa transformed herself, and appeared to be a little blue-eyed Swedish girl of about ten.

Greg goggled. "I guess if you can do Coke cans, you can do that. Wow, are you guys good——"

"Let's go take a walk, Dad——" TiiNa invited him. They didn't have to ask twice. He threw on a coat and wrapped a scarf around his neck.

FriiDa looked at them with an expression of intense concentration as they left, then she looked at NaDii and said,

"Wouldn't you love to be able to do that?"

"A kid who can do that could get away with——just about anything——" NaDii said. "You were already thinking that, weren't you?"

"I'm afraid I was." FriiDa said.

"Well, then I'm glad they're good kids." NaDii said flatly.

"I ***hope*** so——" FriiDa said, not sounding as certain as NaDii.

Greg and the kids made it through the lobby without being spotted by any of the media types camped out there. It was a little bit of a struggle, at first, for TiiNa to stride along like Greg, but she got the hang of it in a few minutes. Bobby seemed to come by it naturally.

"Let's walk over to the ***Konserthuset***, Dad," Bobby said, "If I'm going to be performing there tomorrow, it would be nice to know there is a way to get there without being mobbed by a circus like the one at the hotel."

They spoke and looked at the sights. A few blocks later, they turned into the entrance marked KONSERTHUSET.

Greg stepped in and asked to see the director. Lars Svensson, a gentleman of middle years, appeared a few moments later. Bobby and TiiNa took off their hats and reverted to their normal appearance.

"Hi! I'm Bobby Firestone. This is my sister TiiNa and my Dad, Greg. We were wondering if we could practice on your piano for a little while."

The Director was normally a reserved individual, but could not conceal his astonishment. "Right over here," he said as he led them to a grand piano standing in the empty hall. "We are preparing for a program in four hours, but right now, it should be fine for you to practice."

"Thanks!" Bobby said. "We need to get used to an unfamiliar keyboard and," he added, "the gravity is a little different. Still getting used to that."

Bobby and TiiNa warmed up with a four-hands version of Scott Joplin's ***Maple Leaf Rag***. In a few minutes they had the feel of the instrument.

Then they practiced the second movement of the Fourth Symphony.

"The little one——she plays as well as her brother." Svensson said to Greg.

"Yeah. Her brother wasn't this good until he was at least five——" Greg said, as though it were the most normal thing in the world.

The next day, the rest of the Firestone-DriiBo party staged a diversion, piling into stretch limousines headed for the Concert Hall amidst a horde of reporters seeking Bobby and Chii, while a nondescript family, who gave the names 'Gunnar Larsson and his kids Arvid and Inga' if anybody asked, walked through the crowd of reporters and out the front door.

Thus disguised, Greg, Bobby and TiiNa completed their walk to the ***Konserthuset*** arriving in plenty of time to meet with the orchestra and get acquainted. Director Svensson showed Greg to a seat, and went back to the last-minute activities before the concert was to start. Several times, he wondered what the mysterious solo performance was that Bobby had asked about earlier, but didn't find time to pursue the thought.

Bobby and TiiNa completed the Fourth Symphony to thunderous accolades, and the audience called for an encore as he left the stage. Bobby, expecting this, stepped back out onto the stage, walking up to one of the microphones.

"Ladies and Gentlemen. May I take a moment of your time?" he asked.

Everybody waited raptly for what he had to say.

"I would like to begin by saying that although I live on Placet, the HaChii home world, my father is from Earth." (there was polite applause.)

"He grew up in the United States of America. And today is an anniversary of something very important, in the history of the United States and your world. On this date, December 7th, 647 years ago, it was also a Sunday. People were sitting at home or going to Church. Some of them were even at concerts."

He paused for a moment to gather his thoughts.

"In the USA, people were at peace and recovering from a terrible economic disaster. And then, on that quiet Sunday, the peace was destroyed as airplanes from the Empire of Japan attacked the American naval base at Pearl Harbor. Over twenty-four hundred

Americans died that day, and millions of others by the time that conflict was finally over. I would like to play a piece of music dedicated to the memory of all those who laid down their lives in and because of that conflict. And may nothing like it ever happen again in Europe, on Earth, or any of the planets of our Confederation. Thank you——"

And he sat down at the piano and began to play Robert Schumann's ***Traumerei,*** simply and beautifully. The audience froze in respectful silence. Halfway through, Greg looked at NaDii with tears streaming down his face, and asked her, "Why am I crying for people who died over 600 years ago?"

And she gestured to the rest of the audience, most of whom looked just like Greg and some of whom were sobbing openly.

"We don't cry tears," she said, "but right now I feel the same way, there's a big lump of pain in my chest, and I'm not even human. Does that make sense?"

"Yes. Yes it does——" Greg choked out. And then he was silent throughout the rest of the performance.

After the concert, Director Svensson stopped Bobby as he came backstage. With eyes still brimming over, he said. "That was the single most moving thing I have experienced in my life. Thank you for a wonderful concert."

Monday was the lecture at the Karolinska Institute. Professors O'Brien and Lafeber were watching the talk via q-net.

Chii gave her talk first, exploring the fractal realm and using three-dimensional projections of simple systems, then more complex ones, ending with the replicas of HaChii and human bodies from the initial information in the DNA. Greg, unaware that the human organism being produced in synthetic form was based on his own DNA, turned a bright pink when the structure metamorphosed into his own (naked) body. He wished he could disappear into a hole as a number of people in the audience turned and looked at him in curiosity and astonishment.

NaDii, however, was hugely amused. "Now everyone knows what I like about you," she said.

Bobby shrugged into his three-piece suit--white shirt and bow tie, the vest his Mother gave him, and the tailcoat and trousers his sister had made. He had worn this at the concert, and he would wear it at the Nobel presentation.

As he walked to the front of the room to give his lecture, Chii passed him coming back, and he whispered to her. "You've got some ***serious*** explaining to do for my Dad——"

"Oh! I forgot that was him——" she said, "do you think anyone could tell?"

He looked over his shoulder at her and gave her an eye roll that could be seen across the Solar System.

Bobby's talk went well. He described the creative process more than the mathematics, which had already been thoroughly covered. At the end, he took questions and answers. The last question was the best, and probably the one he was least looking forward to.

"The human model Chii developed. It resembles your father remarkably--at least the parts we can compare--how did that happen?"

"OK--I knew somebody would ask that--When Chii did the test on the HaChii DNA sequences, she had examples from all over to choose from. But she didn't have any human samples. So she kind of--broke in--to ***my*** system and found sequence files for my family members. And guess which one of them was a standard human? And he's the one she used to make the test. So--I guess my girlfriend knows a ***lot*** more about my Dad than she has any right to——"

That got a laugh from the audience.

"But, you know, ***now*** we have ***all kinds of standard humans around,*** so which one of you wants to give her a sample, to replace the one from my Dad? Show of hands? Anybody? Anybody?"

"I thought not!" he concluded.

And that was the end of the Nobel Lecture.

Professor Lafeber analyzed the lecture afterwards, speaking over the q-link to Bobby's message pad. "The lecture was quite good. I liked the way you handled the Q & A session at the end. And I ***loved*** the way you handled the last question. For that, alone, I would give you a 'B+' in the course——"

Bobby seemed a bit disappointed in the 'B' grade. But he wasn't going to object. It ***was*** a rehash of his Abel lecture, after all.

"But I found something else on the q-net. You gave a concert last night that has been posted there. And I looked at that little speech you gave at the end of the concert, that little, heartfelt speech, when you did the encore—— Did you know it has 'gone viral?'"

Really?

"That's an 'A.' In fact, if you count the music, it's an 'A++.' I showed it to three members of my family, and there was ***not a one*** who didn't break down in tears. ***I did,*** and it happened again every time I showed it to someone else. And the cameraman was taking shots of your audience as you performed. I have not seen as emotionally overwhelming a performance in my lifetime."

"So I am very pleased to give you an 'A' grade for Public Speaking. It's been an honor to meet you."

"Thank you, Professor Lafeber."

Stockholm Radisson Blu Royal Viking Hotel: Tuesday, December 9, 2588. Billy Bob Wilson looked at the 'viral video' for the third time. He still couldn't help misting up——

"Ulf," he said to his roommate, "I'm worried what happens if we do this. Yes, this kid is some kind of superhuman mongrel, and we've got to ***do*** something, but we could turn him into a martyr. There are even guys in my outfit that will look at this and have sympathy for him——"

"Billy, my friend," Schultz said, "we need to purge those elements out of our organizations. If they are not removed, we will lose our purity of purpose. And if we lose that, we lose ***everything***——"

Bobby and Chii were invited to a dinner in the Nordic Museum the night before the Nobel ceremony. There was plenty of champagne and a harpist playing classical music. The first was forbidden to the young Laureates, and the latter made very little impression on Bobby. He knew that they would be together again at the rehearsals in the ***Konserthuset*** the next morning, but for now, this was one of the few times they would be able to be together and talk at all. Chii pulled out her message pad and showed Bobby a picture. "Here is a picture I took today. I am carrying the ***item*** with me at all times, but I cannot show it to you. See here, the indications are all very positive. Now I have to close this file before the wrong people see it."

Bobby did not speak, only nodded his head. Chii erased the image.

December 10, Nobel Day. Steeling themselves for the inevitable media frenzy, Bobby and Chii decided to walk downstairs together. They had met Jadwiga Pawłowska, the Nobel Prize in Physics Laureate, who was just down the hall from their suite, at the dinner in the Museum, and agreed to all walk downstairs together. They had spoken with Jadwiga and she felt they would negotiate the lobby to their transport more successfully as a group, than individually. Also, Jadwiga felt protective of the two young foreigners.

The rehearsals would take most of the morning. At least for Bobby, this included performing some music he would play at the ceremony, and that was better than what the rest of the Laureates would be doing. The rehearsals, he had heard, were mostly practicing when to stand up and when to sit down. At least he got to sit down on a piano bench and do something that required more brains than a trained monkey——

His mother fussed with his clothing. She straightened up his bow tie, and made sure the vest he was wearing was buttoned carefully, then put on his tailcoat, and looked at him with pride. Bobby had a ring on one finger NaDii had never seen before, but she didn't have time to ask him about it. "See you this evening." she said.

Bobby did not know it, but the vest he was wearing was bulletproof. NaDii hoped it would never be needed, but it had the latest technology embedded in it, and yet looked perfectly ordinary. Grandmaster MorPhii had warned her, and she had not overlooked his warning.

There was a knock at the door. Chii and Jadwiga were standing there. Chii was breathtaking in a ball gown even more impressive than the one she had worn for the Abel ceremony. Her mother had outdone herself. Bobby had eyes only for her, but thanked Jadwiga for accompanying them, and they walked together to the elevator.

Somehow, they made it out of the lobby and to the transport vehicle that had been arranged to take them to the ***Konserthuset*** in only about 20 minutes. He had earlier only ***heard*** the phrase 'running the gauntlet,' but now, he understood it more personally——

For the next two hours, Bobby, Jadwiga and Chii all got plenty of practice standing up and sitting down. At last, Bobby had a chance to walk up to the concert Grand on the stage and sit where he felt comfortable. He brushed back his tails, sat at the piano, and glanced for a moment at Jadwiga. Then he began to play Chopin's ***Polonaise in A flat major, opus 53***. Its significance was not lost on the Polish Physics laureate, and she dabbed her handkerchief at her eyes while he played.

At the hotel, two American representatives found themselves trussed up and locked in a closet, as men they did not know turned the contents of their room upside-down. The door had been broken in, and things had gone downhill from there. They waited in puzzlement, hoping that the cleaning crew would soon be in to clean the room, and they could be released. Meanwhile, the invaders had left, having apparently found what they were looking for.

Guests were arriving at the ***Konserthuset*** for the Ceremony**.**

Each one presented an invitation, which was scrutinized at the door, and then they were passed in after a cursory inspection and security check.

Outside, two lookouts in brown Hunting jackets communicated via secure q-link connections to headquarters in Hamburg.

"***Fliedermaus*** is in. ***Eagle*** is in. Have the flyer ready when it is needed. ***NordKommando*** out."

The ceremony was following the script perfectly. It had reached the high point of the night.

HRH King Gustav Adolf XIV of Sweden handed the diploma, medal, and a certificate confirming the prize amount, first to Jadwiga Pawłowska, of Poland, for Physics, then to Oliver Tyndale of Great Britain, for Chemistry, then announced 'Physiology or Medicine,' and Bobby walked up to the King holding Chii's gripper in his hand. The King handed Bobby his diploma and certificate first, then hanging the medallion on a ribbon around his neck.

In the audience, two men in black tuxedoes removed the buckles from their belts., One handed, to the other, one of the two pens from his pocket, and they each affixed together the buckles and pens.

They looked at each other, and their eyes said, ***ready?*** but they were otherwise silent as they stood up, took aim, and fired.

Bobby took two hits to the chest, and stumbled back, stunned, then recovered himself. People on either side of the shooters began to rise, in slow motion. Some were moving to flee, while others were reaching to block the two gunmen and grab the weapons. They didn't have time.

As Chii started to turn towards the audience and the King backed up from Bobby, each gunman fired a second round. Bobby's head jerked backwards in a spray of blood, his medallion flew free, his body went limp and he fell.

A blur of motion like heat ripples moved towards the two gunmen, and they felt their guns torn from their grip by invisible hands. The two weapons turned towards the assailants, seemingly in mid-air, and fired.

Where nothing had stood a moment before, TiiNa appeared, one smoking gun in each hand, and looked at the two men's bodies with a pitiless, cold expression in her eyes.

From up on the stage, Chii screamed. The King bent down to look at Bobby, and then turned away, horrified.

Chii called for Bobby's parents. Then she called for Father Boyle.

For the second time, Father Boyle and Chii stood with the Firestones and said the prayers for the dying together.

NaDii bent down and held Bobby's hand while Chii prayed and the priest gave him the Last Rites. Greg held hands with Father Boyle and Chii. A siren wailed in the distance. Guards helped the

King off the stage and took up protective positions around the remaining Laureates, as though their services were of any use now.

A guard stepped in front of TiiNa. She looked up at him, reversed the guns in her hands, and handed them to the guard. "I wasn't fast enough," she whispered, "they killed my brother before I could stop them." she said.

Then she looked at herself and exclaimed, "Where is my ***dress?***" She covered herself with her hands as best she could, and walked back to the place where she had been seated. Her dress, the miniature replica of Chii's Abel prize gown, lay on the floor, as though it had fallen from the sky. She started to put it back on.

Chii held Father Boyle's hand as he prayed. She looked down at Bobby, who lay on his back. The first two shots had struck Bobby in the center of his chest, but had not penetrated the vest. The next two had gone into his forehead, and exited the back of his cranium. Blood ran the length of the stage, and was dripping off the edge. There was no longer any pulsation in the flow of blood. Bobby was not breathing. His pupils were fixed and dilated. Two paramedics appeared and loaded his body onto a gurney, trying to gather up what tissue they could. They put an oxygen mask over his face and tried to force the breathing mixture into his airway, then hurriedly took him away. Elsewhere in the hall, other paramedics were doing the same for Billy Bob and Ulf, each of whom had received a bullet in the center of the mouth, which had gone upwards and embedded themselves in the ceiling.

NaDii stood up and looked into Chii's eyes. "Medicine on this planet is very good; perhaps they can——"

Chii just shook her head. TiiNa walked up onto the stage and took Chii's gripper in her hand, and silently gave it a squeeze.

"Mr. and Mrs. Firestone?" a guard had walked up to them, "Will you come with me; we're going to the hospital."

TiiNa tugged at the guard's hand. "We need to go, too."

Enroute, NaDii took Chii's gripper in her own, and told her,

"I know you wanted to marry Bobby. He wanted to marry you, too—— I'm sorry you didn't have time to——get old enough to——"

Chii silently held up her left gripper. Around her arm was a small, golden bracelet. NaDii had not noticed it before.

"Father Boyle married us Friday. We were going to tell you and Greg about it after the awards ceremony. I am very sorry we did it secretly."

NaDii put her arms around Chii. "You should have had a life together. A whole life. Children——"

Chii hugged NaDii back. "Mrs. Firestone--NaDii--there ***is*** something else I have to tell you——"

But then they arrived at the hospital.

CHAPTER 28 - Requiem

Greg, NaDii, Chii and TiiNa were placed in a waiting room while the doctors worked on Bobby. For a while, nobody said anything. Then, Chii put a gripper into her bodice and pulled out a cylindrical case, something like a purse, suspended on a strap.

Greg looked up from his tears and NaDii turned toward Chii as she opened its clasp and lifted the lid of the case. There, resting cushioned in cotton, was a mottled blue egg about three times the size of a chicken's egg.

"I've been carrying it with me everywhere, ever since we left FriiDa's yacht," she said.

Greg choked out, "Bobby's?"

"Yes. Mine and Bobby's." Chii said, softly.

TiiNa reached out a hand and closed the lid. Turning the clasp, she said, simply, "Let no one else know about this."

"I have to let my Mom and Dad know," she said to TiiNa, "and Vrii."

TiiNa thought for a moment. "Maybe you're right. It's safer in ***your*** family than ours. While I live, my family is still a target. If no one knew it was Bobby's, perhaps it would be safest with you——"

Chii hid the case inside her blouse again.

A doctor came through the door. "I'm so sorry," he said, "The damage was too great."

"I thought so," TiiNa replied. None of the other family members could speak.

"What of the two men I shot?" she asked the doctor. Greg and NaDii's heads swiveled towards TiiNa. "What??!!"

"You did that?!" the doctor said. "I assumed it was one of the guards."

"If I had been a second quicker, Bobby would be alive," she said. And finally, TiiNa, who had been emotionless since the incident, broke down and began to cry.

Greg and NaDii reached toward her, with horror, sympathy and astonishment mixed in their expressions.

With a great effort, TiiNa pulled herself upright and stopped sobbing. "What about those men?" she demanded, through her tears.

"Oh, they are very ***thoroughly*** dead." the doctor said.

"Good!" TiiNa answered, as her steely control reasserted itself.

"And so is one of the finest minds of the twenty-sixth century," Chii mourned, "and that is ***not*** good. My poor, dear love——" she slumped against NaDii and whimpered.

The doctor placed a hand on Greg's shoulder. "I know this is hard, but I need you to come in back, and formally identify the body."

Greg walked in. NaDii, Chii and TiiNa followed. A police officer was present. He introduced himself as officer Ingemar Lillquist.

"This is my son, Bobby Firestone," Greg began, then he corrected himself. Looking at the officer, he said, "This ***was*** my son, Bobby Firestone."

"Was he a resident of Stockholm or a citizen of Sweden?"

"No." Greg answered.

"Of what nation was he a citizen or resident?"

"He was a resident of Placet, in the HaChii Confederation, but he had dual citizenship in the HaChii Confederation and the United States of America."

"For what reason was he here in Stockholm?"

"He was r-receiving the Nobel Prize." Greg choked out.

"I'm sorry," the officer said, "I know the answers to most of these questions, but I have to ask them if a crime has been committed."

"A crime has most definitely been committed!" Greg said with some vehemence.

"A terrible crime, that has brought shame to our whole city," the officer stopped, and wiped away tears, "and yet I must ask these questions."

After he finished with Greg's part of the report, he asked NaDii and others present if they wanted to add anything to the report.

TiiNa stood in front of the officer and asked, "Will you need to arrest me?"

"Why in the world would I want to do that?" the officer asked. ***How old is she?*** Lillquist mouthed to Greg, who held up four fingers.

"I killed two men today. They were the men who shot Bobby." she replied, as matter-of-factly as if it had been the time of day.

"How——Why——" Officer Lillquist was completely boggled by the direction the testimony had gone.

"I took their weapons. It was too late to save Bobby." she replied.

"You had disarmed them. Why did you kill them?" the officer asked. He seemed to think that might have been excessive, although it was clear from his expression that he thought the whole story was unbelievable.

"I thought they probably had other weapons, and they needed to be stopped. The guns. Their barrels were disguised as pens. I saw pencils in their pockets, and something else——" TiiNa replied.

"Excuse me a moment." Officer Lillquist walked over to the doctor. "May I examine the bodies of the two men reputed to be the shooters?"

He was gone for a few minutes. When he came back, he held the two pencils.

"These are blowguns," he said, "Each man had one in his pocket. I can't be sure until forensics is done with them, but I suspect the darts are poisoned. What was the other thing you saw?" he asked.

"Trails where the bullets went," TiiNa said, "I think the bullets were rockets."

"The bullets they used to shoot your brother?" officer Lillquist asked.

"Yes. Rockets. They had little smoke trails. And it wasn't that loud. It was more like 'Tap---Tap' than 'Bang--Bang.'"

"I suppose that's important." He noted it down.

The doctor whispered to the police officer. Lillquist looked pained, then nodded, and turned to the Firestones.

"There is a transport vehicle here from the Coroner's Office." he said.

"What does that mean?" NaDii asked, looking at Greg.

"He was murdered. They have to do an autopsy, to determine the cause of death," he said to NaDii.

"Isn't that ***obvious***?" she cried.

"Well, suppose they find one of the bullets, and it ***is*** a rocket, like TiiNa says. There aren't that many places that make those. It might help people figure out who did this."

"They know who did this, and TiiNa took them out," NaDii said.

"No, NaDii, we don't," Chii said, "Those two couldn't have done this alone. And they're not around to say who helped them."

"I'm sorry," the officer said, "They have come to take Bobby."

The coroner's office people rolled in a gurney, and moved Bobby's body to it. They were starting to cover him up with a sheet, when Chii walked over and asked them to stop for a moment. She picked up Bobby's hand, put it into her mouth, and bit down gently. Then she put it down, took the gold ring off his finger, and handed it to Greg. "OK." she said. NaDii leaned on Greg and whimpered.

They covered Bobby and rolled him away.

The Firestones stepped back out to the waiting room, at a loss where to go or what to do. There, waiting for them, were Father Boyle, MeBlii and ChuuRii, Vrii, BoTii and DriiLa, Greg's mother, Enya and his human friend Rob Harker. There was also a HaChii woman none of them had met before, holding a bundle of cloth up to her chest, in her right arm.

Rob stood there with tears streaming down his face and said,

"We know about Bobby. This was supposed to be a happy day——" Rob choked, and couldn't speak for a few moments.

"I was going to introduce you to MriiYa," she put her free gripper around Rob's shoulder, "and Greggie. Now, Bobby's never going to meet him——"

"It was going to be a surprise," MriiYa said.

Greg and Rob hugged each other and just sobbed for a while. NaDii walked over and took a look at MriiYa's baby. The little blue-green face peered out, owlishly, one little hand holding aside the edge of the flannel blanket.

"My God!" TiiNa said, looking up at MriiYa. Then she noticed MriiYa's necklace, a crucifix. "Lord, protect this baby!" she prayed, "There are terrible people out there who don't want any of us hybrids to live."

And she recovered her composure a bit. Looking at Rob, she said, "Keep this a secret, if you possibly can. Bobby didn't keep a low profile, and look where he is now——"

Rob looked back at her. "I spoke to Father Boyle. I know where Bobby is now; he's with God. But you're right. I don't want Greggie to be with him yet."

ChuuRii and MeBlii gave their condolences to Greg and NaDii, and told TiiNa how sorry they were about her brother. TiiNa asked where RiiMa was, and found she was being babysat by NaDii's sister Brii, back at the hotel.

And finally, MriiYa looked at Chii. "Who is this?" she asked.

"I'm Chii Ix——" she stopped for a second, looked very intensely at her parents for a moment, and completed the statement.

"I'm Chii **Firestone**. I'm Bobby's wife——I mean——" she choked and couldn't speak, "I'm Bobby's ***widow***." she held up her bracelet.

DriiLa and BoTii looked at each other, then the priest. Father Boyle nodded.

"Father Boyle married us last Friday. I'm sorry; we were keeping it a secret until after the Nobels. But I suppose that doesn't matter now."

"No it doesn't" BoTii said, "You ***are*** Chii Firestone. I can't imagine losing DriiLa but I almost did, last Summer. The only reason I didn't was Bobby."

"I would be honored to have a daughter named Chii Firestone." DriiLa said, "Never mind the legal authorities. It's OK that you married Bobby. I'm just so sorry that you lost him."

Vrii put her grippers on her sister's shoulders. "I'm sorry I never told you how proud I am of what you've accomplished. You and Bobby fit together like--look, I know, TiiNa told me--like jigsaw puzzle pieces——"

Chii looked mystified.

"Vrii told me what TiiNa told her." BoTii said, "and we looked the other way, because you're a smart girl, and we didn't think you'd make any mistakes——"

Now, Chii was ***really*** puzzled. She looked at TiiNa.

"I watched you one night last Summer." TiiNa whispered, "and then I shot my mouth off to Vrii about it. Sorry. You guys were ***perfect.***"

She regarded her small sister-in-law with astonishment.

"Mom and Dad," Chii said. "I hope you're not mad at me."

"FFurff, no, Chii!" DriiLa said, "After last Summer, I was half-way in love with him, myself. I can't ***believe*** he's gone——"

"Well, Mom and Dad, I still have a ***little piece*** of him——" and she drew the case on its strap, out from inside her bodice.

"Look, here——" and she opened the lid of her case.

DriiLa and BoTii craned over and looked, DriiLa's gripper around BoTii's shoulder. "Ordinarily, I would be very upset," BoTii said, "But this not an ordinary day. I'm going to use a phrase from your human friends, and say ***thank God*** this happened before he was——killed——"

"Yes. Thank God," Chii said, and looked at Father Boyle. Pointing at MriiYa's necklace, she asked, "Do you know where I can get one of those?"

"They have them at all the spaceports." Father Boyle said. MriiYa nodded.

When they got back to the hotel room, it was late evening. The press had been cleared out of the lobby by Royal Guards. They received a military escort to their room. When Greg, NaDii, TiiNa and Chii walked in, his Majesty, King Gustav, awaited them, flanked by two aides.

Chii walked over to the room message system and dialed her parents' room. BoTii's voice answered. "I'm staying over with the Firestones tonight." she told her father, "Is that all right?" And her father agreed.

The King stood up, addressing Greg and NaDii. "The government of Sweden is at your disposal. If there is anything we can do to help——"

Greg shook his head. "How can anyone help, ***now?"*** he said bitterly.

The King's expression was bleak. "I don't know," he admitted, weakly, "Funeral arrangements, perhaps——"

Greg looked at NaDii. "Bobby never talked about death. I have no idea what he would have wanted."

Chii placed a gripper on Greg's shoulder. "***I*** can tell you——"

"***Really?*** What did he say?" Greg said, surprised.

"We were talking about medicine on the q-net——our Nobel prize was for Physiology and Medicine, after all——and Bobby said his body would be of no use to anybody sitting in a box in the ground, but a medical school could learn a lot about how hybridization worked between humans and HaChii, if they could use his body for research."

"Research? That sounds like Bobby," NaDii said, "It sounds too much like him, ***not*** to be true. Thank you. I never would have thought of that myself."

"We were willing to offer a formal state funeral," King Gustav said, "but I can't see how he could donate his body and still have one of those——"

"Your Highness?" Chii said, "How about a memorial service? Without the body present?" She turned to Greg and NaDii, "Would that be acceptable?"

"I trust your judgment, Chii," NaDii said, "As for a medical research institution, Your Highness, do you think the Karolinska Institute would accept the donation of Bobby's body?"

The King broke down and sobbed. His aide, on the right, spoke for him. "I'm sure the Karolinska Institute would be honored to accept such a donation."

The King recovered himself somewhat. He gestured to the aide on his left, who opened a pouch he had been carrying. Inside it were three objects. King Gustav took them out and handed them to Chii. There were her medal, diploma and certificate for the Nobel Prize.

She accepted them wordlessly, set them on a table in front of the King, and said, "Thank you. I appreciate that you remembered. But I'd give them all away if I could only have Bobby back."

"There is one other thing," King Gustav said. May I speak to TiiNa?"

TiiNa stepped forward.

"I understand that you, like your brother, have dual citizenship in the HaChii Confederation and the United States of America. Is that correct?"

"Yes——your Highness," TiiNa answered, "It is. Bobby valued his US citizenship and I have never thought about it much, but if Bobby thought it was important, so do I."

"Yes. I supposed that you would." King Gustav replied, "What I have to ask you next is——a bit awkward, I'm sorry——"

"Go ahead," TiiNa said.

"There are two gentlemen here from the United States' Federal Bureau of Investigation. They believe that at least one of the men who shot Bobby was a citizen of the United States, and they have asked me——to ask you——if you would let them talk to you about what happened."

"Of course." TiiNa replied.

The King gestured to one of his aides, who pushed a few buttons on his message pad. A moment later, there was a knock on the door.

The agents were admitted into the room. The taller one said, "Is there a place where we can speak privately with Ms. Firestone?"

Greg and NaDii pointed to one of the bedrooms adjoining the meeting room in the suite. The agents beckoned TiiNa into the room and closed the door.

Inside the room, the shorter agent took a picture from an inside pocket of his coat. He showed it to TiiNa. "This is Billy Bob Wilson." he explained, "Is he one of the men who shot Bobby?"

"Yes," TiiNa said, "He was the one on the right. I believe I shot him first——"

"That's right," the other agent said, "That's what the cameras showed. He belongs——he ***belonged***——to a terrorist organization in the United States called the ***United Klans of America.***"

"Then they have to be dealt with." TiiNa replied, with ill-concealed fury.

"We most heartily concur," said the first agent, "and that leads us to another question. Please feel free to refuse to answer if you do not want to, but we have looked at the camera images over and over, and there is one thing we just do not understand."

"Go ahead and ask," TiiNa responded, "I think I can guess your question."

"TiiNa," the taller agent said, "Just how did you disarm those men?"

"I took the weapons out of their hands," she said simply.

"But——"

"And they could not see me——"

"Ahh——"

"And your cameras could not see me either."

"Pardon me?"

TiiNa began to disrobe.

"Little girl, you don't have to do that——"

And then, there was just the pile of clothes on the floor. No TiiNa.

Momentarily, there was an impression of heat ripples in the air, but just barely. Each man felt a tug at their jackets, which fell open.

And then, TiiNa was standing in front of them again. In each hand she held the sidearm that had been in the agent's holster a moment before, by the barrels. She handed them back to the agents, one at a time.

"Like that——" she answered.

Each agent looked at the gun in his hand, and returned it to his holster. The shorter one was the first to recover the use of his tongue.

"My God——What just happened there?"

"Bobby had already discovered a very effective method of camouflage, some years ago," she began, "and he could imitate any background, so that you could not see him from a specific point of view."

"But he was observable from other angles and positions?" the agent asked.

"Yes. However, about a week ago, I discovered how to make the chromatophores in my skin into a hologram."

"A three-dimensional picture?" asked the taller agent.

"Not exactly. It's more than that, but the point is, from whatever angle you look at me, you see exactly the same light wavefronts that would arrive at your eyes from behind me, if I were not there. It took a little practice, but I was getting pretty good at it, and I was going to show it to Bobby once——this Nobel nonsense——was over."

"And then," she said bitterly, "I never got the chance."

The agents looked at each other. "We've got to call headquarters."

"You call," TiiNa pointed at the taller agent, "while I speak to him." and she pointed at the shorter agent.

As the taller man stepped to the back of the room and began speaking to someone on his q-link message pad, TiiNa addressed the shorter agent:

"A while back, Bobby and I realized that these--talents--would make us very attractive to three-letter agencies like yours. And we resolved to conceal them, so we could get on with our lives and not be bothered by people who wanted to turn us into secret agents."

"I fully understand——" the agent replied.

"But we did ***not*** get on with our lives, did we?" she said, "Tonight, one of us does not have a life to get on with at all——" and at this point, tears began to run down her cheeks, "and I have changed my mind ***completely***. If you need an agent who can remove these--she used a HaChii epithet for an excretory process that was impossible for humans--from the face of the Earth, I am more than willing to co-operate with you."

TiiNa began to put her clothes back on.

"She's only four years old," said the taller agent. "somehow, we're going to have to get permission from her parents——"

"Leave that up to me." TiiNa told the agent.

She stepped outside. King Gustav and his aides had left. Her parents and Chii remained.

"Mom and Dad, we have to talk." she said.

December 11 dawned, gloomy and raining, in Boston, Massachusetts.

Professor O'Brien's message pad beeped. He opened the message and found himself face-to-face with a picture of Bobby Firestone.

"Hello, Professor O'Brien. If you are receiving this message, I have not logged in to my system in 24 hours. Given the character of recent threats on my life, it is likely that I am no longer alive."

The Professor halted the message. Like most of the world, he had heard what had happened to Bobby. It was just too much to bear.

An hour later, he came back to the message screen. He resumed the message.

"——no longer alive. I am——***was***——***will be?***—— transferring files to your account that will show what I was working on when the bad guys took me out——"

——.. (data transfer follows, the screen told him)

"——if you can accept the following project ideas ***in lieu*** of course credit, I would——I mean I suspect my family would—— appreciate it if I could be awarded my diploma posthumously. Several of these projects will probably take a large number of researchers, working for several years, to implement. Some are highly speculative. Feel free to use your judgement as to which should be done first, and which should be saved for later. There are more projects than course credits in the curriculum, so if you can choose the ones you think would be most expeditious first, provided you find them acceptable, I will trust your prioritization so as to make the achievement of my degree possible in the shortest time after my demise."

He opened the folder full of files. There were 200 projects in Physics, 150 in advanced Mathematical topics, and one in Astromony. Professor O'Brien called the Mathematics and Physics departments of five major US universities, and arranged, one-by-one, a consortium of professors who could begin to sift through the project descriptions. "Ladies and Gentlemen," he addressed the assembled personnel via the q-net, "We owe this to the memory of Robert Firestone. Let us begin."

December 14 began in Stockholm the way December 11 had begun in Boston.

A solemn procession worked its way down Södermalm to Saint Eric's Cathedral. NaDii, Greg, TiiNa and Chii walked to the front of the church, genuflecting before the altar, and seated themselves in the center of the front pew. The King of Sweden and the King of Norway and their wives entered the pew from the right, and sat down next to the Firestones. The President of the United States and her husband entered from the other side of the pew and sat to their left. They were joined a moment later by the Prime Minister of the HaChii Confederation.

There were more Royal Guards than anyone had seen in Stockholm in several lifetimes. And then, there were the agents from three-letter organizations out of other countries that nobody was seeing right now, even though they were present in massive numbers.

A symbolic coffin stood at the altar, with a picture of Bobby on a stand in front of it. Resting on top of the coffin were a gold Nobel medallion with a bloodstained ribbon, the Nobel diploma, and the certificate, along with his Abel plaque and diploma. DiiRa, along with Lars Svensson, the director of the Royal Philharmonic, walked up to the coffin, and each placed a stack of sheet music alongside the other items.

His Holiness, Pope Patrick the First, flanked by Father Boyle and another priest, walked to the front of the altar.

The world stood silent for a moment, and the funeral Mass began.

After the Mass, the Holy Father asked to speak to Chii alone. They stepped past the holy water fonts into a small side room. John Ryan closed the door.

"Chii, I heard about the egg," he said.

"Secrets travel fast." she answered.

"Father Boyle and my nephew Rob were both there when you showed it to your parents," he answered, "you think I wouldn't hear about that?"

"I suppose so," Chii answered.

"Father Boyle told me you got baptized when you were married," he stated.

"Yes. That's something I wanted," she said.

"Up to now, the Church hasn't had a lot of oviparous members——"

"I suppose not," Chii replied, wondering where this line of inquiry would go.

"Did you know Father Boyle baptized RiiMa and TiiNa in the egg?" the pontiff asked.

"I had no idea. Is that an acceptable policy?" Chii asked.

"It was ***my*** policy. And I'm the Pope, so now it's Church policy." he answered.

"I guess you know that I have the egg with me," she stated.

"Yes. And every moment you go anywhere outside of maybe a fortress, you are both at risk, if the wrong people find out," he said.

"Then I guess you better do the baptism. That was what you were going to ask, wasn't it?" she asked the Pope, extracting the case and opening its lid.

He went outside to a holy water font, and came back with a handful of water. Setting the egg on the table and splashing the water over it, he said,

"***Ego te baptizo in nomine Patris, et Filii, et Spiritu Sanctii,***" tracing a cross with one wet finger, and then, he placed the egg back in the case.

"That's it?" Chii asked.

"That's all we need to do for now. If you would like a more formal ceremony after the egg has hatched, I'm sure Father Boyle would be glad to do it. OK? Now go back out to your family. They're waiting for you."

"Thank you, Holy Father——"

"Jack——" he said to himself, after she had left, and spent the next half hour praying for her and her baby to be safe.

CHAPTER 29 - Aftermath

Saturday, May 30, 2589: The morning had turned leaden and oppressively hot, on this late Spring day, as two people walked in to the tiny town of Benton, Alabama on 4th street, having come from the direction of US 80. An adult male, apparently the father, and a little girl with blonde pigtails, apparently the daughter, stepped into the local store-plus-lunch-counter.

"Howdy," the man said, "you know a good place that could put us up for the night, while our flyer is repaired?"

The storekeeper recommended a motel two blocks away, and asked them if they wanted breakfast. "Grits and gravy," the man said, "scrambled eggs," the little girl said.

After the meal, they took a walk around town. At various places, they saw signs that said "UKA meeting tonight" and identified the Grange Hall on the west side of town as the place of the gathering at 7:00 PM.

That evening, they checked in to the motel. The man told the manager they were taking a walk to go get dinner, and would be back later.

They left together. Twenty minutes later, the man walked into the Grange Hall alone.

Several speakers harangued the audience about the evils of humans working with HaChii, the threat of mongrelizing between human male and HaChii females, and tried to outrage their audience with stories of HaChii males raping human females (which certainly never happened in the mining business).

The 'father,' new Agency officer Robert Harker, pretended to be an enthusiastic supporter of all the viewpoints presented, while his 'daughter,' new Agency officer TiiNa Firestone, explored and observed the scene in the Grange Hall from all viewpoints, unseen.

Dang! Rob thought, Looks like there's going to be a sudden rise in the suicide rate here in Benton, my, my——Lots of that going around in the Southland, lately——

Saturday, May 30, 2589, Earth reckoning: Gracedon, Gracet, HaChii Confederation. The egg was beginning to hatch. Chii, who had bought a home next door to her parents, invited them and Father Boyle over as the shell began to crack. Every day, Chii had been talking to the egg, telling it stories about Bobby, singing songs and playing music from recordings.

Today it was 234 HaChii days since the egg was laid--well overdue by HaChii reckoning--but at last, the hatching process had begun. The shell was cracking, and finally, they could see the first views of little blue hands pulling apart fragments of shell and widening the opening.

At last, a little blue head popped out and looked at Chii. "Hi!" he said, "Are you my Mommy?"

Two days after Robert Firestone, II hatched, Greg and NaDii arrived in the runabout. They landed it in a field behind Chii's house and walked over.

"Nice place you've got here, Chii," Greg said as they walked in the door.

"Can I hold him?" NaDii asked, and Chii handed the tiny bundle over to his grandmother.

"Hello, little guy!" NaDii said.

"Hi, pretty lady," the baby answered. NaDii turned gray and almost dropped him in shock.

Greg held out a finger, and the baby grasped it.

"When did he start talking?" his grandfather asked.

Chii pointed at the eggshell, still in its incubator box on the table, "As soon as there was enough air for him to take a good breath. He wasn't even fully hatched out."

"Hello, little fellow," Greg said to his grandson. "What's your name?"

"RoBii!" the tiny hatchling exclaimed, "Mommy told me when I was ***little***."

NaDii looked at Greg, "My Dad Bii is going to love that name. And he's going to (she looked at Greg) 'flip his wig,' when he finds out RoBii's talking."

Greg looked back at her, "I'd buy him a wig, just to see that."

At the Karolinska Institute, researchers had been investigating how Human and HaChii characteristics were combined in the only Human-HaChii hybrid they had ever had a chance to examine (i. e., *dissect*). They also had the Firestone-DriiBo equations and the associated iterative computer program to play with. Naturally, from time to time, they consulted with Chii.

In her Nobel lecture, as in the original paper, Chii had used a human DNA sequence and a HaChii DNA sequence to generate the coefficients of the equation. Since the only human DNA sequence she had found was that of Gregory, a human male, she had decided to seek out DNA of a HaChii male as a comparable example, and, as it turned out, a file for NaDii's uncle Xii Iz ChaJii, was included with the family records Chii had spirited out of Bobby's computer.

The HaChii nudity taboo was just as real as the human one. Mercifully for Uncle Xii, he was not present in the audience when Chii's recapitulation-of-ontogeny program metamorphosed from an embryo into ***his*** adult, naked body. Greg Firestone had not been so lucky.

But the researchers were interested, not in embarrassing males with a nudity taboo, but in how the hybrid DNA of Bobby had formed his body, and more remarkably, his outstanding brain. Using a sample of Bobby's DNA they worked backwards to find the coefficients of the Firestone-DriiBo equation for Bobby. Then they processed it forward to confirm that the final structure matched all that was left intact of Bobby Firestone.

That left only one puzzle for them--the greatest of all. How had the human DNA of Gregory Firestone been integrated into the HaChii DNA of his son, and would it work consistently if other Human-HaChii hybrids arose?

They had Gregory's DNA sequence. Fortunately, they also had NaDii's sequence in the family record. The question now was, how had the two combined?

Human DNA has four bases, sometimes called nucleotides, cytosine(C), guanine(G), Adenine(A) and Thymine(T). If it were untwisted and laid out flat, the DNA molecule would look like a railroad track with ties going across from one rail to the other. There are two types of base-pairs, or 'ties' that connect across the 'rails.' One type of tie is formed when C and G lock together, the other is formed with A and T lock together. The ladder rungs are about the same size, but C's only lock with G's and A's with T's.

Of course, the ties can be connected to the rails either way, A-T or T-A (or C-G, G-C). So there are four arrangements that might be possible for any single tie you find as you roll down the DNA railroad.

HaChii DNA has two more bases. The chemicals have their own names in HaChii chemistry, but the humans decided to call this base pair H and X. 'H' as in Ha, and 'X' not as in the Roman 'exs' but the Greek Chi, Thus, the H-Chi, or HaChii, base pair.

Again, H-X or X-H combinations can be placed into the same space as A-T or C-G, so that makes six arrangements that might be found 'connecting the tracks' in HaChii DNA.

You might think that these combinations occur randomly, so any given stretch of track should have a pretty even assortment of all six (or four) forms.

But no. Sometimes all you see is A-T, A-T, A-T, for miles and miles, like DNA with obsessive-compulsive disorder. It's not very interesting, and it doesn't code for any kind of structure in a multi-cellular organism.

In HaChii DNA, the same is true, with the same results. A long string of C-G C-G, or H-X, H-X wouldn't do anything interesting. But unlike human DNA, in HaChii DNA, there are stretches of the DNA railroad consisting of only H-X and C-G ties with no A-Ts, only H-X and A-T ties, with no C-Gs or only C-G and A-T ties, with no H-Xs. From a human point of view, the third type is the most interesting, because it is the pattern of DNA for all Earth-based life. But the question was--did C G A T-only stretches of DNA have any special significance in HaChii structure?

One way to find out: Knock out the sequences, run the Firestone-DriiBo equations with the new DNA sequence, and see what happens——

Researcher Ole Ingvarsson contacted Chii via q-net. He asked her, as the only living member of the Firestone-DriiBo team, whether she would be interested in the results.

"Yes, of course, I am interested in your research," she answered. ***It could be very important to me,*** she thought, ***Best if he doesn't know about RoBii (and he is my secret) but the more I know, the better,*** she thought.

"Well, let's see together how this plays out," Ole said to Chii, and they both observed the computer program as it rolled out the development of a HaChii with no long stretches of C G A T DNA.

It became immediately apparent that the development of appendages off the main body trunk had been degraded. Grippers at the end of arms and walking-tentacles were stunted, almost absent. The head was micro cephalic, with almost no brain. Other appendage development (this was a male) was so inadequate that its gender was not easy to judge, even after maturing the model to full adulthood.

"That's an interesting result," Chii responded, "Could you try it on the DNA of an animal with a tail, like a Thorb?"

"We don't have a lot of HaChii animal DNA sequences here," Ole lamented.

"I had a pet racing Thorb," Chii responded, "His name was Thorbert. Let me look in my files. I think I have his DNA sequence here someplace—— Ahhh! Yes! Here it is——" and she transmitted him the file.

"OK," Ole said, "This may take some time——" and the program to make the sequence into coefficients for the equations began running.

"So, Mr. Ingvarsson," Chii said, "This list of defects sounds a lot like what happens when a haploid egg hatches."

"That's interesting," Ingvarsson said, "I think you're right. Look here. I've just searched up a description of what happens when a heat-shock haploid egg develops enough to hatch, and the list of defects is almost a perfect match for the 'knock-out' model without the pure-CGAT sequences." Then, he turned his attention to another section of his screen. "Aha! The coefficients are calculated. Now, we roll the program to see how the Thorb turns out——"

They both watched. Soon, it started to look like a Thorb. Then, it didn't.

"Wow!" Chii said, "by the time it hatches, it doesn't look like Thorbert at all. His nose, the tips of his crawlers, and the end of his tail, are all missing——"

"Something else is missing, too——" Ingvarsson noted.

"Oh, so it is. He's more a Thorbette than a Thorbert——" Chii concluded.

"Now, Let's get Thorbert's original DNA again," Ole said, "and take away the DNA that came from his father."

"You can do that?" Chii asked.

"If Thorbert came from a reputable breeder, probably yes," Ingvarsson said, "If the breeding male is a stud Thorb, he's usually an older, well-established male who has been put out to stud after his racing career is over. The females are bred as soon as they are old enough. The older male has shorter telomeres on his chromosomes because they break off and get reduced with age. So--even with the telomere-restoring stuff that goes on in HaChii meiosis, if there's a paired set of chromosomes, the one that has the shorter telomeres is probably from the male."

"That's clever!" Chii said, "so let's take out the chromosome with the shorter telomeres in each pair——"

"Done——" Ingvarsson replied.

And in a few minutes, they watched the organism develop.

"Wow! ***Still*** not Thorbert, and with all the same stunted parts——"

"Let's try doing what happens sometimes, where all the haploid chromosomes duplicate themselves from the egg, and then those spindle things pull the pairs together and make double chromosomes."

"Yeah. But they're all still duplicates of each other——" Ole argued, while setting up the experiment. "Well, that wasn't very hard, here goes——"

And a few minutes later, the same results——

"If there's something missing in the mother's chromosome," Ingvarsson said, "it would usually be 'filled in' by the equivalent part of the father's chromosome. But in this case, both chromosomes have the same defect, so nothing changes."

"Are there any chromosomes that are mostly C G A T in the HaChii genome?" Chii asked.

"Interesting question; let me look." Ingvarsson did a search.

"Wow! there are 28 chromosome pairs in the HaChii nucleus." Ole Ingvarsson exclaimed, "Nine of them are over 95 percent C G A T-sequence DNA, the rest are H X C G A T."

"Those mitotic spindle thingies," Chii said, "they are what figures out which chromosomes to pair up when the first cell division occurs after the egg is fertilized. Do you have any program that can simulate what they would pull together if you had human chromosomes in there with a bunch of HaChii duplicates?"

"We have a mitosis simulator for Human mitosis——but I don't know if we have anything that work along the rules that HaChii cells would use to pick out what chromosomes to pair up with others——"

"I'll check with some of the Universities on Placet," Chii said, "they might have something. Thanks, Mr. Ingvarsson. Get back to you in a couple days——"

"Thanks, Chii. There's probably a paper in this! Bye——"

"Hello, Professor O'Brien," the Director said.

"Hello, Professor Chakrabarti." O'Brien replied, "What news from MIT?"

"Project 150 is progressing faster than we had a right to hope. Truly the proposals of Mr. Firestone point the way where many decades of blind fumbling have not. Please do something for me."

"What is that?"

"Clear a spot just in front of your monitor,"

"How big?"

Chakrabarti held his hands about half a meter apart. "Like so?"

O'Brien shoved the papers and books aside; a space of about the size requested was available.

There was a momentary glow in the air; then a white rat materialized directly in front of the monitor. It stood there, whiskers twitching, apparently too terrified to move.

O'Brien picked up the rat, stroked it absently. "Did you send him from your lab?" the professor asked.

"No. That is the beauty of it." Chakrabarti replied. "This rat came from the Harvard Radiation Lab. He disappeared out of one of their cages ten years ago, and no-one could figure out how he had escaped. I remember it was quite a mystery for us, at the time. We always assumed someone had sneaked in and stolen him."

"Ah——Then we are ***very, very close*** to our goal," O'Brien concluded.

2589, June 4. Early morning in Gracet, where Chii lived near her parents: RoBii was taking his morning nap. ***This is a good time to call Doctor Ingvarsson at Karolinska,*** she thought. She linked back to his earlier call and messaged a request to speak to him.

"Good Morning!" she said brightly.

"Maybe where you are," he said with a tone of irony, "It's evening here and we are having a lightning storm Thor would be proud of. If my lights go out and we lose our connection, don't be surprised."

"Well, I'll be quick then. I checked all the major research institutions on Placet and elsewhere in the Confederation. None of them had a program that would emulate the way the cell selects which chromosome to combine with its partner in the first mitosis after fertilization,"

"That's too bad. I was hoping——" Ingvarsson interjected.

"So I wrote it," Chii finished.

"Oh. Good," Ingvarsson said, "So you know the chemistry that assembles the chromosomes?"

"***Selects*** them," she said, "and then puts them together. Yeah. I got the details of the Chemistry from Placedon Medical School. Coding the program wasn't too hard after that."

"OK. Send me the program, please?" he asked, thinking, ***Not hard work for you, maybe——***

"Sure," and Chii activated the transmission, "but I've already tried it out."

"What results did you get?" Ingvarsson asked.

"I've run the program with Greg and NaDii's DNA ten times. As long as the timing is right, and an unfertilized egg starts dividing, it looks like human DNA gets accepted into a HaChii egg almost every time, instead of the replicas of the HaChii chromosomes--at least for those nine chromosomes that are mostly C G A T, without any H-X. Most runs, for those C G A T chromosomes, eight out of nine matched with Greg's DNA, not the replicas of the original haploid set. One run even matched up human chromosomes with **all nine** of them. The mitotic spindles in HaChii DNA seem to——prefer——something that doesn't match ***exactly*** as compared to something that is identical. It seems to be a way to avoid inbreeding."

"Human DNA doesn't do that." Ingvarsson replied.

"HaChii cells can be fertilized by more than one sperm," Chii told him, "The egg has to be--'smart'--enough to pick and choose which father's chromosome it--'likes'--to maximize genetic diversity."

"So a HaChii infant can inherit features from two different fathers?" Ole asked, in a somewhat disbelieving tone.

"It doesn't happen often," Chii told him, "but apparently our distant ancestors--'played the field'--a lot more than HaChii people do today. Among us now, sex with two males at once is considered——***kinky***——I think you humans call it, is that right?"

"Most humans would agree," Ingvarsson said, looking somewhat embarrassed, "it doesn't happen often with us, either."

"I'll send you the ten DNA profiles that resulted from the runs I made. You might look at what happens when you run sequence four through the Firestone-DriiBo equations," she said, "It's not ***exactly*** Bobby, but it's pretty close, considering you have thousands of different possibilities."

"How many of that one--number four's--chromosomes matched up with human DNA?" Ingvarsson asked.

"Eight out of nine. I figure that was what happened with Bobby, too," she said, "And his sister must have been nine-for-nine."

"Bobby had a sister?" Ingvarsson asked, "I didn't know that——"

"Yeah. She performed in a concert with him the weekend before the Nobel——" and she choked up.

"Please, don't cry!" Ingvarsson pleaded, "I forget sometimes that this is research for me, but it was someone you knew very well——"

Now that's an understatement if I ever heard one, she thought. "I'm sorry," she hiccupped, "It's just hard to talk sometimes, when I think about Bobby. Anyway, his sister TiiNa is on Earth right now, in some sort of exchange-student program. My sister Vrii did that last year. I think TiiNa's learning how to play chess."

Just then, she heard a loud crash of thunder from behind Dr. Ingvarsson, and the window on her screen went black.

2589, Early evening, June 4: TiiNa, at that moment, was in Germany, where she had been playing in chess tournaments and taking lessons from Earth's grandmasters by day, hunting for friends of Ulf Schultz, by night.

On Earth, where she was already known, it was safer to travel as a human. Here, she was a little blond girl with pigtails called Martina Feuerstein. Her identity as a chess prodigy exchange student from the United States worked well as a cover. And she was quickly picking up a working knowledge of German, as well as chess. That was, of course, proving quite useful in both of her two rôles.

She was doing well by day, already ranked with a rating over 2300. She hoped to match the number of this year by the time she left Earth in the Fall. She was also doing well by night. The 'suicide' rate among members of the Hamburg VDEM organization was approaching 100%. Scary girl.

At this moment, she was in the Schellingsstraße building of the Hamburger Schachklub Chess facility. They didn't usually meet on Thursdays; this event was an exception, a special meeting for foreign (***they have no idea how foreign!*** she thought) exchange students and local players. Players were still arriving, and there was an old upright piano standing in the corner. Bored, she sat down and began picking out a tune.

For some other little girl, that might have been 'twinkle, twinkle, little star,' for TiiNa, it was the Goldberg Variations. She lost herself in the music, and for a timeless span was not aware of her surroundings. About eight minutes later, she stopped and looked around her. She was surrounded by everybody in the room. They beamed at her and began to applaud. ***Uh, oh——got to watch that, don't want to attract too much attention to myself.*** Fortunately, she could maintain her appearance as Martina without any conscious thought, but she really ***had*** to watch blowing her cover in other ways; Martina was supposed to be a ***chess*** prodigy. Too Many other talents would not look too good on her résumé, right now. "Kleine Mädchen," (Little Girl) her host whispered to her quietly, "I just recently listened to a recording of that Bach piece by the Firestone boy. God rest his soul——but even ***he*** didn't do it as beautifully as you."

She ducked her head. The praise made her feel good and terrible at the same time. Thinking again of her brother, she resolved more firmly than ever to excel at the rôle of death angel for which she had been recruited.

Chakrabarti called O'Brien at about the same time the storm was rolling in Stockholm and the chess prodigy was playing piano in Hamburg.

"Dr. O'Brien?" he said, without preamble, "Do you still have our little friend with you that I sent last week?"

O'Brien held up a small cage with a watering bottle and food dish. "He is in good health, for the world's oldest rat, wouldn't you agree?"

"We have something additional to demonstrate, if you don't mind," said Dr. Chakrabarti, "Could you clear a little more space in front of your monitor, and put Ralphie down there?"

"Ralphie? He has a name?" O'Brien said as he extracted the rat from his cage and set him down on the tabletop, "Hold still, Ralphie——"

And there was a similar airglow to the one that had delivered him the previous week, just for a moment. And there were now two Ralphies, side-by-side, in exactly the same pose. For a moment, the twitches of the whiskers, the sniffing of the noses, the turning of the heads, was exactly identical, and then their movements began to diverge. The two Ralphies jumped off the edge of the table in different directions. "Hey, come back here!" O'Brien demanded, without much effect.

He rummaged around amongst cushions and piles of books, and eventually came up with a rat in each hand. "Which one is the Alpha model?"

"Damned if I know," Chakrabarti responded, "You have shuffled the deck pretty thoroughly now, and with quantum entanglement, it doesn't really matter anyway. You are now the possessor of the world's ***two*** oldest rats."

"Outstanding!" O'Brien said, somewhat chagrined, and put them both into the now-too-small cage, "I dub thee Alfie and Ralphie," and closed the cage.

"So now, 'all the ducks are in a row,' as you Americans say," Chakrabarti declared. "When we move any object from any point in space-time to any other point in space-time, we duplicate it, and remove the original. Also we could transport a duplicate, leaving behind the original."

"Or transport the original and leave behind the duplicate," Dr. O'Brien concluded.

"Which is exactly what we propose to do. As you and I have the exact space-time co-ordinates for the origin, and we know exactly what object we wish to transport, the only remaining issue is where to place the destination," Chakrabarti said.

"If I put together a three-way q-link connection," Dr. O'Brien inquired, "Can you direct the object to the location of the third party?"

"Just as simply as I directed Alfie and Ralphie to you, just now." Chakrabarti responded.

"Then stay on this link, I'm going to place a call."

Chii's message center beeped. She checked the cradle where RoBii was sleeping, and, confident that he had not been disturbed, she opened the connection. She was expecting Ole Ingvarsson, calling back with some question. Instead, she found herself looking at Dr. James O'Brien, her advisor for the online courses she had been taking, and another gentleman she did not recognize.

"Good (O'Brien checked his wristwatch) ——Morning, Ms. DriiBo." he said, "I have two pieces of good news for you this morning. First, all the requirements for your Bachelor's degrees in propulsion engineering and mathematics, and Bobby's in physics and mathematics, have been met. It would have been an embarrassment ***not*** to grant a degree in propulsion engineering to the inventor of the Firestone-DriiBo Drive, I might add—— So, these diplomas (he held them up in his hand) are now registered with Bentley University's Online College. You can pick up the diplomas and transcripts, any time."

"Well, thank you, Professor O'Brien. After--certain events--a lot of the motivation for my seeking the sheepskin (They don't really make it from a sheep, any more, do they?) went away, but I figured I should follow through if I had started it, so thank you——" Chii said.

"No sheep were harmed in the making of these diplomas, I assure you," O'Brien chuckled.

"You said there was another piece of good news?" Chii asked.

"Yes. Let me introduce you to my colleague, Dr. Anish Chakrabarti, of Harvard University," Dr. O'Brien proclaimed.

"Hello, Dr. Chakrabarti," Chii responded.

"Hello, Chii Ix DriiBo," Chakrabarti greeted her. She decided not to correct that with the confusing title of Chii Firestone. That marriage was still secret from the world at large, although Professor O'Brien was an exception.

"Is there something I can do for you?" she asked.

"Actually, it is ***I*** who can do something for ***you***, I think," he answered, "We have been working on some projects your partner Robert Firestone sent to us. One of them concerned q-based transporter and replicator technology."

"***Really?*** He never spoke to me about that idea!" she was genuinely startled.

"Oh. He gave us many more tasks to work with," Chakrabarti replied, "But this one has been of exceptional importance to us. We have succeeded by following the guidance he gave to us, and now, we get to repay his trust."

"Oh——Kay——" Chii said, "And is there something I can help you with?"

"Yes. Something simple," Chakrabarti said, "Could you move some of the toys on the floor so there is a clear space about one meter wide, just in front of your monitor?"

"Sure——?" and she cleared the space.

"Now, stand back," Chakrabarti warned. She took two steps back from the space she had cleared.

There was a momentary glow in the air in front of her. Suddenly, there was a person in the space, stumbling back as though he had been hit in the chest. He straightened up, looked around, looked at Chii.

"Chii! Where am I?" he asked. It was Bobby, in his tuxedo. The two projectiles that had been stopped by his bulletproof vest fell free. He dropped the half of a Nobel diploma that had been transported with him, and the pages fluttered to the floor.

Chii screamed, and threw her arms around him. Bobby hugged her back.

After a few silent moments, Dr. Chakrabarti cleared his throat, and Chii looked back at the screen. "Robert Firestone, thank you for your mail message to Professor O'Brien. We have now, from your project number 150, got the ability to transport an object from anywhere in space-time to anywhere else in space-time, although it is easiest if the destination is in the same time as the transport device is activated."

"This is really Bobby?" Chii asked, still holding him.

"Yes. The person you saw killed is——was——a duplicate. As much as any object in the quantum universe we inhabit is real, this is really your friend, Bobby," Chakrabarti explained.

"No," Chii replied, "This is my ***husband***, Bobby. And from now on, you can call me Chii Firestone!"

They both looked at the screen. Bobby, having apprehended what had happened, said, "Things looked really bad for me just a moment ago. It looks as though my automatic mail delivery program paid off——"

Professors Chakrabarti and O'Brien, realizing that this was a different situation than they had imagined, said their goodbyes and promised to get back in touch in a few days. Then they closed the link.

He looked at the surroundings and the screen. "***Was*** that just a moment ago?"

"We're on Gracet, Bobby," Chii said, "My house. What 'just happened to you,' that's six months ago, now, and I am so glad to see you. But Bobby, there's someone you just have to meet——"

For this, Chii figured, it's worth waking up the baby.

Author Note:

Bobby and Chii are back together and their family can move forward, but Bobby's little sister TiiNa is with her Dad's sidekick Rob, out in the world and taking on the terrorists with a vengeance ...literally!

In the next book, TRIROON, her work of battling the forces of intolerance takes on a new urgency. For a sneak preview, check out the following pages, where TiiNa tells you more of her story in her own words:

Excerpt from Book 2 of this Series -- "Triroon"

PROLOGUE

My name is TiiNa Firestone. Not 'Tina,' although that's a perfectly acceptable name where I am right now. I also go by 'Martina,' but on my home planet, I'm TiiNa; that's my ***real*** name and don't you forget it.

At this moment, I'm standing on a street corner in Berea, Kentucky, waiting for the light to change. Anybody looking at me right now will see a little Caucasian girl with blond pigtails, blue eyes and freckles. The blue eyes are from my Dad. He and my brother have brown eyes, but there must be a recessive gene for blue in there, somewhere. But they're nothing like my Mom's eyes, so they must be from Dad.

The rest of me is a lie.

If you were to reach out and touch one of my little, pink, shell-like ears, your finger would stop about a quarter-inch short and run into a surface that feels both leathery and gelatinous at the same time. But you wouldn't see that surface. All you'd see is a very normal-looking Earth girl with an upturned nose and freckles, maybe Swedish-or-Irish-American. Which is all right, my Dad is at least half Irish. Me? I'm not really a white girl at all. If you saw me in my natural appearance, I'd be a faded version of the color of the Kentucky bluegrass you see growing around here. My wig is pretty good, but it's a wig--I have to keep it taped to my head so it doesn't slip. But blonde, blue-eyed Caucasian is what I'm looking like right now because that's what works for the neo-Nazi types I'm hunting.

I'm holding hands with a man while we wait for the light to change. Everybody thinks he's my Dad. Actually, he's my father's closest friend, Rob. They worked together for five years as asteroid miners. Rob's a lean, rugged guy, somewhere in his early forties. My Dad has a picture of him, holding his helmet in one hand, cigarette hanging from his lips, and wearing a patched pressure suit that looks like the veteran of several wars, none of them short. He quit smoking when his son was born, about six months ago. I hope he can make it stick. Filthy habit, even if it does support a bunch of farmers around here.

Now, he's working with me. Second generation co-workers, I guess.

Good Vibrations

Me? I'm an enigma. In some of the neo-Nazi literature I've been reading lately, they still waste their time fuming about hybrids between black people and white people. I guess they really flipped their lids when my brother was born. But I digress. In that 'literature,' somebody with one black and one white parent is referred to as a 'maroon.' OK, mostly 'moron' is what the literature says, as well as other, less flattering terms. Following the same line, you're a 'quadroon' if you have one black grandparent and all the rest are white, and you're an 'octoroon' if one great-grandparent is black and all the rest are white. By that accounting, I'm a 'triroon' from Mom's point of view, since about a third of my DNA is human and the rest is HaChii.

I'm four and a half years old, but I look about like a nine year old human girl--when I'm looking human, that is. At home, I can pass for a HaChii if I keep my mittens on and wear contact lenses. But there, too, I look like a nine-year-old. I'm growing, and it's a lot faster than human or HaChii kids do. Then again, my brain runs faster, too. I'm not the standard model for either species, and if my brother hadn't been hatched ahead of me, nobody would've known what to expect when I came along.

I was raised Roman Catholic. There are maybe half a dozen Catholics living in the HaChii Confederation; me, Mom and Dad are half of them. Rob's uncle Jack had a lot to do with that; he's a priest. He probably wouldn't approve much of what I'm doing for a living right now, but I thank him and his Church for one idea. If I'd been raised HaChii, without any religion, I would never have heard the phrase "Angel of Death."

My hands and feet are another feature I got from my Dad. HaChii have tentacles with grippers at the end, I have large, very human-looking, five-fingered hands. They're kind of big for a nine-year-old, even; I can bridge an octave with either hand, easily. It makes me a pretty good piano player. But right now I'm traveling around this planet as a childhood chess prodigy. It's a great cover, as long as I don't let slip too many of my other talents. Let me give you a for-instance: we stopped in England on the way from Germany back to the States. There was a museum in London that was setting up an exhibit replica of a house with things in it from the 1940's, which the English call 'their finest hour.' Skip the part about how a decade can be an hour, they had interesting stuff, and had a living room, dining room and bathroom almost completely set up when we were going through. Me, I naturally looked at the plumbing in the bathroom. Always fascinated me, plumbing--I think it's a thing four-year-olds everywhere find entertaining, maybe mostly because they've just learned how to use it.

Anyway, there on the floor is a rectangular box with a little window, and you could see a wheel with numbers on it through the window. I looked around and nobody was looking, so I picked it up. When I held it by the sides and squeezed, the wheel rotated and the numbers moved past a pointer in the glass window. The set of numbers on top of the marks were called ***pounds***. I know that was the name of their currency at the time, and couldn't figure out how this thing could be a cash register, but on the bottom of the marks was another set of numbers labeled ***stone***. I don't know how that could measure anything, stones are all different sizes and don't have much monetary value. I squeezed the box a little and saw that 280 ***pounds*** was equal to 20 ***stone***. Since both scales started at zero, that means a ***stone*** is 14 ***pounds***. I saw that if I squeezed a little harder I could get the numbers to wrap around; they didn't go past 300 before they started over at 0. I figured if I pushed it much further I might damage it, so I was just starting to set it down when a woman curator hollered at me not to touch it, and I dropped it the last few inches. I saw it drifting down to the floor in the Earth gravity, and it made a 'clack' sound when it hit the floor. She was right, I shouldn't have been playing with the stuff in the exhibit; it's over 500 years old and probably pretty fragile. I'm sorry I dropped it. I hope it wasn't damaged.

When I asked him a few minutes later, Rob explained to me that it was a scale you would step on to measure your weight. I've seen those, of course, but they don't have mechanical, moving wheels. They just have numerals that light up on a screen, and they measure kilograms. Rob has one of those at home. I've seen him step on it and he says he has to watch his weight. I don't know why he has to bother. I can look at him and tell he's 85 kilograms, give or take a half. Rob says everybody can't do that, but it's not hard for me. That little box of his, though, it's hard to squeeze 300. I can just barely do it. I suspect ***pounds*** are something like kilograms, although squeezing 300 on the mechanical scale seemed a lot easier than squeezing 300 on Rob's bathroom scale.

Rob caught me once and told me not to let anybody see me doing that. He said most people's hands aren't that strong, and especially not nine-year-old girls. That sounds insulting to the girls I've met, but I suppose Rob may be right. I'm not very much like human girls, even though my hands look similar. Rob's usually right about what humans can do and can't do. I like working with Rob. My Dad named my brother Bobby after Robert Harker.

I should tell you about Bobby. I suppose I'm the only little sister on 17 planets whose big brother was never mean to her. He never even said an unkind word to me, and I pulled some things on him that were real doozies.

He only knew a few of the things I spotted while I was spying on him. I can spy pretty good without getting caught, because I have the same skin thing that Bobby had. HaChii skin has chromatophores, that change the skin color when emotions change. It was originally intended for communication between our animal ancestors, I suppose, but it's a nuisance to most HaChii today, because they wear their emotions on their skin, so to speak. If you know what to look for, you can read happy, excited, frightened, angry, embarrassed and all kinds of other things from the skin of the HaChii you're talking to. Very few HaChii can lie with their skins; mostly they can't control it. Humans have it a lot easier. Lying, I mean.

Bobby, on the other hand, found out before I was even born, that he could put any color or pattern on his skin that he wanted. He saw some kind of Earth animal called a cuttlefish, using dynamic camouflage, and figured out how to do it himself. He could merge into any background and not be seen from the front. I figured how to do it watching him. Then I discovered something better, when I studied optical physics and found out how holograms work. (I said my brain ran faster than average, didn't I? That means I'm a fast study too.) Once I figured out how to use the chromatophores in my skin to form a hologram, I could look like almost anything that's roughly the right size and shape, or I can look like nothing.

That's right. I can mimic the wave fronts coming at any side of me, so that what you see on the other side looks like the waves went through me. If I do it well--and I do ***everything*** well--I'm invisible. Like H. G. Wells' *Invisible Man*, except I can turn it off and be visible again, any time.

Have I left anything out? Oh, yes. I was telling you about Bobby. Bobby was murdered by neo-Nazi terrorists about six months ago, when he was nine and a half years old. They blew his brains out when he was up on stage receiving his Nobel Prize. (I said I was a fast study, right? I was nothing near as good as Bobby.) Poor Bobby... He was the very first human-HaChii hybrid, and that seemed to push a lot of folks right into the loony bin. Trouble was, some of them weren't too loony to organize, plan, and carry out an assassination.

At least some of them were loony enough, though, to write hate letters before they carried out that plan, and I'm returning their mail to them, one by one. Mom doesn't know I found those letters in a drawer where she was collecting them. They must have scared her to death. Or maybe they didn't scare her enough. Bobby was too 'out in the open' and didn't keep a low profile, Now he's dead. Anyway, I ***read*** all of those letters. Memorized every word, every postmark, every name the writer was stupid enough to include. I said I was a fast study, didn't I? And I've got help. I was recruited by a **vigilante branch of a three-letter organization I can't name.**

I'm like Bobby in a lot of ways. He was wicked smart, but I might just be smarter. I know how to keep a low profile. I know how to keep an *outrageously* low profile. More about that later; the light just changed. 'Bye...

About the Author:

Patrick J. O'Connor graduated from Northern Illinois University BS (Physics) 1968 and MS (College of Engineering/Engineering Technology) 1998. Also Master's Degree National-Louis University (Management) 1983.

Taught at DeVry University from 1968 to 2007. Senior Professor 1985-1989. Program Chair 1989 - 1999. Dean of the Electronics and Computer Technology Program from 1999 - 2007.

Co-Author (with Leah O'Connor) of Physics Experiment: "Planck's Constant using LEDs." Published in 1974 in American Physical Society's "The Physics Teacher" and presented at Argonne National Laboratories to the AAPT (American Association of Physics Teachers).

Won a bronze medal for astrophotography awarded by Adler Planetarium, which exhibited a photo he took of the comet Kohoutek in 1973.

Member of CACHE (the Chicagoland Computer Hobbyist Exchange) in the 1970s-80s.

Member of the Triple Nine Society in the 1980s.

Did computer graphics/animation for Disney on the Radio Shack Color Computer in the 1980s.

Author of textbooks "Digital and Microprocessor Technology" 1981 and 1989 editions, and "Understanding Microprocessors: How Computers Work" 1985. Co-Authored "Voice Data Telecommunications" 1986 with Michael Gurrie.

Sigma Pi Sigma member (Physics National Honor Society) since 1973. ISCET member (International Society of Certified Electronics Technicians) Journeyman in Electronics, Journeyman in Computers. Second Class FCC radiotelephone operator's license.

Columnist/contributing editor for TRS-80 Computer User and Interface Age magazines during the 1980's. Also had a column in Computer People and wrote articles for Kilobaud magazine during that decade.

Designed Ray Bradbury and Wernher Von Braun's Hugo Awards, given at Noreascon 4 in 2004.

President and webmaster of Chicagoland Costumers' Guild. On the board of directors of the International Costumers' Guild. Editor of their newsletter from 2008-2012.

DRAMATIS PERSONAE

Firestone Family:

NaDii Ix ChiiBii--HaChii Asteroid miner and mother of Robbie Firestone
Gregory Firestone--Human Asteroid miner and father of Robbie Firestone
Enya Firestone--Gregory's mother
Bii Iz ChaaJii--NaaDii's father
Chii Ix SiiFii--NaaDii's mother
Brii Ix ChiiBii--NaaDii's youngest sister
Robbie (Bobby) Firestone--son of Greg and NaDii
TiiNa Firestone--daughter of Greg and NaDii

MeBlii Ix BaShii--Asteroid miner and work partner of NaDii Rob and Greg
Robert Harker-- Asteroid miner and work partner of NaDii, MeBlii and Greg
Dr. Subrahmanian O'Reilly--human physician, Vesta Infirmary
Dr. Fii Iz ChaDii--HaChii physician, Vesta Infirmary
Dr. RuFii Ix ChaDii--HaChii physician and talk-show host; sister of Dr. Fii
FriiDa Ix KaaLo--HaChii entrepreneur and former college room-mate of NaDii
Denny Harris--ex-asteroid miner and homeless person
BriiLaa Ix GiiDii--Asteroid miner and work partner of Denny, Fred and TuuRii
TuuRii Ix HaaBuu--Asteroid miner and work partner of BriiLa, Fred and Denny
Fred Gemsbok--Asteroid miner and work partner of Denny, BriiLaa and TuuRii
ChuuRii Iz QuiiGaa--Sole male HaChii asteroid miner and boyfriend of MeBlii
John Cardinal Ryan--Archbishop of Chicago and Robert Harker's uncle--Promoted
Mary Ryan Harker--Rob Harker's mother and sister of Cardinal Jack Ryan
DiiRaa Iz SuuZaa--Music critic for the *Daily Vibe* and music promoter
Officers Grii and Jii--HaChii police detectives
Father Seamus Boyle--Pastor of the Chapel at Placedon Spaceport
Vrii Ix DriiBo--***polyadok*** champion of Gracet, sister of Chii
Chii Ix DriiBo--precocious math genius, Bobby's girlfriend
Oscar VI--King of Norway
BoTii Iz AaBii--Father of Chii Ix DriiBo and Vrii Ix DriiBo
DriiLa Ix FraaTroo--Mother of Chii Ix DriiBo and Vrii Ix DriiBo
RiiMaa Ix MeChuu--daughter of MeBlii and ChuuRii
MorPhii Iz PaaWul--GrandMaster, ***polyadok*** Planetary Champion of Placet

Professor James O'Brien--on-line college advisor to Bobby and Chii
RaGii--cabin steward on FriiDa's yacht, ***Good Vibrations.***
Ulf Schultz, ***Verbindung Der Echten Menschen,*** Northern Field Commander
Billy Bob Wilson, ***United Klans of America,*** Grand Kleagle, Eastern Sector
Lars Svensson--Director of the Stockholm Symphony Orchestra and Konserthuset
Ingemar Lillquist--Stockholm police investigator
MriiYa Harker--wife of Rob Harker
Gustav Adolf XIV--King of Sweden
Ole Ingvarsson--Researcher at the Karolinska Institute in Stockholm
Anish Chakrabarti--Chair, Harvard Physics Department

Made in the USA
Middletown, DE
02 September 2021